Amish Christmas Cookie Tour

Jennifer Beckstrand

Rachel J. Good

Mindy Steele

ALLY PRESS

Contents

Peanut Butter Christmas Cookies

Jennifer Beckstrand

Jennifer Beckstrand is the #1 Amazon and *USA Today* Bestselling author of *The Matchmakers of Huckleberry Hill* series, *The Honeybee Sisters* series, *The Petersheim Brothers* series, and *The Amish Quiltmaker* series for Kensington Books. *Second Chances on Huckleberry Hill*, the delightfully romantic eleventh book in the *Matchmakers of Huckleberry Hill* series, came out in May of 2023. Jennifer also writes sweet contemporary and historical romances. Her third Western, *Maggie and Max*, just hit the shelves, and Larkspur Ranch, the much anticipated second book in the Dandelion Meadows series, comes out in 2024.

Find out more about Jennifer:

Website:

www.jenniferbeckstrand.com

Facebook:

www.facebook.com/jenniferbeckstrandfans

Facebook group:

www.facebook.com/groups/550930369229378

Twitter:

@JenniferBeckst1

Pinterest:

www.pinterest.com/jgbeckstrand

Amazon:

www.amazon.com/Jennifer-Beckstrand/e/B0073GHCOG

Instagram:

j.beckstrand

Bookbub:

@JenniferBeckstrand

www.bookbub.com/authors/jennifer-beckstrand

Jennifer's Books

Apple Lake Amish Series

Book 1: *Kate's Song*
Book 2: *Rebecca's Rose*
Book 3: *Miriam's Quilt*

The Matchmakers of Huckleberry Hill Series

Huckleberry Hill
Huckleberry Summer
Huckleberry Christmas
Huckleberry Spring
Huckleberry Harvest
Huckleberry Hearts
Return to Huckleberry Hill
Courtship on Huckleberry Hill
Home on Huckleberry Hill
First Christmas on Huckleberry Hill
Second Chances on Huckleberry Hill
Happily Ever After on Huckleberry Hill

The Honeybee Sisters Series

Book 1: *Sweet as Honey*
Book 2: *A Bee in her Bonnet*
Book 3: *Like a Bee to Honey*
The Honeybee Sisters Cookbook

The Petersheim Brothers Series

Book 1: *Andrew*
Book 2: *Abraham*
Book 3: *His Amish Sweetheart*

The Amish Quiltmaker Series

The Amish Quiltmaker's Unexpected Baby
The Amish Quiltmaker's Unruly In-law
The Amish Quiltmaker's Unconventional Niece
The Amish Quiltmaker's Unlikely Match (2024)
The Amish Quiltmaker's Uninvited Guest (2024)
The Amish Quiltmaker's Unattached Neighbor (2025)

Cowboys of the Butterfly Ranch series

Rachel and Riley
Maggie and Max
Jessie and James

Dandelion Meadows Small Town Romance

Dandelion Meadows
Dandelion Meadows Christmas Kisses

Chapter 1

Mary Yutzy glanced at the clock on the oven and breathed a weary sigh. An hour until closing and the crowd at Austin Petersheim's Plain and Simple Country Store had yet to thin out. Mary smiled as she watched her *schwester* Hannah help a customer with a quilt he wanted wrapped for Christmas. Hannah loved socializing with customers and meeting new people. She was kind and friendly, and her enthusiasm for the store and life in general never seemed to wane. Hannah and Austin's relationship had been bumpy at the beginning, but when Austin had finally come to his senses and realized he loved Hannah, neither of them had doubts ever again. They were deeply in love, and it made Mary very happy to see Hannah's never-ending smile and seemingly endless supply of enthusiasm for the store and her new husband.

Mary boxed a dozen sugar cookies for Mrs. Wheatley and sent the older Englisch woman to the cash register to pay for her purchase. With a lot of help from Hannah, Mary and her *bruder* James ran the bakery inside Austin's Plain and Simple Country Store. They took orders for Christmas cookies and rolls and whole wheat bread and a host of other baked goods for Englisch and Amish alike. Austin's store had been open for just a year, but it was almost always busy, and business was better than Hannah or Austin ever could have dreamed. This December promised to be their biggest month yet.

Everybody wanted homemade baked goods for their Christmas parties and dinners. Mary loved making people happy with her sweet baked treats.

She glanced at the clock again, but it hadn't moved much, and she wasn't going to make it rotate faster with wishing. Much as she wanted a warm bath and a nice comfy bed, she still needed to go home and make dough for tomorrow's cinnamon rolls.

Austin loaded more apples into the bin while Hannah finished wrapping the quilt for the Englisch customer. He thanked her profusely and walked out of the store with the quilt box tucked under his arm. Austin caught Hannah's eye, and they shared a look that was deeply personal and exquisitely intimate. Mary's heart soared and then fell to the floor, shattering against the polished wood.

Hannah had found the love of her life.

The love of Mary's life stood just out of reach.

Mary gazed at the sugar cookies she'd decorated this morning with tiny red poinsettia petals and tried very hard to muster some Christmas cheer. It was December 1st, and in the next three weeks, there would be Christmas *singeons*, caroling to shut-ins, and lots and lots of Christmas baking. Mary loved the Christmas program at the school every year, and she loved helping Mamm decorate the house for the season. Home was filled with the heavenly scents of fresh pine garland and gingerbread the whole month of December.

Christmas had always been her favorite time of year, but she missed Jerry Zimmerman too much to find any joy in it this year.

Summer two and a half years ago, Jerry had jumped the fence and gone to New York City to work at a homeless shelter. He hadn't told

Mary of his plans, and she had felt betrayed and abandoned and heartbroken. That Christmas, ten-year-old twins Alfie and Benji Petersheim, of all people, had cooked up a scheme to lure Jerry back to Wisconsin. Jerry had stayed for two glorious weeks, and Mary had fallen in love with him all over again. She would have said yes in a minute if he'd asked her to marry him. Instead, he told her he had doubts about the Amish church and didn't even know if he wanted to be baptized. He needed more time. So he'd left her and gone to Mexico as a missionary, assuring her that he would return when he figured out his faith. That was two years ago.

He'd written her every week, but he hadn't come back. Mary was beginning to fear he never would.

She pressed her lips together, remembering their last conversation. Jerry had promised Mary that if she wanted him to join the Amish church, he would, just so he could marry her. But would he be miserable for the rest of his life if he got baptized into a faith he didn't believe in? How could she ask such a thing of him? She wouldn't hold him to that promise, even if it meant losing him. If Jerry didn't get baptized, they couldn't be married in the Amish faith. Mary would either have to marry Jerry outside of the church or give him up. Neither option made her happy.

Would she have to choose between Jerry and her family? In the end, her heart would break, no matter what she chose.

Mary missed Jerry most acutely at Christmastime. His early letters had been filled with romance and talk of marriage, but he hadn't mentioned marriage in any of his letters for the last six months. She was worried beyond words. He'd promised he'd come back, but would he want to get baptized and marry her or would he decide he was happier living his calling in Mexico or New York or somewhere else?

"May I have two sugar cookies, please."

Mary gasped and turned around at the sound of the voice she knew as well as her own. "Jerry!" she squealed. She ran around the counter and ignoring all modesty, launched herself into his arms.

He caught her and wrapped his arms around her waist, but there wasn't much enthusiasm in his touch or his expression. "*Ach, du lieva,* Mary, it's *gute* to see you." He was dressed as an Englischer, in blue jeans, a faded black Packers t-shirt, and a baseball cap. His clothes and Englisch haircut made Mary's heart sink.

He smiled as if he was just going through the motions as if he didn't know how to be happy anymore. "I hope you don't mind that I came over. Rebecca Petersheim told me you'd be here, and I didn't want to wait even a minute longer to see you."

"I don't mind at all," Mary said, taking a step back. Three Englischers plus Perry and Ida Miller were staring. "I'm so happy to see you." She took a *gute* look at him, gulping in his presence like a parched traveler with a glass of ice water. He looked older and weary, as if the last two years had taken his joy and his youth, but his good looks still stole Mary's breath. His thick, dark hair was shorter, though more unruly, he looked like a pile of skin and bones, and worry lines had etched themselves at the corners of his dark brown eyes. And was that a new scar above his eyebrow?

Mary pretended not to notice, pretended not to worry. Pretended that the man she loved hadn't changed one little bit. Her heart weighed heavier than a stone. She didn't know what she had expected, but this was not it.

He lifted his hand and caressed her cheek. She leaned into the warmth of his touch. "Seeing you is like eating a piece of German chocolate cake after two years of celery."

"Seeing you is like all my dreams coming true at the same time."

His smile faltered as if he didn't have the strength to keep it up any longer. "Mary, we need to talk."

She didn't like the sound of that. Was he going to break up with her? Did he love New York City more than he loved her? Did his devotion to Gotte make it impossible for him to be devoted to her? She tamped down her rising panic. He'd just gotten here. Couldn't they just enjoy being together for a few minutes? "When did you get back?"

"Just today."

"I missed you so much. Where are you staying? Are you at your parents' house?"

Something akin to longing flickered in his eyes. "Mary, before we get ahead of ourselves, we need to talk."

What he meant was, he needed to talk and she wasn't going to like what he had to say. Her stomach tied itself into a tight knot. Hadn't she endured enough heartache already?

Hannah and Austin both caught sight of Jerry and rushed over to the bakery counter. Hannah was one of the few people who knew how desperately Mary had missed Jerry. "Jerry, we're so happy you're back," she gushed, not giving any indication that she thought his clothes were inappropriate. "It's been ages since we've seen you. Just ages. *Frehlicher Grischtdaag.*"

Jerry gave Hannah the same unhappy smile he'd given Mary. "*Ach,* I guess we're saying that now that it's December. Merry Christmas to you too."

Hannah tensed and glanced at Mary, no doubt as concerned as Mary was. "Are you...are you here for a while?"

Austin, who wasn't the most observant person in the world, didn't seem to notice anything amiss. He shook Jerry's hand. "What do you think of the new store?"

Jerry looked around, that serene and fake smile still plastered on his lips. "It's the most *wunderbarr* place I've ever seen. Mary's been keeping me updated on your business and how much it's grown. You should be very proud."

Austin looked down and traced a circle on the floor with his foot. "Not proud. But pleased."

Jerry's mouth tightened until it looked as if it would suddenly snap off his face, like a taut rubber band. "I forgot. You must avoid pride at all costs." He turned to Hannah. "Mary told me you made the sign above the door. It looks beautiful."

Hannah gave Austin a wry look. "Scilla Lambright didn't like it. She painted the word 'organic' at the bottom, and Austin let her."

Austin winced. "We almost broke up because of it."

Hannah folded her arms and cocked her eyebrow. "I was pretty mad, and you were pretty *dumm*."

"*Jah*, I was. I admit it." Austin put his arm around Hannah's shoulders. "How have you been able to put up with me all this time?"

Hannah patted Austin on the cheek. "I overlook all your flaws because you're so handsome."

He chuckled. "I thank Derr Herr for that."

Rebecca Petersheim blew into the store like a gust of wind. She was a wiry, determined, no-nonsense woman with glasses and strong opinions. She was also Austin's *mater*. "Austin, have you seen Alfie and Benji?" she said, propping her hands on her hips as if getting ready for a fight. Her gaze flicked in Jerry's direction. "Oh, *hallo*, Jerry. It looks like you found Mary." She looked around their little circle and melted long enough to give Hannah a hug. "My sweet Hannah! Is Austin treating you well? Because if he isn't, just say the word and I'll take care of it."

Hannah giggled. "*Jah*, Rebecca. Austin has many flaws, but he is usually a wonderful *gute* husband. When he isn't, I tell him about it."

Rebecca nodded curtly. "You're strong enough to stand up to Austin. He can get cocky, and someone needs to put him in his place occasionally."

Austin waved his hand in front of Rebecca's face. "I'm standing right next to you. You don't have to talk about me as if I'm not here."

Rebecca wasn't deterred. "It's *gute* for you to understand your shortcomings. You are one of my favorite sons, and you are quite remarkable, but your head would swell to twice its size if I didn't do my best to keep you humble." She unzipped her coat. "I'm here to get some Christmas cookies and find Alfie and Benji. Have you seen them?" Alfie and Benji were ten-year-old twins, Rebecca's youngest sons, and they were always getting into one kind of trouble or another.

"I haven't seen them," Mary said. "Were they coming to the store today?"

Rebecca sighed in exasperation. "They weren't happy about Jerry moving into the upstairs bedroom."

Mary's heart lurched. "You're staying at Petersheims'?" It was bad news because it meant his parents were still not speaking to him, but it was *gute* news because it meant he might be in Bienenstock for a few days.

"*Jah*," Jerry said, drawing his brows together. "I'm sorry, Rebecca."

Rebeccca swatted away his concern. "Nothing to worry about. Alfie always has a chip on his shoulder about one thing or another, and the cellar has been a sore spot for several months. Benaiah's *dat* had a stroke three years ago and had to move in with us. With one fewer room, I moved Alfie and Benji to the cellar to sleep. Alfie has been mad at me ever since, even though there's a very nice air mattress down there and all the canned goods they can eat."

Mary covered her mouth with her hand to hide a smile. Rebecca painted a very cheery picture of the cellar. Alfie talked as if he and Benji were forced to sleep in a haunted cave.

"They didn't come home from school today, and their backpacks, a whole box of crackers, and Dawdi David's binoculars are missing. I think maybe they've run away."

Austin snorted. "Only Alfie would be enough to run away in the middle of winter."

"That's why I'm not worried. When they get cold enough, they'll come home."

Hannah grimaced. "But will they come home with all their fingers and toes?"

Rebecca's unconcerned attitude was oddly comforting. "Alfie likes to learn things the hard way. Losing his pinky toe would be a *gute* lesson in patience and gratitude." She pointed to the bakery display. "Hannah, will you box me a dozen of those Christmas cookies?" She patted Jerry on the shoulder. "We're having spaghetti and Christmas cookies for dinner tonight if you want to join us. We're eating in half an hour."

"*Denki*, I will try to come."

"If Alfie and Benji don't show up, you might have to eat their share." Rebecca looked only mildly irritated at the thought of her two boys not showing up for dinner. Nothing seemed to ruffle her. She was the perfect *mater* for five sons.

Hannah went behind the bakery counter, and Austin stepped away to ring someone up at the cash register. Jerry reached out and took Mary's hand as if he were going to shake it. "Mary, we need to talk."

Oh, how Mary wished she could keep Hannah in her pocket for times like this. Hannah would know what to do if Jerry broke up with her. Mary had always admired Hannah's courage and strength, the way she said what was needed and never backed down from a conflict. Mary longed for some of Hannah's confidence right now. She had been waiting patiently for Jerry for two years, and at the very least, she deserved an explanation for why Jerry was giving up on their relationship. But was she brave enough to stand up for herself? She glanced in Hannah's direction, hoping Jerry didn't sense her hesitation. "I have to help clean up in about thirty minutes."

"That will be enough time."

He'd need much less time than that to break up with her. *Mary, I don't want to marry you, and I don't want to be baptized. I'm going to New York to minister to perfect strangers because I don't love you enough to stay here.*

"Is there a backroom where we can go for some privacy?"

"We could go to the storage room." With dread growing at the base of her throat, Mary motioned for Jerry to follow her down the stairs. She took her time going down the steps, not especially eager to have this conversation.

Jerry paused on the bottom step. "Oy, anyhow. Austin and Hannah have really made this place up nice."

"*Ach*, they put in so much work." The basement had been unfinished, damp, and dirty when Austin bought the house. Austin and his *bruderen* had installed three exit windows on three sides of the basement by cutting holes through the foundation cement. The basement was still a little dark, but it looked much less like a dungeon than when they'd started. Mary pointed to the four rows of storage shelves loaded with merchandise and supplies for the store. "I worked down here for days."

"I'm impressed."

She laughed at the look of admiration on his face. "Don't be. I measured and marked boards and sheets of plywood for cutting, and Austin and his *bruderen* did the hard part. I saved them some time, I guess. When the windows were in and the shelves were done, they worked on the main floor and the upstairs." She ambled to the wall that separated the storage room from the rest of the basement. "After the store opened, they started work on this." She opened the bright white door and strolled into Austin and Hannah's apartment.

Jerry's eyes got rounder. "Do Austin and Hannah live here?"

Mary switched on the battery-operated light that stood in the middle of the living room. "*Jah.* Two bedrooms, one bath." The kitchen and living room were one big space with a butcher block bar separating the kitchen from living area.

Jerry stepped into the space and smoothed his hand along the kitchen countertop. "*Ach, du lieva.* This is really something."

"It's the perfect place for a newlywed couple. Hannah has never been happier."

Jerry eyed her with an unreadable expression on his face. "That's saying something. You and Hannah have always been the happiest people I've ever met." He pressed his lips together as if he'd said the wrong thing. He was probably thinking about how hard it was going to be to break her heart.

Mary briefly showed him the whole apartment then led him out the door and into the storage room. She shut the door behind them and turned on another cabinet light bulb that stood next to the first row of shelves. It was time to stop stalling and get it over with. Wasn't it better to rip off the Band-Aid than to try to pull it off slowly? "What did you want to talk about, Jerry?" she said, hoping he couldn't hear the dread in her voice.

Jerry turned his face from her as if it was too painful to look into her eyes. "Do you remember what I told you two years ago?"

Mary spoke past the lump in her throat. "You said you needed to go to Mexico. You said you didn't know if you wanted to get baptized." She paused to bolster her composure. "You promised me that it didn't matter what you wanted, that you'd come back and join the church if I asked you to. You promised to marry me, even though you didn't know if you wanted to." Mary thought of Hannah and squared her shoulders. "I don't want you to sacrifice your happiness for me. If you don't want to be baptized or married, I won't hold you to a silly promise you made two years ago." It broke her heart to say the words, but she meant every one of them.

"It wasn't a silly promise. If it's what you want, I'll marry you as soon as I can finish baptism classes."

Mary shook her head. "I won't let you give up your happiness just to ensure mine. I could never really be happy if you aren't happy, no matter how much I love you."

He looked positively stricken with longing. "Do you love me, Mary? After all I've put you through? After making you wait for two years?"

"I will always love you," she said, even though it would make it harder for him to leave her. He wanted to save the world, and he hated the very thought of doing harm to anyone. "I would never hold you to a promise you don't want to keep."

He took off his cap and angrily scrubbed his fingers through his short-cropped hair. "Ach, Mary, it's not that simple. I would never, never hurt you, but I'm a different person than I was two years ago. You think you want to marry me, but you really don't." He cupped his fingers around her shoulders and squeezed tight. "You would be much better off if I left Bienenstock and never came back. I want to give you a chance for happiness, and that chance is not with me."

Even though she had known it was coming, panic welled up in the hollow of her chest. "What do you mean? Of course, it's with you. I'll never be happy again if I can't be with you."

"That's not true. I'm broken. I'm jaded beyond repair. I have no hope left." He dropped his hands to his side as if in surrender. "I've lost all faith in humanity, and if we married, you'd grow to hate me because I'd make you miserable."

Mary had no idea what "jaded" meant, but the way he said it sounded terrifying and desperate. She snatched his hand and held it tight. "I want to help you. Let me help you."

He smiled bitterly. Mary tensed. She'd never seen such a cynical expression on his face before. "You don't happen to have seven hundred dollars in your pocket, do you?"

"I…I don't, but I have some money in the bank."

He held up his hand to stop her. "I don't want your money. I don't want your help. There's nothing you can do."

"Surely our love is strong enough to fix this together."

His face lost all expression. It was as if he'd instantly built a brick wall between them. "This can't be fixed, Mary. I just don't believe in Gotte anymore. If there was a Gotte, why would He allow His children to suffer? Why would He let people die? There is a huge pile of grief and pain that Gotte can stop, but He lets it happen. Every day. He lets kids die every day of drug overdoses shootings and suicide. If He truly loved us, why would He let that happen?"

"I…I don't know."

Jerry's eyes looked like two ice cubes. "You see? You can't help me. And you don't want to marry me. Even if we married, I would never agree to bring children into the world. It's just not safe."

She was reeling like a leaf in a windstorm. "How can you say that?"

"How can I not say that? You don't understand what I've been through."

She wouldn't let him get away with that. "Then talk to me. Help me understand why you feel this way. Don't just stand there and tell me we can't be together. I want to know why. I deserve to know why."

"I told you why. I've lost my faith in humanity. You don't want me in your life. I don't care about anything anymore, and you don't want to marry a man who doesn't care." He backed away from her and avoided her gaze. "I came back specifically for you, Mary. I came back to explain because I don't want you to be sad. I want you to get on with your life and forget about me."

Mary took a shuddering breath. "You sound to me like someone who cares."

"The only thing I care about is your happiness. It buries me in grief to think I've caused you so much pain, and that's why I have to leave." He turned and put his foot on the first step. "I told Rebecca I'd try to be there for dinner. I've got to go. I hope life is kind to you, Mary."

She couldn't let him leave this way, couldn't accept that this was the end. Maybe it was a foolish yearning, but no one was beyond the reach of Gotte's healing. She loved Jerry better than her own soul, and she refused to let him go without a fight. In desperation, she grabbed for a thin thread of hope. What if she pretended to hold him to his promise after all? "You can't leave."

"I've got to go. *Mach's gute.*"

"Did you mean what you said or not?"

A tiny line appeared between his eyebrows. "Always."

"You promised you'd marry me, even if you don't want to. You said if I wanted to marry you, you'd marry me. In the faith." She stiffened her spine. "I'm going to hold you to that promise."

If she hadn't been so distraught, she would have laughed at the look on his face. His eyebrows shot up his forehead, and his mouth fell open. He was beyond surprised. "I...thought...I thought...you're so unselfish, Mary. You said you wouldn't hold me to it."

"You've underestimated me," she said, a sick feeling in her stomach. She had to tell him a version of the truth. "Spend Christmas with me. Help me at the bakery. Go caroling and skating and sledding. At the end of December, if you still want to leave, I'll release you from your promise."

He bowed his head in resignation. "It's not going to work, Mary."

"Then you have nothing to lose."

"It will just make it harder in the end."

"I'm not afraid of hard," she said. "I'm afraid of not trying."

He expelled a long, deep breath. "Okay then. I'll stay until the end of December, but only because I have a shred of integrity left."

"You care more than you claim."

He didn't answer, just shook his head and tromped up the stairs. Mary was left in the basement with tears streaming down her cheeks, frantically thinking of ways to help Jerry believe in her and Gotte again before December 31. She flinched when she heard a muted thud from behind the third row of shelves. Sidling to the end of the row to investigate, she saw Alfie and Benji Petersheim sitting on the floor on a rolled-up sleeping bag, clutching their knees to their chests and looking guiltier than two cats that had just eaten the pet bird. Benji had a ring of cracker crumbs around his lips, and half a cracker stuck out of Alfie's mouth. "Alfie and Benji, what are you doing down here?"

Alfie shoved Benji in the shoulder with his hand. "Oh, *sis yuscht*. You couldn't keep quiet for two more minutes?"

Benji reciprocated by shoving Alfie, and Alfie fell off the rolled-up sleeping bag and onto the cement floor. "I wasn't trying to be noisy. My foot fell asleep. I don't want it to fall off. I won't be able to play baseball if I'm a cripple."

"Lots of cripples play baseball. And your foot could have waited two more minutes."

Mary's lips twitched upward involuntarily. No matter how bad things were in her life, Alfie and Benji always made her smile, or wince, as the case may be. "Why are you *buwe* hiding in the storage room with a sleeping bag? Your *mamm* is very worried about you."

Alfie blew air from between his lips. "She is not. She doesn't love us anymore. She doesn't care if we die of spiders or have to get our feet cut off because of frostbite."

"I see."

Benji wiped the cracker crumbs off his lips. "We ran away to teach her a lesson, but I don't want her to feel bad. Do you think she'll feel bad?"

Alfie stood and nudged Benji not-too-gently with his foot. "We don't care if she feels bad. We've been stuck in that cellar for three years. She deserves to feel bad."

"I don't see how your situation has improved much," Mary said. "You're in Austin's basement, and all you have to eat is a box of crackers. You must be thirsty."

Benji stood up. "We were planning on sneaking up to the store after Hannah and Austin went to bed and eating the day-old cookies and getting drinks from the sink."

Alfie gaped at Benji as if he'd just committed a deep betrayal. "Why don't you stop talking before you give away all our secrets."

Mary dabbed at the tears on her face. "It's too bad about your bedroom. Jerry is staying with you. You were going to get your old room back, and now he's there."

"We're not mad at Jerry," Benji said. He glanced at Alfie. "Right? We're running away, but we're not mad at Jerry. We like him. He saved Alfie from a tree once."

"He didn't save me. I could have climbed down myself."

"No, you couldn't have."

"Yes, I could."

Mary couldn't help but smile, even with tears still in her eyes. "*Ach, vell*, you boys need to get home. Your *mamm* is worried, and she's making spaghetti for dinner."

Benji lit up like a propane lantern. "Spaghetti. That's my favorite."

"Much better than cookies."

Alfie dug his elbow into Benji's ribs. "We can't go home, not even for spaghetti. We're running away."

Benji pointed to the sleeping bag. "But we can't stay here. Mary knows where our hideout is."

"We'll find a better hideout. We can go to that cave down by the pond."

Benji frowned. "It's too cold to sleep outside, and I miss Tintin."

"You saw him after school."

Benji lifted his chin. "I still miss him. He'll wonder where we are."

"You boys really should go home." Mary slumped her shoulders. "I know you're mad about Jerry sleeping in your old room, but I don't wonder that he'll soon be gone. You'll have a room upstairs in no time."

Benji's eyes filled with pity. "We heard him say he doesn't want to marry you."

"Did you?"

Alfie folded his arms and leaned against the shelf behind him. "We heard everything. Like you waited for him for two years, and he's jaded and doesn't believe in Gotte. And now he doesn't want to keep his promise, but you said he has to keep his promise and go caroling with you."

Mary's throat felt so thick, she thought she might choke. "Something like that."

"And he's lost his faith in humidity," Benji said.

Mary smiled half-heartedly. "Humanity."

"What does that mean?"

She shrugged. "I think it means that people keep disappointing him, that he doesn't think there are any *gute* people in the world. Maybe he doesn't believe bad people can change and that it's useless to try to help them."

Benji nibbled on his fingernail. "Aendi Lisa says she moved away from Michigan because of the humidity."

"I don't know how to help him." Mary didn't intend to say that out loud, but as soon as the words came out of her mouth, she burst into tears. She couldn't help herself. The burden was just too heavy to bear.

Alfie and Benji just stared at her, obviously uncomfortable, with no idea how to handle a blubbering girl. Benji took a step toward her and gave her an awkward pat on the arm. "Can't we help her, Alfie? She looks really sad, and she's getting little wrinkles around her mouth."

Mary closed her lips and tried to relax her mouth. She hated to think she was looking old before she'd turned twenty-one.

"What can we do?" Alfie said. "We can't even convince Mamm to give us our old room back."

"Well, we helped Mary and Jerry get back together last time. And we found wives for Austin, Abraham, and Andrew."

Mary stifled a disbelieving cough. Alfie and Benji gave themselves too much credit, but they weren't lacking in confidence, for sure and certain. Andrew and Mary Coblenz had met...*ach, vell,* come to think of it, Andrew and Mary had started dating after Alfie got himself stuck in that tree. And Abraham and Emma got together when Alfie and Benji's dog got too friendly with Emma's chickens. There was no doubt Alfie and Benji had a role in getting Austin to finally notice Hannah, and in a roundabout way, the twins had been the reason Mary and Jerry had gotten back together two years ago.

Hmm, maybe it was Mary who didn't give *them* enough credit.

Benji swiped his hand along one of the shelves and sent dust floating into the air. "If we help Mary with her problem, Jerry will realize he's in love with her, ask her to marry him, and move out of our old room."

Benji had Alfie's full attention now. Alfie caught his breath. "That could work."

"They belong together. Their names rhyme."

Alfie nodded slowly. "I didn't think of that."

Benji put his arm around his *bruder.* "Jerry is in love with Mary. He's just lost his faith in humidity."

Alfie made a face. "And he needs seven hundred dollars."

Mary swallowed her pride. She needed all the help she could get, even in the form of two ten-year-old boys who were prone to mischief and smoke bombs. "Will you...Can you help me? I don't know what to do."

Alfie stood up straight, as if pleased Mary would ask him to do such an important thing. "We'd be glad to help."

"But we're not very *gute* at earning money," Benji said.

"We tried to raise money to buy Dinah's *mamm* a wheelchair, and all we could come up with was selling the tomatoes we grew in our garden.

ter, and it's Christmas, and nobody wants tomatoes at Christmas."

"I like tomatoes at Christmas," Benji volunteered.

Mary plopped herself down on Alfie and Benji's sleeping bag. They sat on either side of her. "Don't worry about the money. I don't know that seven hundred dollars is going to renew Jerry's faith in humanity."

Benji scrunched his lips together. "That's the first thing he asked you for. If you got him the money, I bet he'd love you forever."

Ach, vell, it wasn't the worst idea in the world, but it was a ten-year-old's idea, and Mary had to be more practical than that. "I don't know where to get seven hundred dollars. Have you got any other ideas to help Jerry be happy again?"

Benji pointed up at the ceiling and shot to his feet. "An Amish Christmas cookie tour!"

"What?"

"That's how we could earn money. Our cousins in Pennsylvania did one and they earned a million dollars, or maybe two thousand." Benji was still thinking about the money.

"What besides money?" Mary prompted.

Benji looked as eager as Mary had ever seen him. "The cookie tour is a *gute* idea, Mary. You sell tickets and then people go to all the Amish businesses and stores and homes, and we give them a Christmas cookie at each stop. Austin will like it because it will bring people to the store to spend money. You have to make dozens and dozens of cookies. It's a lot of work. Jerry would have to help you bake cookies, and that would mean you'd have to spend a lot of time together."

Alfie scratched his chin. "We could be your cookie tasters."

As crazy as it seemed, the cookie tour wasn't a bad idea. Mary also had cousins in Pennsylvania who participated in a Christmas cookie tour every year. It was a *gute* way to attract new customers to Amish businesses and spread some Christmas cheer at the same time. "But isn't it too late to organize a cookie tour? It's already December first."

Benji made an I-have-no-idea face. "We don't know. We're just kids."

"Our *mamm* could make peanut butter cookies and sell Petersheim Brothers peanut butter when people come to our house for the cookie tour," Alfie said. "And I bet the Honeybee Sisters would make honey cookies. Englischers would go to their house for a cookie and some fresh honey and Bitsy could show them her cats."

How many Amish merchants would have to agree to the cookie tour to make it worthwhile? Then again, how hard would it be to set a date, figure out a way to sell tickets, and do a little advertising? When Austin opened his store, they'd passed out flyers to the entire town, and the mayor put the opening on the town website. Mary couldn't believe she was considering it, but maybe working on a project like this would make Jerry happy. It most certainly could pull the community together. Maybe Jerry would have so much fun, he'd decide to be baptized. Maybe if he and Mary baked cookies together, he'd realize he was in love with her. The project wasn't going to make anybody rich, but surely the money wasn't important. Jerry's happiness was what really mattered. She simply had to get the old Jerry back. Her broken heart depended on it. "Do you think it will work?"

"It will work," Benji reassured her. "Cookies make people fall in love all the time." He thought about it for a second. "And you should go sledding. Cookies and sledding."

Alfie leaned back against the cement wall. "We could set something on fire for you. That worked last time."

Mary shook her finger at him. "No fires and no smoke bombs."

Alfie eyed her resentfully. "Nobody knows who lit that smoke bomb in front of the library."

Mary giggled. "Nice try, Alfie, but everybody knows it was you. You're just lucky you didn't get caught."

Benji and Alfie shared a mischievous look. "We're fast runners."

Mary pinned Alfie with a stern gaze. "Fire is a very bad idea. Promise me no fires."

Alfie wrinkled up his face like a dried prune. "Don't look at me. Benji is the one who set the shed on fire and burned Mamm's folding table. And how were we supposed to know the Christmas tree would catch fire like that? We never in our lives ever meant to set a fire."

That was probably as close to a promise as Mary was going to get. "Will you help me with the Christmas cookie tour? Taking flyers to houses? Telling your friends?"

Alfie and Benji looked at each other and nodded. "We could do that," Benji said. "We'll also plan other activities to help Jerry get back his faith in humidity."

Mary narrowed her eyes. "No fires, no smoke bombs, no blood, and no tree climbing."

Benji stuck out his bottom lip. "The tree worked pretty *gute* last time."

It was taxing trying to reason with a ten-year-old. "If you die in a tree, you'll never get to move back into that room you've been working so hard for."

"I suppose that's true."

Alfie rubbed the side of his face and left a dark smudge. His hands were filthy. "Don't worry, Mary. The mayor said we're Bienenstock's finest citizens. We'll make you proud."

"It's a sin to be proud," Benji scolded. "And it's 'cinizens,' not 'citizens.'"

Mary tapped her palms to her knees then stood up. "You'd better get home now before Jerry eats all your spaghetti."

Alfie squared his shoulders. "We're not going home. We're still running away. We just need to find a better hideout and get better snacks. Mamm needs to know she can't treat her sons like this. Right, Benji?"

Benji was mute.

"Right, Benji?"

"It's cold outside," Benji mumbled.

Alfie scowled. "Aren't you mad that Mamm takes us for granite?"

Benji pressed his lips into a tight line. "I really like spaghetti, and it's getting dark. Can't we run away tomorrow? We could take Tintin with us."

Mary stifled a smile as she watched the battle of emotions on Alfie's face. Alfie was stubborn, but he was also smart enough to know that a warm plate of spaghetti and a warm bed were infinitely more desirable than a chilly night in the snow or on Austin and Hannah's storage room floor. "It might be fun to take Tintin. He's a *gute* dog."

Benji brightened. "*Jah*! Tintin would be so fun. He could hunt for food and scare away the bears."

Suddenly, Alfie was fully committed, as if the plan had been his idea all along. "We need Tintin, and tomorrow morning we could sneak into the kitchen before Mamm gets up and steal better snacks. And matches, because we need to build a fire out in the wild."

Benji's eyes filled with worry. "But we won't really steal."

"It's not stealing. It's our food too." Alfie picked up the sleeping bag and threw it over his shoulder. "Should we take the Doritos or the Fritos?" He strolled to the end of the aisle with Benji right behind him.

"We should take both, because some days I'm in the mood for Doritos and some days I want Fritos."

Mary watched from between the shelves as Alfie and Benji climbed the stairs discussing the advantages of Fritos versus Doritos. Fritos won out because they don't make your hands as dirty. The twins were sincere, incorrigible, and adorable. Maybe it was unrealistic to think they could do anything to help her, but they *had* somehow managed to get Jerry home two years ago, and Mary hadn't even been able to do that. There was no such thing as false hope if she was willing to open her heart to all possibilities—even the possibility that a pair of ten-year-olds could bring Jerry back to her and make all her deepest longings come true.

Chapter 2

"It's too cold. Let's go back."

Alfie turned around and pinned Benji with the stinkiest look he had ever given anybody. Benji was a *gute bruder*, but sometimes he didn't have enough of a commitment. "We've been gone for thirty minutes, Benji. Mamm won't even know we've run away unless we're gone for twenty-four hours."

"Tintin is cold too," Benji said, pointing to their dog who was running around and around them as if he couldn't be happier to be on an adventure with his two boys.

Alfie growled. "He doesn't look cold. He looks happy. Aren't you happy, Benji? We're finally going to prove to Mamm she can't push around her two youngest sons."

Benji stopped long enough to tie his bootlace. "But if we help Jerry and Mary get together, Jerry will move out, and we'll get our old room back. We don't have to build a fire or miss dinner or sleep in the snow."

Alfie reached into the plastic grocery bag he'd brought and pulled out the can of Spaghettios. "We don't have to miss dinner. And we can have Doritos for breakfast if we want. Mamm isn't here to tell us no. She isn't here to boss us around or make us sleep in the cellar."

Benji caught up to him. "I guess, but she's also not here to kiss us goodnight and open that can for us."

Alfie blew a puff of air from his lips in disgust. "We don't need Mamm to open cans for us. We're almost teenagers. We can take care of ourselves."

"But we didn't bring a can opener," Benji said.

Alfie stopped, realized Benji was right, and almost drop-kicked his bag of snacks. "Why didn't you tell me?"

"I just thought of it."

"Well, we can still eat the Doritos, and I brought a whole loaf of bread."

Benji shifted the sleeping bag on his shoulder. "Did you bring butter?"

Alfie gritted his teeth. Benji sure had a bad attitude. Alfie should have left him home to rot in the cellar. "It doesn't matter. This is going to be the funnest time of our life, and when we get home, Mamm will be so happy to see us, she'll put Jerry in the cellar and let us sleep in the room that is rightfully ours."

"I don't mind if Jerry sleeps in our old room. He needs a nice warm bed and people who love him. He's lost his faith in humidity."

"What about me?" Alfie snapped. "Maybe I've lost my faith in humility. Why can't I have a nice warm bed and people who love me too?"

Benji put his free arm around Alfie. "I love you, and our air mattress in the cellar is warmer than sleeping in the snow."

"It's warmer, but it's a house empty of love. Mamm doesn't understand us. When we don't show up for church tomorrow, then she'll understand." Alfie stepped over a rock in his path and pointed toward the pond. "We can build a fire in our cave and sleep nice and warm there."

Amish Christmas Cookie Tour

Elgin Pond was the perfect spot to camp. Not twenty feet from shore, there was a little cave just tall enough for Alfie and Benji to stand up in and wide enough for them to sleep side by side with Tintin between. They occasionally fished there in the summer and skated on the pond when it got really cold. The pond was a three-minute walk from the road, so a lot of other people liked to come here in the summer, but Alfie and Benji usually had it to themselves in the winter. They liked to come and build a wall of snow around the opening of their cave and pretend they were hiding from wolves and bears.

Tintin flinched as if someone had thrown a rock at him then took off in the direction of the cave, barking as if he'd spied a rabbit to chase. Alfie's heart lurched. There was a small campfire already burning right outside the opening of the cave, with thick, white smoke curling up into the sky. Whoever built that fire hadn't used dry wood. Damp wood always smoked something wonderful.

"Do you see that?" Benji said.

"*Jah*. Somebody's in our cave."

Benji frowned. "Let's go home. It might be a robber or a man with a pitchfork."

Alfie was angry enough to be brave. They needed that cave. "Mamm will never appreciate us if we go home now." He swallowed hard. "Maybe he'll go away if we ask him to."

Or maybe whoever was in there would stab them with his pitchfork.

Leaving Benji no choice but to follow, Alfie picked his way down the icy slope and around the shore to the cave. They crept up to the cave and peeked around the edge, which didn't make a lot of sense because Tintin was making so much noise, there wasn't any use in sneaking. A solitary figure in a worn blue coat sat cross-legged on the floor of the cave with his arms outstretched toward the fire. Brown strands of hair poked out from under his ratty green beanie, and his dark beard was trimmed close around his face. He startled Alfie and Benji when he looked up as if he'd been expecting them and gave them the kindest, liveliest smile Alfie had ever seen. "Well, look at you," he said. "Do you need to share my fire? It's super cold out here this morning." He extended his palm and invited Tintin to lick his hand. Tintin wagged his tail and let the stranger pet him.

Alfie checked to make sure there weren't any pitchforks, then sidled out from behind the wall. "Um, hey, this is our cave, and we need it."

Benji crept past Alfie until he was standing just a few feet away from the stranger. "You made a really good fire."

Benji didn't know anything. That fire was smoking like a chimney. The stranger hadn't even used dry wood.

Benji stuck out his hand and the stranger took it. What in the world was he doing? "My name is Benji Petersheim, and this is my brother Alfie."

"Nice to meet you," the man said, his smile widening. He had a raspy voice, like his throat was full of gravel. He was missing two teeth on the top, and his other teeth didn't look like they were going to be in his mouth much longer.

"Benji, we're not supposed to talk to strangers," Alfie scolded. All of a sudden, Benji didn't seem concerned about pitchforks.

Benji made a face. "Why not? Mamm talks to strangers all the time when they come to our house to buy peanut butter."

The man reached out his hand to Alfie. What could Alfie do but shake it? "You're right, Alfie. You can't be too careful these days. You're smart to bring your dog. I bet he's good protection." The stranger patted Tintin on the neck and smiled again. Alfie could tell he liked dogs. Someone who liked dogs couldn't be all bad. "My name is Campbell Smith. And now we're friends."

Alfie frowned. Knowing someone's name didn't make him a friend, but he didn't want to be rude and contradict him. Mamm would be mad if Alfie was disrespectful to an elder, even an elder who didn't seem that old. Then again, when was Mamm ever going to find out? "We don't know you. We can't be friends."

Campbell Smith nodded thoughtfully, like he wasn't mad that Alfie had been rude. Like he was thinking through what Alfie had said. "That's very smart, Alfie."

Alfie pulled his shoulder back. Campbell Smith had already called him smart twice. Not even Mamm had noticed what a good head Alfie had on his shoulders.

"It's good to be careful," Campbell said, "and I know I must look pretty bad. I've been hitchhiking for three days, and my ride dropped me off here last night."

"What does hishhiking mean?" Benji asked.

"Hitchhiking means I start walking to where I want to go, and I stick out my thumb when a car comes by. Sometimes the driver stops and gives me a ride. A truck driver picked me up in Green Bay and took me all the way to Pittsfield. From there I snagged a ride with a family in a van, a plumber, and a guy in a pickup truck. He made me sit in the back, and it was cold, but I was grateful for the ride."

Alfie had never heard of hitchhiking, but it sounded kind of fun. He'd have to try it the next time he and Benji went to school or even church.

Campbell Smith rubbed his hands together to generate some heat. "I'm super glad I found your cave to sleep in and super glad I had some matches on me, even though I don't smoke anymore. Thank you for letting me use your cave."

"You're welcome," Benji said, which was a thing to say. They hadn't given Campbell Smith permission to use anything.

"When I got out of the truck and stumbled onto this cave, it felt like a miracle."

Benji nodded. "We gave Mary Yutzy a Christmas miracle once."

Campbell Smith's eyebrows traveled up his forehead. They were so bushy, they looked like two caterpillars crawling up sideways. "Then you know about miracles. If we do our best and trust in the Good Lord, He always makes everything work out just right, no matter what."

Alfie scoffed. "No, He doesn't. He won't give us a new bedroom, and that's all I've wanted for three years."

Campbell pulled his knees up to his chest and laced his fingers around his shins. "Well, Alfie, it's cuz you're not looking at things with a heavenly perspective. God works in mysterious ways, and He isn't usually so obvious as to just give you what you ask for. He ain't a vending machine, even if some people treat Him like one. When you ask for something, or want something really bad, God usually gives you what you need, not what you want. He might not give you a new bedroom, but He might give you a warm place to sleep and parents who love you enough to take care of you."

"Our *mamm* doesn't love us. She makes us sleep in the cellar."

Campbell Smith pursed his lips as if he were trying not to smile. "That must be hard."

"We're going to die of spiders."

There was a sorry pile of twigs and sticks sitting next to Campbell. He picked up a stick, pointed it at Alfie, and tossed it onto the fire. "Your teeth are chattering. Get closer to the heat. You too, Benji."

Benji didn't even hesitate. He set down the sleeping bag and slid his backpack off his shoulders, sat down, and scooted as close to the flames as he could get without catching fire. Alfie set his bag in the dirt and made sure to sit across the fire from Campbell, even though that put him outside in the breeze. Tintin sat on his haunches opposite Benji. They had the fire surrounded on all four sides.

Benji reached into his backpack. "Are you hungry?"

Campbell sighed as if he had been waiting for Benji to ask that question. "So hungry. I haven't eaten since Thursday."

Benji pulled a whole package of Oreos from the backpack.

Alfie just about had a heart attack. "Where did you get those?"

"Mamm keeps them in the top drawer under the pencils."

Alfie's jaw dropped. That's where Mamm hid the Oreos? He'd looked for her stash too many times to count. "Why didn't you tell me?"

"Mamm told me not to." Benji handed the whole package to Campbell then pulled two squishy-looking bananas from the front pocket and handed them to Campbell. "You should probably eat something healthy before you eat the cookies."

"Thank you so much," Campbell said, looking truly grateful. And why wouldn't he be? Benji had given him a whole package of Alfie's favorite cookie ever in the whole world and hadn't offered Alfie a single one.

Alfie threw a twig into the fire, but there really was no hope. "Do you live around here, Campbell Smith?"

Campbell's eyes were twinkly, like Mary Yutzy's, as if he felt happy and warm, even though he was sitting in a cave and it was December. But he did have Oreos. "Now that we know each other better, you can call me Soup."

Benji leaned back on his hands. "Soup? Is that your nickname?"

Campbell nodded. "Yes. You know, like Campbell's soup?"

"Our *mamm* only buys Campbell's soup. She says it's the best." Alfie tried his question again. "Do you live in Bienenstock?" Once he said it, he realized it was a *dumm* question. If Soup lived in Bienenstock, he wouldn't be sitting here in their cave.

Soup finished the first banana. "I'll tell you boys, and I'm not proud to say it, but I don't have a home. Five years ago, I did some bad things, and my mom kicked me out of my house."

A lump grew in Alfie's throat. Soup's *mamm* had kicked him out? At least their *mamm* had let them sleep in the cellar, even though Alfie had set two smoke bombs and gotten stuck in a tree and burned down a shed, and melted her card table. "Didn't she love you?"

"I think she loved me very much, but when someone won't stop hurting you, you have to get them out of your life."

Benji's bottom lip trembled. "You…you hurt your *mamm*?"

"She tried to help me, but I got addicted to drugs, and I started stealing money from her. She asked me to leave. She had to protect herself and my brother." His smile faded to nothing. "Not a day goes by that I don't regret how I broke my mom's heart."

Alfie swallowed hard. Had he hurt his *mamm* by running away? He had wanted to teach her a lesson, but maybe she was home right now, lying on her bed crying her eyes out because Alfie and Benji were gone. Would she kick him out of the house? What if she didn't love him anymore?

Campbell Smith sat quietly for a few minutes. It seemed he wasn't even considering getting out of their cave. It didn't seem nice to ask him to leave, especially when he didn't have anywhere else to sleep.

"So do you always live in caves?" Benji asked.

"No. Sometimes I sleep on the street. Sometimes I sleep at the shelter." He cleared his throat. "I've been in jail too."

Alfie's heart nearly jumped out of his chest. "Jail! Are you a criminal?"

Soup chuckled softly. "I guess so, but that was a long time ago, and I'm trying to be a better person. I'm trying to make amends for all the bad things I done to people. I know I've got a long ways to go, but I want to be someone my mom can be proud of."

"What are amends?"

"It means I'm trying to fix mistakes and give back what I took from people, whether it be money or trust."

Benji nodded. "Like when Mamm made us pay for the card table or when Andrew made us smooth out the tire tracks after the fire truck drove on Bitsy's lawn."

Soup's lips curled upward. "Just like that. I came to Bienenstock to find someone and ask for their forgiveness. I screwed up and betrayed his trust, and I think I singlehandedly destroyed his faith in humanity."

Benji's head shot up. "Jerry Zimmerman?"

Soup caught his breath. "You know him?"

"Of course we know him. He's the only guy around here who's lost his faith in humidity."

Chapter 3

"Baking is a lot more creative than I expected," Jerry said, his lips curling slightly as he sprinkled a few more mint chocolate chips into the cookie dough. "These triple chocolate chip cookies are going to be *appeditlich*. I don't wonder but we'll sell out."

The Amish Christmas cookie tour was turning out to be a wonderful *gute* idea. The community was enthusiastic about the idea, Mary was trying out new recipes, and Jerry was much less gloomy than she'd seen him all week. He still acted as if he had a cloud hanging over his head, but the cloud wasn't as black as it was on Saturday. It was all Alfie and Benji Petersheim's doing. Mary would have to give those boys a big kiss and a free donut a day for the rest of their lives.

Jerry stole her breath when he leaned close to her ear and whispered, "Am I allowed to sample the dough, Chef Mary?" He drew back and winked at her, then nudged his arm against hers. It was more affection than he'd shown her in years.

For sure and certain, Jerry was trying to be cheerful, but he had never been of a lighthearted disposition. It was almost as if he felt guilty for being happy when there was so much suffering in the world. It was why he'd left Bienenstock in the first place, because he'd wanted to make a difference, to help people who couldn't help themselves. Whatever he'd seen out there had shoved him to the ground and stomped on his tender heart. The thought made Mary want to cry. But she wouldn't cry because she was determined to savor every minute she had with Jerry and enjoy every smile he gave her, no matter how fleeting it might be. He seemed happy to be helping her with cookie dough, and his mood gave her confidence that better days were ahead. Mary would hold fast to even a thin thread of hope. Hope was all she had.

On Saturday, Mary had taken Jerry with her to visit twenty-seven homes and businesses in the area to ask them to participate in Bienenstock's first annual Amish Christmas cookie tour. She'd planned on holding the cookie tour Thursday after next and ending on Saturday night, December sixteenth. Tickets were twenty dollars a person, and that ticket got customers a punch pass good for one free cookie at every location. Fourteen Amish neighbors who didn't own businesses agreed to host visitors for the cookie tour and make cookies to hand out. The Millers and the Troyers had offered to give people tours of their homes, which Mary hoped would bring in a lot more customers. Englischers were curious about the Amish, and a home tour was a very attractive incentive to buy a ticket.

Folks were going to get a cream cheese cookie at Kanagy's Diary; cookies, honey, and beeswax at Bitsy Kiem's farm; peanut butter cookies at the Petersheim house; and a warm chocolate chip cookie at Austin and Hannah's market. Even Raymond Glick at Glick's Family Market had agreed to participate, though he greatly disliked the Petersheims and just about everybody else in town. As a businessman, he saw the benefit of drawing customers to his store with the promise of a free cookie.

Rebecca Petersheim blew into Austin's store with a chilly breeze carrying a medium-sized box. She nudged the door closed with her foot.

Jerry quickly wiped his hands and strode around the counter. "Here, Rebecca, let me help you with that."

Rebecca gratefully handed him the box and took off her scarf and coat. "*Denki*, Jerry. I wanted to send this box with you earlier this morning, but I hadn't finished applying the labels, so I had to wait." Jerry set the box on the bakery counter.

Hannah looked up from the cash register. "*Gute morgen*, Rebecca. What have you got for us?"

"It's eight more jars. Austin said you were out."

Hannah took a jar of peanut butter from the box. "Completely out. I could use another dozen, if you can spare them."

Rebecca was always overjoyed when people bought her peanut butter. She nodded and propped her hands on her hips. "I'll make another batch as soon as I get home. You're selling more this month than last Christmas."

Mary came around the counter and draped her arm over Hannah's shoulder. "Hannah is a business genius. She created a fancy Christmas gift basket with Petersheim Brothers Peanut Butter, Honeybee Sisters Honey, and two jars of homemade jam tied up with a pinecone and a red Christmas ribbon. She put together twelve baskets, and we sold all twelve in less than two days."

Hannah grinned. "I wouldn't say I'm a genius."

"I would," Austin said, just coming up the stairs. "It's a wonderful-*gute* Christmas gift. If it weren't for Hannah, I would have gone out of business months ago yet. It wonders me if I ever would have started a store at all."

Rebecca nodded pointedly at Austin. "I'm just grateful Hannah agreed to marry you. She could have done much better."

Austin's jaw dropped. "I thought I was your favorite son."

Rebecca reached out and patted Austin's cheek. "You are definitely one of my favorites, even though you can be quite dense sometimes."

Jerry laughed. Mary loved the sound of it. "He got a lot smarter after he married Hannah."

"*Jah,*" Rebecca said. "He's turned out quite well. And he's always been handsome." She pointed to the bowl of cookie dough Jerry and Mary were stirring. "What are you making today?"

Jerry grabbed a spoon from the drawer, scooped a spoonful of dough from the bowl, and handed it to Rebecca. "Try it. We're making triple chocolate chip cookies for the Christmas Cookie Tour. We're going to form the dough into balls and freeze them, then bake them on the first day of the cookie tour. That way, they'll be warm out of the oven when we hand them out. We're also making plain chocolate chip cookies, snickerdoodles, and molasses crinkles to sell. I think people will like them."

Watching Jerry's face, Mary couldn't help but melt like a pat of butter on a summer's day. His eyes glowed with warmth as if he didn't mind making cookie dough, as if maybe he'd set aside his troubles for the pleasure of this moment with the people who loved him best.

Mary smiled up at him. "I am thinking about trying some stained-glass window cookies."

"Pastor Andrea used to make those...," he said, the light fading from his eyes.

His look was so mournful, Mary couldn't help but ask, "Is she okay?"

"*Ach,* I haven't seen her for almost a year," he mumbled.

But hadn't Jerry just been in New York working with Pastor Andrea at the homeless shelter? Mary didn't want to ask and ruin the moment.

It seemed no one else wanted to ask either, and they stood in awkward silence until Rebecca, who was braver than all of them, huffed out a breath and changed the subject. "I'm going upstairs to see your Christmas quilt display. Austin says it's breathtaking."

Austin burst into a smile. "It really is. Hannah and Mary made it look like a Christmas wonderland up there." He gestured to Jerry. "Will you come down to the storage room and help me move a couple of heavy boxes."

Jerry seemed to recover from the gloom that had briefly overtaken him. He gave Austin a stuttering smile. "*Jah*. We need another bag of flour too."

Jerry and Austin tromped down the stairs as Rebecca climbed up to the second floor. Hannah watched until Jerry and Austin were out of sight. "*Vell?* Jerry seems a little less depressed today."

"He's discovered he likes making cookies. I don't know if I should get my hopes up or plan for the worst. But maybe I'm just going to jump in with both feet and enjoy being together."

Hannah brushed some flour off Mary's sleeve. "That's a wonderful *gute* idea. I know you don't want to hear this, but if Jerry loses his head and leaves for good, he doesn't deserve you."

"It doesn't make me feel any better, but you're nice to try."

Hannah giggled. "I think what you meant to say is, 'Hannah, keep your mouth shut.'"

"Of course not. I want to hear your opinion, no matter how much it hurts."

"*Ach, vell*," Hannah said, "I hope it doesn't hurt."

Mary grimaced. "It pinches just a little." They whispered because there were two Englisch customers in the store. The man was squeezing the tomatoes, and an older woman was checking out their selection of organic dairy products.

The door blew open again, and Alfie and Benji Petersheim marched into the store with an old man following behind them. The old man gave Mary a friendly, gapped-tooth smile and a purposefully casual, yet awkward, wave as if he feared he was breaking some rule just setting foot in the store.

Alfie and Benji came to the store often, but not in the middle of a school day. Mary narrowed her eyes. "What are you boys doing here? Aren't you supposed to be in school?"

Benji crossed his feet and nibbled on his fingernail, but Alfie seemed unashamed, like a puppy that had just chewed someone's favorite slippers to shreds. "We had something more important to do today."

Mary tilted her head to one side and tried for a stern look, but it was almost impossible to be cross with Alfie and Benji. They were just too cute. "You're not running away again, are you?"

"It's too cold," Benji said. "We only lasted two hours and then we gave up and went home."

Alfie scowled at Benji. "We did not give up. Soup needed the cave more than we did, and all our Oreos were gone." Alfie motioned to the old man when he said "soup," but Mary had no idea what he was talking about.

Oh, wait. Mary took a closer look. That wasn't an old man with Alfie and Benji. His clothes were ragged, he wore a frayed and filthy Green Bay Packers beanie on his head, and he was missing some teeth, but he wasn't as old as he looked. There were no gray streaks in his shaggy, chin-length chestnut hair, and his face was smooth with no wrinkles. He could have been around Jerry's age. His cheeks were red with weather burn, and he had several days' growth of whiskers on his face, but there was a kind, wounded air about him, and Mary took pity on him. Whoever he was, he looked friendless, homeless, and pathetic.

Mary felt extraordinarily sorry for him, and he hadn't said a word. In fact, he had migrated to the pellet stove and was warming his hands, leaning so close it looked as if he were going to kiss the chimney pipe.

Alfie fisted the man's coat sleeve and pulled him toward Mary and Hannah. It was strange to see a ten-year-old leading a grown man around. "This is Campbell, but his friends call him Soup."

Campbell had a hundred-dollar smile, even though he was missing two teeth in the front. "Sorry to barge in, but Alfie and Benji said it would be okay. They say their brother owns this store and wouldn't mind if I came." He lowered his eyes but didn't lose his smile. "I'm sure I look a little rougher than your usual customer."

"He came cuz he wants to talk to Jerry," Benji said. "To apologize to him for ruining his faith in humidity."

"It's humility, Benji," Alfie hissed.

Mary's stomach twisted into a tight knot. "You know Jerry?"

"Yeah. I came all the way from Green Bay to see him. Is he here?"

"Alfie and Benji Petersheim, why aren't you in school?" Rebecca stood on the bottom step with her arms folded and fiery darts shooting out of her eyes at her two incorrigible sons. "You'd better start explaining before I make you muck out the barn for the rest of your lives."

Alfie tried really hard for a smile, but he only managed to look constipated. "Mamm, what are you doing here?"

Rebecca cocked an eyebrow. "Didn't expect to see me?"

Benji was less devious than Alfie, and he always tried to smooth things over and make peace, especially with his *mater*. "We had to miss school, Mamm. You always tell us it's more important to help our fellow man than to be smart."

Rebecca didn't soften one little bit. "Don't put words in my mouth, young man. No son of mine is going to grow up to be a *dummkopf*. How can you help your fellow man if you don't know how to read?"

"I know how to read," Benji mumbled.

Rebecca snapped like a turtle. "Don't change the subject."

Alfie was clever, and he had an answer for everything. "They're not doing anything at school today but assigning parts for the Christmas program."

Rebecca looked skeptical. "They're not doing anything else? No arithmetic? No spelling? No reading?"

Alfie forged ahead, probably because he couldn't defend himself. "That's right, and me and Benji don't want to be in the Christmas program anyway."

Benji's face fell. "I want to be the friendly farmer."

Alfie glared at Benji. "You can be the friendly farmer next year. We have to help our fellow man."

Rebecca pulled a tissue from her coat pocket and licked it then strode across the room and wiped a smudge off Benji's cheek with the moist tissue. Benji grimaced. "You boys are a mess, and no son of mine will be a Christmas program slacker. I'm taking you to school right now and you're going to apologize to your teacher and beg her for parts in the Christmas program."

"But Mamm," Benji whined. "Campbell Soup has to talk to Jerry."

Rebecca finished mopping up Benji's face and zeroed in on Alfie next. "To think I took pity on you this morning and drove you to school in the warm buggy. You betrayed my trust, and that's worse than anything else."

"I'm sorry, Mamm," Benji said.

Alfie made a face when his *mamm's* damp tissue touched his skin. "It's more important to help your fellow man than to tell your *mamm* all your secrets."

A vein bulged in Rebecca's neck, and she pulled her tissue back from Alfie's face. "There is nothing more important than telling your *mamm* the truth, young man." She shook her finger adamantly. "Don't you ever let me hear you even breathe such a thought again. And for goodness' sake, you don't have to choose between two goods. You can tell your *mamm* the truth and help your fellow man. Every. Day."

Benji glanced at Alfie and swiped his hand down his cheek, putting another smudge on his newly-cleaned face. "I told you so."

Rebecca took one look at Benji and growled in frustration. She pulled another tissue from her pocket and cleaned Benji's face again. "How did you two get all this way from the school? It's an hour walk."

Alfie stood up straighter. "We hitchhiked."

"You...hitchhiked," Rebecca spoke in a relatively calm voice, but Mary could tell she was on the verge of a heart attack.

Benji nodded. "You should try it, Mamm. You just walk on the road and stick out your thumb, and people pick you up. Campbell taught us."

Rebecca's head snapped up, and her gaze found Campbell Soup like a well-aimed bullet. If looks could strike someone to the ground, Campbell would have immediately been flat on his back. "You took my boys hitchhiking?" she said, barely containing her rage. The two customers still in the store abandoned all pretense of shopping and stared at Rebecca.

Campbell smiled through gritted teeth and took two steps backward, for sure and certain attempting to escape Rebecca's wrath. "I'm sorry. I really need to talk to Jerry, and these boys said they'd help me."

"You let my boys hitchhike like two vagabonds?"

"It's okay, Mamm," Benji said. "A nice lady picked us up and drove us all the way to the store."

Rebecca practically snarled at Benji. "Don't change the subject, young man." She again turned her wrath on Campbell Soup...was that really his name? "Did you stop to consider that my boys could have been murdered or kidnapped or run over?"

Campbell looked down at his feet as if he were a ten-year-old delinquent just like Alfie and Benji. "I'm sorry you're upset, but we were perfectly safe. I do it all the time."

"That's no excuse, young man." Rebecca propped her hands on her hips and looked Campbell up and down. "Who are you, and how did my boys end up hitchhiking with you this morning?"

Benji sidled close to Rebecca and wrapped his arms around her elbow. "He's our fellow man, and we're helping him. He ruined Jerry's faith in humidity."

"Humility," Alfie growled.

"Humanity," Campbell said, his eyes darting between Rebecca and Alfie. Rebecca's anger flared to life behind her eyes, and Campbell shut his mouth tight. Mary had never seen Rebecca so angry, even when the twins had set Emmon Gile's shed on fire and burned it to the ground.

"What are you doing here?" Jerry's voice was like a cold, sharp knife. Mary hadn't even heard him come up the stairs. Campbell turned around. Austin stood behind and slightly to the left of Jerry with a curiously worried look on his face, while Jerry was as straight and stiff as a post, flour sack slung over his shoulder, his hair and face dusted with the fine white powder. He set the flour sack on the floor, balled his hands into fists, and stared at Campbell as if Campbell were the Devil himself.

Mary's mouth went dry, and her heart felt as heavy as a boulder. She'd loved Jerry for years and had never seen him get angry or irritated or even mildly annoyed. He was kind and compassionate and would never dream of hurting another living soul. Now, here was the man she loved, with fire blazing in his eyes and hot anger melting his bones. Mary thought it entirely possible that Jerry would lash out with all his rage and do Campbell some sort of harm.

Campbell must have seen it too. He raised his hands and backed away from Jerry, even though moving away from Jerry put him closer to Rebecca. "Jerry, hey. Um, it's good to see you."

"You need to leave now and never come back," Jerry said softly. It sounded more like a threat than a suggestion.

A shiver traveled down Mary's spine. She couldn't think of one word to say that might calm the tension in the room. Hannah was completely silent. Even Rebecca seemed to have been struck *dumm*.

Frowning, Benji unhooked himself from his *mamm* and wrapped his hands around Jerry's arm. "Jerry, this is Campbell Soup. He needs to say sorry."

Jerry's gaze connected with Benji's, and he softened ever so slightly. "Benji, you are a *gute* boy, but Soup needs to go."

"But he wants to apologize," Alfie said quietly as if he feared saying it louder would further provoke Jerry.

A muscle in Jerry's jaw pulsed up and down. "He doesn't need to apologize. I've forgiven him." He pinned Campbell with an intense gaze. "For everything."

Mary didn't know what Campbell had done to Jerry, but it was as plain as day that Jerry hadn't forgiven Campbell for anything. Jerry was the most miserable creature Mary had ever seen.

Campbell took a tiny step forward. "Look, Jerry…"

Jerry stiffened like ice in the dead of winter. "No, Soup. Go now or I'll call the police."

Mary held her breath. The threat of the police was serious. What had Campbell done?

Campbell shook his head and started walking backward, nudging past Rebecca on his way to the door. The Englisch woman still in the store squeaked and shuffled out of his way. "Look, Jerry, I'm really sorry. If you'd just let me explain…"

Jerry's glare should have struck Campbell dead. "Go. I won't ask again."

Campbell bowed his head in defeat and turned and slid out the door. Alfie darted after him. "Me and Benji will make sure he gets back okay."

Rebecca shouted and stopped Alfie in his tracks. "You're not going anywhere except back to school and then straight home to muck out the barn for the rest of your lives."

Jerry pulled Benji close to his side and gave him a squeeze. "It's okay, Benji. Are you hurt? Did he hurt you?"

Benji looked puzzled and distressed. "He didn't hurt me. He was nice. Why don't you like him? Why do you want to call the police?"

"We rode in a police car once," Alfie said.

Rebecca wrapped her arms around Alfie. Mary didn't know if she was trying to hug him or smother him. Surely…surely, she wasn't trying to smother him. "If you ever go hitchhiking again, I'll give you the spatula." She nudged him away from her, cupped her hands around his shoulders, and looked him in the eye. "Do you understand? No hitchhiking and no talking to strangers. I thought I taught you better than that."

"You did teach us better, Mamm," Benji said. "You said that sometimes we don't realize that strangers are angels so we should always be nice to them. And you said we should help our fellow man. We just wanted to help."

Jerry pressed his lips into a hard line. "Be *froh* the boys are safe. Soup is dangerous and untrustworthy."

"Dangerous?" Rebecca gestured for Benji to come to her, and she gathered both boys in her arms. This time it was definitely a hug. "You are *gute* boys," she said, lingering with her arms around them. Then her expression changed from loving mother to angry bear. "But you broke two commandments today. You lied, and you didn't honor your *fater* and *mater*."

Alfie had apparently had enough hugging, and he wriggled from his *mater's* grasp. "Can't you be happy that we kept the other eight?"

She gave him the stink eye. "Don't try to squirm out of your sins, Alfie Petersheim. Besides, I'm not so sure you didn't break four or five other commandments today. Just remember I'm watching you. All the time."

Alfie scrunched his lips to one side of his face and slumped his shoulders. "*Jah*. We know."

Jerry pointed to Alfie and Benji. "This is very important, boys. Stay away from Campbell. He's a very bad man."

Benji half-closed one eye and scratched his head. "Mamm says there are no bad people, just bad choices."

Jerry sighed impatiently. "Just stay away from him. He's made some very bad choices."

Alfie stuck out his bottom lip. "But we like him. We let him share our Oreos, and we sat around the fire. He taught us how to hitchhike, and he gave Tintin part of his breakfast."

"LaWayne," Rebecca corrected. "I named that dog LaWayne."

Mary stifled a smile. Tintin had been a stray dog that Alfie and Benji had secretly adopted a couple of years ago. Their *mamm* had agreed to let them keep the dog if they agreed to name it LaWayne. The boys still called their dog Tintin when Rebecca wasn't around.

"LaWayne," Alfie said, before shutting his mouth. Mary wouldn't have been able to pry it open with a crowbar. Alfie liked to argue with his *mamm*, but he knew better than to contradict her about the dog. Rebecca thought Tintin-LaWayne was a nuisance.

Rebecca wasn't one to get distracted for long. "I don't care what you think about Campbell. You are not to go near him again. Do you understand?"

"Okay," Benji groaned.

"Alfie?"

"Okay. We won't go near him." He emphasized "near" as if that word carried some sort of loophole. Mary wouldn't be surprised if Alfie went home and looked up "near" in the dictionary, just to figure out what he could get away with.

Rebecca put her coat back on and snatched the boys' hands. "I'm taking you two to school, and if you've missed out on parts for the Christmas program, you have no one to blame but yourself."

She was still lecturing them about friendly farmers and Christmas songs when they left the store and closed the door behind them.

Austin laid a hand on Jerry's shoulder. "You okay?"

Jerry nodded slowly. "If Campbell ever comes in again, get rid of him as soon as you can. He'll steal all the money out of the cash register if he gets a chance."

Worry lines etched themselves around Austin's eyes. "Okay. One of us should always be here just for safety."

Mary eyed Jerry as if seeing him for the first time. Who was this suspicious, angry, resentful man standing next to her? Did she even know him anymore? He stared right back, something raw and fresh shining in his eyes.

Hannah cleared her throat. "Um, Austin, we should inventory the milk so we can send Will our order."

Austin's gaze darted from Jerry to Mary. "Uh, for sure and certain. I'll get a notebook."

Hannah and Austin practically crept to the refrigerated section, whispering as if they were in a library and didn't want to disturb anyone. Mary rang up two loaves of bread and a tomato for the Englisch man, and he left the store. With a furtive look, the woman slipped out behind him. They probably wouldn't see her at the Plain and Simple Country Store ever again.

Jerry hovered around her at the cash register watching her put the money in the correct slots in the till. He scrubbed his hand down the side of his face. "I guess you want to know what that was about."

Mary wasn't sure what to say. Should she scold him for being so unforgiving? Give him a lecture about anger and bitterness? Hold his hand and assure him she understood what he was going through? Try to give him comfort?

She drew in a deep breath and laced her fingers through his. Her gaze connected with Hannah's, and they nodded to each other. "Let's go upstairs and sit." She pulled him up the stairs to the rooms where Austin and Hannah sold Amish handicrafts, quilts, crocheted dish rags, and painted milk cans. In one of the rooms sat a beautiful cherry-wood table and chairs Austin's *bruder* Andrew and their *dat* had built. Hannah had set a "SOLD" placard on the table just this morning. An Englisch couple from Shawano had paid for it, and they were coming on Saturday with a truck to pick it up. Mary gestured for Jerry to pull out a chair, and they sat down.

Jerry literally perched on the edge of his seat as if it was impossible for him to let his guard down for even a second. "I'm sorry, Mary. You haven't seen my angry side, but there's no use hiding it. That's what I'm like now, angry, mad all the time, and hopeless. I just don't care anymore. You don't want to marry me. I'll make you miserable from the very first day."

"I don't believe it."

"It's true. I can't make you happy, Mary."

Mary couldn't keep her voice from shaking. "I don't believe any of it. You say you don't care, but in truth, you care so deeply that the emotion is eating you away from the inside. This is not who you are, and you could never make me miserable." She reached out and caressed his cheek. He flinched but didn't pull back. Then he closed his eyes as if savoring her touch. "I have loved you forever, Jerry. Do you know how happy you made me the day you came into my life?"

He opened his eyes and scoffed. "I've made you miserable, Mary, and believe it or not, that thought tortured me every day. First I left Bienenstock without telling you, then I went to Mexico for missionary work. Tell me the truth. You felt I'd abandoned you. You wondered if I really loved you, wondered why I hadn't chosen to stay if I loved you as I said I did. Don't deny you felt the rejection clear to your bones."

Mary bowed her head. "It was hard, I admit it. But I never stopped hoping, never stopped loving you. If anything, my love for you grew with each letter."

He shook his head. "I've been gone for two years, Mary. You have borne the brunt of my selfishness. How you must hate me for abandoning you!"

"I don't hate you. I just told you, I love you with all my heart."

He buried his face in his hands. "All those wasted years. It was all for nothing, and now I'm not fit to be your husband. I don't deserve you. I was never *gute* enough before, and now I'm even less worthy. I left you and went to Mexico to find my life's purpose. All I found was loss and violence and despair."

"You never said any of this in your letters."

He wiped an errant tear from his face. "I didn't want to tell you. It would have crushed you."

"Maybe I'm stronger than you think." Mary took his hand again and kissed his knuckles. Jerry wasn't unworthy. He was wounded. And wounds could be healed with time, care, and affection. And Jesus. Jesus could heal anything.

The corner of his mouth twitched. "You are much stronger than I thought."

"Then talk to me. I want to know everything."

He pulled his hand from her grasp. "The honest truth is that I don't recognize this bitter person I've become. I'm ashamed of myself for feeling anger and resentment, but I can't help it. I'm just so mad. I'm mad at the world, I'm mad at myself, I'm mad at Gotte."

"Your emotions are just feelings. They're neither good nor bad. Don't be ashamed of your feelings, and don't beat yourself up for having emotions. That makes you human, like the rest of us. I like that you have one or two flaws. I couldn't marry a man who's perfect. It would be very aggravating to never be able to win an argument."

Amusement flitted across his face, followed by frustration. "Mary, I can't marry you."

She ignored the prick in her heart. "If you're going to reject me, then I deserve to know why."

"I would never reject you. I'm protecting you from a life of misery."

"Don't you think I should decide for myself?"

He closed his eyes momentarily and huffed out a breath. "As you know, I was in Mexico for a year. I wrote you nice, comfortable letters about building schools for orphans and installing water systems for some of the villages, but reality was much harsher. We were often robbed at gunpoint. One of the missionaries was severely beaten for his wallet. The villagers are so poor and under the thumb of some very evil people. There was only suffering everywhere I looked, and it didn't matter how many schools I built or how much food I handed out, the efforts seemed so futile, like trying to stop a river with my arm. Gotte wouldn't do anything. He abandoned all of us, and I grew bitter at his lack of interest in our little corner of the world."

Mary wanted to argue, to insist that Gotte was faithful still, but Jerry had opened his heart and she refused to say anything that would make him close it up again. "I'm sorry there was so much suffering."

"I gave up hope, but I was ashamed for losing my faith, so I never told you. Maybe I should have returned to Wisconsin then, but I was more confused than ever, and I didn't want you to see me like that. As I told you in my letters, I went back to New York and started working with Pastor Andrea again at her homeless shelter. Three months later, she asked me and two others to move to Green Bay to open a halfway house."

Mary's insides dropped as if she were on a plunging roller coaster. "You moved to Green Bay?"

His eyes confirmed the truth. "I didn't lie to you, but I didn't want you to know I was so close. I didn't want you to come and see me, not looking like that." He pressed his fingers to his forehead. "Not looking like this."

Mary tried to mask the hurt in her heart. "So you've been in Green Bay for almost a year?" An hour away this whole time, and he hadn't told her.

"It was a small halfway house, and Pastor Andrea asked me to run it. I was in charge of everything; the money, the supplies, the food. I felt like my life meant something again, like I could really, truly make a difference." His expression darkened. "But I was naïve and unqualified. Pastor Andrea chose the wrong person, and I failed her."

The raw pain on his face was heartbreaking. It was clear that Jerry despised no one more than himself.

"That's where I met Campbell. We called him Soup. He's an addict, but he said he'd been clean for six months."

"What does 'clean' mean?"

"It means he was off drugs and alcohol. He lived at our facility because his mom had kicked him out of the house." Jerry hung his head. "We became friends. We were the best of friends actually. He was funny and kind and a truly *wunderbarr* person. He was really trying to change his life."

"And he betrayed you somehow," Mary mumbled, more to herself than Jerry.

"One night, he came to me in an absolute panic. He told me he hadn't used drugs in several months, but that he still owed a former drug dealer a thousand dollars. He claimed if he didn't pay, the dealer would kill him. I pulled every last penny I had from my small bank account and another three hundred dollars from the halfway house's funds. I was still short three hundred dollars, but I figured seven hundred would be enough to save Soup's life. Soup assured me that he was coming into some money the following week, and that no one would ever know I'd taken the three hundred dollars to begin with. Soup and I were going to go together to meet the dealer and give him the money."

Jerry closed his eyes and winced, as if the memory itself was painful. "That night, Soup never showed up. I went to the meeting place myself, hoping he would be there, but it was just his dealer and two other men. The dealer was furious that I only had seven hundred dollars, and he and his two buddies beat me up. They took the money, stabbed me in the gut, and broke my jaw."

Mary gasped. Jerry had been through more than she could ever have imagined.

"I spent three weeks in the hospital with my jaw wired shut and a drainage tube stuck in my abdomen. I got a bad infection, and I couldn't eat anything except what I could suck through a straw."

"I'm so sorry," was all she could say, because "Why didn't you contact me?" was water under the bridge, even though the thought of his languishing in the hospital by himself was inexpressibly painful. Even more painful was the thought that he *could* have called her and chose not to.

He must have guessed what she was thinking. "I didn't want you to see me like that, Mary. I was ashamed. I deserved everything I got, and I didn't want you to know how far I had fallen."

"Nobody deserves to suffer violence. Nobody."

He shook his head. "I did everything wrong, broke every rule. You never give an addict money and never believe any story he tells you. I knew better than to walk blindly into a dangerous situation, but I did it because Soup was my friend. I thought I was protecting him, and I thought he would have my back. Before I got out of the hospital, Pastor Andrea fired me, as she should have. After that, I had nothing."

Mary looked down at her hands and tried to ignore the sting. "You had me. You will always have me."

He seemed irritated by her words. "I don't deserve you."

Mary wasn't usually one to get angry, but up until a week ago, her temper had always been shorter than Jerry's. She had always been the one who was passionate and enthusiastic, the one who sometimes let her enthusiasm, or her aggravation, run amok. She was the one who tried to milk the most out of life and relationships. The one who laughed too loud, had too much fun, or bawled like a baby when she felt like it, not caring what other people thought of her. Jerry had always been more reserved, more measured and steady. He was the flagpole, and she was the flag, waving in the breeze and attracting all the attention.

She wanted the old Jerry back.

A new thought hit her so hard, she felt dizzy.

Jerry was intent on proving he wasn't the old Jerry anymore. Did he want her to reject him so he had something else to beat himself up about? Or would it be easier for him if *she* made the decision to let him go? Maybe he even believed he was being unselfish, but Mary knew better. He wanted to wallow in his self-loathing the rest of his life, and throwing Mary's love away only proved how little he loved himself.

Mary could not, would not, let that happen. She loved Jerry too much to let him go so easily. "Do you know why we add salt to cookies?"

Confusion flitted across his face. He hadn't been expecting the sudden change of subject. "Um, *nae*."

"Every good baker knows that if you leave out the salt, the cookies won't taste as *gute*, even with cups and cups of sugar. Do you know why I use semi-sweet chocolate chips in my triple chocolate chip cookies?"

He blew a small puff of air from between his lips as his mouth curved upward. "I don't know, but I like them. Milk chocolate chips with white chocolate chips and mint chocolate chips is too sweet."

She nodded. "That's a very *gute* answer."

He grunted. "A *gute* answer for what?"

She reached out and took his hand. "Life can't be sugar all the time. Sometimes you need salt and lemons and vinegar. Sometimes you need the salty to contrast with the syrupy. The tart balances out the sweet."

"But nobody wants bitter or rancid or moldy. That's what my life has been."

Mary couldn't keep an errant smile from forming on her lips. "I'm not sure what a moldy life looks like, but I know we can't appreciate the sweet unless Gotte gives us bitter. We can't know love unless we know loss and betrayal. We won't learn anything *gute* without first fighting through opposition. What have you learned from your tragic experiences?"

He leaned back in his chair. "I've learned that I can't trust anyone, that Gotte has abandoned the whole miserable world, that people trying to do *gute* are wasting their time."

"That's not completely true, and deep down, you know it. You can trust me. You can trust Austin and Hannah. The people in this community love you. You can trust us, even your parents. I'm guessing you still believe you can trust Pastor Andrea, even though she fired you."

"*Jah,*" he mumbled. "I can trust her."

She was *froh* he would admit to that much. "Maybe you can't see it, but I don't believe for one minute that Gotte has abandoned anyone. You were stabbed, but your life was spared, and you came back to me. I know you saw miracles in Mexico and Green Bay. You're honest enough to admit that."

He fell silent and gazed out the window at the snow glistening in the sun. After a minute, he said, "I suppose you're right."

"Tell me."

"A mugger tried to shoot me, and the gun misfired. And in Mexico the food always went further than was physically possible. Sometimes it was like Jesus feeding the five thousand."

"I missed you something wonderful," she said, "but I was also convinced that you were doing *gute* things. That you were following Gotte's plan. I would never say you wasted your time. I'm certain your service touched many lives."

His countenance fell. "It's all over now."

"Jerry, you are twenty-four years old. Your life is just beginning, and it can be anything you want it to be."

"Even if I don't deserve happiness after what I've done?"

"It doesn't have anything to do with deserving. We all sin and fall short of the glory of Gotte. Your mistakes can be great or small, but Jesus would never cast you off." She looked him squarely in the eye. "Neither will I. If you want to leave, that is your decision, but I won't make it easier on you by giving you permission. You will never have my permission. You must make your own choices."

He obviously hadn't expected that. He eyed her with longing. "It would be easier on everybody if you gave up on me."

She wasn't going to behave as if her world was crumbling, not in front of Jerry. From now on, she was going to pretend he was with her forever. She was going to be happy, like she'd always hoped she would be when Jerry came back to her. She could make her own choices too. She pasted a teasing smile on her lips. "You have to stay until the cookie tour is over. I'm going to teach you how to make stained glass."

Chapter 4

Mary picked up another sugar cookie and dipped her spatula in the bowl of frosting, never taking her eyes from Jerry's face. He always lit up when he talked about Pastor Andrea and her ministry in New York City.

"Pastor Andrea spoke for Marcus at his hearing, and the judge agreed to let Marcus go to a residential treatment center instead of to prison for ten years." Jerry smiled at the memory. "Marcus has been clean for almost a year."

"I love that story," Mary said. "Jesus can truly work miracles for anybody." Mary and Jerry had spent the last week making cookie dough, baking the cookie dough, frosting cookies, and talking about miracles. Every day, Mary had asked Jerry to think of a miracle he'd seen in the last two years, and Jerry had been able to come up with at least one miracle for each day. Lord willing, Jerry was beginning to see that miracles were not as scarce as he'd once thought they were. Miracles were everywhere for anyone who cared to look for them.

Mary hoped she was helping Jerry see with new eyes. She could tell his heart was softening. He no longer wore that look of unfettered misery, and gloom didn't follow him like a black cloud. But he still couldn't talk about Campbell Soup without a tinge of bitterness in his voice, so they mostly didn't mention his name between them.

Mary finished frosting the sugar cookie and handed the spatula to Jerry. "I'm done. You can lick the frosting off if you want."

Jerry's grin had never been wider. "I could drink a whole gallon of your cream cheese frosting."

Mary giggled. "You'd get sick and be no good for the cookie tour tomorrow."

Jerry's tender look sent a ribbon of warmth threading down Mary's spine. "I need to be healthy so I can help you. It's for a *gute* cause, and people are going to want to try one of everything. I don't wonder but we'll sell out the first day."

"That would be *wunderbarr*. We froze twenty dozen balls of cookie just in case."

Hannah rang up another customer and shot a smile at Mary. When the woman left the store, Hannah did a little dance. "That's forty-four tickets sold for the Christmas cookie tour tomorrow. For sure and certain it's going to be a huge success. That doesn't count the punch passes all the other places have sold."

Jerry had flatly refused to let them use the money they raised on the cookie tour to pay back the money he'd taken from the halfway house. Mary didn't know if the other merchants and neighbors would have agreed to that anyway. They had decided to use the money this year to help pay Tabitha Zook's medical bills. Tabitha had been diagnosed with juvenile diabetes and had been in and out of the hospital all winter. It was going to be a very nice Christmas present for the Zook family.

"How many punch tickets do you think have been sold altogether?"

Hannah was overjoyed. "I bet over a hundred. That's a thousand dollars for the Zooks. And it's going to bring so much new business into the store."

Austin propped his feather duster on his shoulder. "You were always so *gute* at math. I should have studied harder."

Hannah's eyes sparkled with amusement. "You didn't need to study harder. You married me for my math skills."

Austin rolled his eyes. "Among other reasons, like the fact that I love you so much, I can't function as a normal person unless you're with me."

The two of them strolled downstairs, debating who loved the other one more. Mary enjoyed hearing their lighthearted banter. It gave her hope for her and Jerry.

She turned to catch Jerry staring at her. The emotion on his face was unreadable, but it made her shiver with pleasure, all the same. "Are you happy or despondent or both?"

"I'm hungry," he said, smiling when she laughed. "*Nae*, I'm happy, but it all feels so temporary, like I can't live in this fantasy world forever where nothing ever goes wrong, where the only problem is if we've made enough cookies for the cookie tour. It feels like I'm burying my head in the sand."

"Why does it need to be temporary? We are called on to yield our will to Gotte, and let Gotte take care of the world."

He cleared his throat as a smile flitted across his face. "But Gotte isn't doing a very *gute* job."

She cuffed him on the shoulder. "You don't believe that anymore, and if you keep saying it, Gotte is going to strike you with an embarrassing rash for being so contrary."

"Gotte doesn't work that way. He makes the sun shine on the evil and the good," Jerry said.

Mary arched an eyebrow. "That's right, and don't you forget it. Your work and my work is to spread love, even here in our fantasy land. Let Gotte do His work and quit second-guessing him."

He glanced behind him, making sure no one was in the store and wrapped his arms around her waist. "You're very *gute* at your work."

Her pulse galloped. She certainly hoped so because she wanted to love Jerry into staying in Bienenstock.

Alfie and Benji Petersheim bounded into the store like the ten-year-olds they were, with bright red cheeks and tufts of wind-blown hair sticking out from under their beanies. Benji wore a navy blue beanie under his straw hat. Alfie wasn't wearing a straw hat at all. Did his *mamm* know? Probably. Rebecca knew everything.

"Mary," Alfie said. "Mamm wants to know if you have any more Petersheim Brothers Peanut Butter on the shelves. We're out, and she needs to make one more batch of peanut butter cookies. It's an emergency."

Mary glanced at the shelf where they stocked peanut butter. "I'm sorry, boys. It's gone. Your *mamm's* peanut butter is just too popular."

Benji's expression was grim, but Alfie looked especially horrified. "*Ach, du lieva.* She's going to have to make the cookies with store-bought peanut butter." Alfie said "store-bought" as if it were a bad word.

Benji peered at Jerry. "Maybe if you had time, could you help Mamm make peanut butter tonight?"

Jerry put a hand on Benji's shoulder. "I wish I could, but I've got to help Mary finish these cookies, and I'm helping Austin get the store ready for the cookie tour."

Alfie was positively despondent. "We've got to figure out a way to make more peanut butter. Mamm will be in a bad mood for weeks if she has to use store-bought peanut butter in her cookies."

Benji scratched his nose. "It wonders me if Soup could help. He just sits in the cave all day."

Mary's heart lurched. Soup? Were the boys still in contact with Soup?

Jerry snapped like a rubber band. "What about Soup?"

Benji's grimace stretched off his face and across the county line. "Um, I mean, um, Soup is wonderful nice. I bet he'd be *gute* at making peanut butter."

Alfie palmed his forehead and shook his head, but he didn't say anything. He was smart enough not to dig himself and Benji a deeper hole.

Jerry stiffened, and his eyes flashed with anger. "Have you boys been in contact with Soup, even when I told you not to?"

Mary's heart sank. Had the boys put themselves in danger? And the bigger concern? It didn't seem that Jerry was ready to show Soup even the tiniest bit of grace.

Alfie answered for his *bruder*, with that innocent mischievousness on his face that always disarmed Mary. "Don't worry, Jerry. We told Mamm we wouldn't go near him, so we stay at least six feet away when we visit the pond."

Benji must have thought Alfie's admission gave him permission to spill the beans. "We sneak out there and take him food and blankets because he's really cold. And firewood. He's living in that cave, and it's cold out there."

Jerry's mouth was thin and tight. "The cave at Elgin Pond?"

Benji nodded. "Tintin goes near him, but Mamm never said anything about Tintin staying away from Soup. She never said anything about LaWayne staying away from Soup neither. Sometimes Tintin sits by him and keeps him warm. They're friends."

Without another word, Jerry marched to the phone that sat by the cash register, lifted the receiver, and started punching numbers.

Alfie and Benji glanced at each other with panic in their eyes. They had probably guessed who Jerry was calling.

"Hello, yes, I'd like to report a dangerous vagrant squatting at Elgin Pond."

Mary held her breath, dread squeezing her heart like a vice. Jerry was livid. There wasn't a trace of mercy in his expression. Didn't he care what would happen to Soup? Didn't he care the police might put Soup in jail or throw him out of the cave and into the cold?

Jerry hung up the phone, his eyes ablaze with angry determination. His gaze connected with Mary's, and he hesitated, as if he saw something that made him doubt himself. "It…it had to be done, Mary. I won't allow Soup to hurt…"

Mary caught her breath. Alfie and Benji had disappeared. They must have slipped out the door, but they'd gone so quietly and stealthily that Mary hadn't even noticed. Apparently, neither had Jerry.

He was at the door in three long strides. He pulled his coat from the hook and shoved his arms into the sleeves. "For sure and certain they've gone to warn Soup." He opened the door.

"Wait," Mary shouted. "I'm coming with you."

"Nae, it's cold, and I don't want you anywhere near Soup."

Mary grabbed her coat and bonnet from behind the counter. "And I don't want *you* anywhere near Soup."

Surprise flashed in his eyes. "You don't think I'd…I would never… what are you afraid I'll do?"

She lifted her chin. She didn't want to hurt his feelings, but he wasn't seeing himself clearly. "You tell me."

In frustration, he ran his fingers through his hair before putting on his hat. "Mary, I'm mad at Soup, but I would never hurt him."

"Maybe I don't believe you." And that was the honest truth.

He reared back as if she'd slapped him across the face. "Is that what you think of me?"

Now was not the time to talk about how much Jerry had changed or how far he needed to go. Now was not the time to feel regret about the raw emotion on his face. "We can talk about it later, but right now, we need to find the boys and find Soup and see if we can set things right."

Jerry gave her one last glance, then held the door for her. They walked out of the store side by side, but they weren't really together. Maybe they would never be truly together ever again.

Chapter 5

Mamm was going to give them the spatula, for sure and certain, but this was an emergency and the fastest way to get to Elgin Pond was by hitchhiking. A nice old lady had picked them up and driven them all the way to the pond, Tintin too, lecturing them the whole way about how dangerous it was to hitchhike and if they ever needed a ride again, they could just call her and she'd take them anywhere they wanted to go. She'd even given them her phone number, and Alfie hadn't had the heart to tell her that they didn't have a phone.

There was a phone in the "factory" where Mamm made peanut butter, but Alfie and Benji weren't allowed to use it, and the one time Alfie had tried to call their Englisch friend Max on Mamm's phone, Mamm had yelled at him for eleven minutes. He knew the exact time because he had watched the kitchen clock while she lectured him about the evils of phones and the outside world and "don't you ever play video games," which Alfie wasn't sure had anything to do with phones, but Mamm wasn't one to waste a *gute* lecture on just one topic.

Benji and Alfie jumped out of Mrs. Kleinhenz's car as soon as she stopped. Benji paused long enough to tell her thank you, but Alfie didn't even turn back. They had to get to Soup and warn him the police were coming so he could run away before he got arrested. Tintin was hot on their heels as they ran down the slope and toward the cave. The trail was ice mixed with mud because it had been kind of warm the last few days. Mamm called it unseasonably warm, but all Alfie knew was that the thermometer at school had read forty degrees when Alfie and Benji had started toward home in the afternoon.

Alfie paused long enough for Benji and Tintin to catch up to him. They peered across the pond. Soup had a nice fire going, which would keep him warm but would also alert the police to his location. There was no time to waste. Alfie took the shortcut and sprinted across the pond, running as fast as he could without slipping on the ice.

The ice crackled beneath his feet, but he wasn't looking down. He had his eyes trained on Soup's cave. Without even asking Alfie, Benji had just given Soup their cave. Soup appeared and threw another log on the fire. "Soup!" Alfie screamed. "Soup! Get out of here. The police are coming."

Soup turned and smiled, cupping his hand around his ear. He was too far away to hear what Alfie was trying to tell him.

"Soup!" Benji yelled. "Get out of here before the police come."

Alfie heard a deafening crack behind him, then Tintin's frightened yip, then a horrifying splash. He turned in time to see Tintin's nose and Benji's hand disappear under the broken ice. Alfie's heart tried to claw its way up his throat. He screamed and ran toward Benji and Tintin. Alfie fell once and hit his knees hard but pushed himself up and kept running. Benji came up sputtering and spitting, his straw hat missing, his beanie already covered with a layer of ice. Tintin braced his paws on the edge of the ice, but he couldn't pull himself out of the water.

A streak of blue and brown ran past Alfie. "Don't let my *bruder* die," Alfie yelled. "Or my dog."

Soup dropped to his stomach and skidded to the hole in the ice like a baseball player sliding head-first into second base. He ripped off his coat and plunged his hands into the water, somehow finding Benji's hand and pulling him upward. Benji coughed, and Alfie had never seen such terror in his eyes.

Alfie started to cry. He lay down beside Soup, and the ice burned through his coat as he reached out and grabbed Benji's other hand.

"Get back, Alfie," Soup said. "I don't want you falling in too."

Alfie was supposed to respect his elders, but he wasn't going anywhere. "I can't pull him up. He's too heavy." Tintin whined and thrashed about in the water, and Alfie's tears felt like trails of ice down his cheeks. He didn't want Benji or Tintin to die, but he wasn't strong enough to save them. Soup was their only hope.

"Help me," Benji gasped, clinging to Alfie's hand. The ice beneath Alfie shifted, and he tried to make himself flatter so it wouldn't crack beneath him.

"Here," Soup said, keeping hold of Benji's arm and throwing one sleeve of his coat into the water. "Benji, grab my coat, and I think I can pull you out."

Benji moaned. "I'll sink."

"You won't sink. I've still got a hold of you."

Alfie snatched Soup's coat sleeve and shoved it into Benji's hand. Benji grabbed on tight with one hand and held onto Alfie with the other. Soup let go of Benji's arm and pulled his coat with both hands, still lying flat on the ice. Soup was strong, but the ice kept making scary cracking noises, and he had to pull very slowly so the ice didn't break underneath the both of them. Alfie backed up as Benji slowly came out of the water. Once his legs were halfway out, he pushed against the edge of the ice with his knees and crawled onto the ice.

"Good," Soup said, panting heavily. They were all gasping for air. Alfie thought his lungs might explode and his arms might fall off. "You two get back to shore and sit by that fire. I'm going to pull Tintin out."

"I want to help," Alfie said.

Soup didn't argue, but it was probably because he didn't have enough air to say anything. He nudged Alfie aside and lay flat on his stomach again, reaching way over the edge to put his arms around Tintin. But how was he going to pull Tintin out in that position?

"Benji," Soup whispered, his voice raspy and breathless. "Hand me the coat. I don't want to hurt Tintin, but if I can tie my sleeve around his collar, I might be able to pull him out."

Benji's teeth were chattering so hard, they sounded like a drum set. He nodded and handed Soup the coat.

"Now go get by that fire," Soup said, sounding weary and angry, and afraid all at the same time.

Benji didn't move and neither did Alfie. He would rather get pneumonia or the spatula than leave Tintin in the water. What if Soup couldn't pull him out by himself?

Alfie's heart jumped like a frog when he heard yelling from the road. Jerry and Mary were already running down the slope, Jerry tearing off his coat as he ran, Mary following close behind. Jerry motioned for Mary to stay back, but she followed him onto the ice, and they both tiptoed quickly toward the hole and Tintin.

Soup saw Jerry coming, but he didn't try to escape or run away. He held tightly to Tintin, even when Alfie heard another terrifying crack from the ice beneath him.

Mary got down on her hands and knees and crawled to Alfie. She grabbed his wrist and yanked him hard. "Ouch!" Alfie said. He didn't know Mary was so strong.

"*Cum,*" Mary snapped. "You and Benji need to get off the ice."

Alfie tried to pull away from Mary, but she wouldn't let go. Who knew she was so strong? "I need to help Tintin," he growled, even though it was Mary and even though Mamm said he should never yell at a girl.

Mary reached out and snatched Benji's arm too. "You'll only make it harder for Jerry and Soup to save Tintin. Too much weight on the ice will surely send you all crashing into the water."

Alfie glanced at his dog and at Jerry, who was already down on his stomach next to Soup. His gut twisted with fear. He wanted to help, but Jerry and Soup were grown-ups, and they were stronger than he was. He hated it, but he had to get out of the way so Jerry and Soup could save his dog.

"Is he going to die?" Benji wailed. His teeth chattered, and ice crystals had formed on his eyebrows.

Alfie could hear his heartbeat in his ears. Benji was shivering something wonderful, and Alfie knew what could happen if someone got too cold. Perry Miller had gone ice fishing two years ago, and they had to cut all his toes off. Alfie had to trust Jerry and Soup. They would save Tintin. But now Alfie had to save Benji's toes. He got on his hands and knees and crawled to Benji, then linked his elbow around Benji's arm. "Benji, we have to get you warm by the fire, or your fingers will fall off."

Benji sniffed twice. "Why will my fingers fall off? How would I eat?"

With Mary beside them, they crawled for a few feet, then stood and carefully stepped to shore. As soon as they were on solid ground, Mary put her arms around them and tried to lead them to the campfire. But Benji, shivering and rattling like a pile of bones, wouldn't budge. "Wait." He pointed to Jerry and Soup.

Alfie was so cold, he felt like he'd been stung by a hundred yellow jackets. Benji must have felt even colder. But they couldn't sit by the fire and get warm until Tintin was safe.

Soup still had a tight hold around Tintin's middle, but it was too icy and slippery for Soup to pull him out without falling in himself. Jerry and Soup talked it over for a minute, but Alfie couldn't hear what they were saying.

"We need to help," Benji said.

Mary held out a hand to stop any thought of going back on the ice. "Wait. Jerry is strong. Stronger than anyone I know."

Alfie caught his bottom lip between his teeth. Jerry used to be a fire-fighter, but he was skinnier than he was two years ago when he'd pulled Alfie out of that tree. Still, he had pretty *gute* muscles, and he had experience rescuing people and cats from trees and such. If anybody could save Tintin, it was Jerry, especially with Soup's help.

Jerry nodded to Soup then grabbed Tintin hard by the scruff of the neck. A loud, grunting yell came from deep in Jerry's throat as if he was concentrating all his strength in one spot at the center of his chest. Slowly, Tintin rose out of the water. Jerry pulled him far enough out that Tintin's back paws finally found a foothold on the ice. Alfie let himself breathe when Tintin scrambled out of the water and trotted to shore as if he'd just had a refreshing leisurely swim.

Tintin launched himself into Benji's arms and knocked Benji on his *hinnerdale*.

"*Cum*," Mary said, her voice clipped and strained. She nudged Tintin off Benji and pulled him to his feet. Alfie gave Tintin a hug, and then the four of them hurried to the campfire. Alfie glanced behind him. Jerry and Soup had made it to shore and were slowly trudging toward the fire, Soup dragging his soaking coat behind him. Jerry had his arm around

Soup as if they were old friends. Or maybe Jerry was making sure Soup didn't escape before the police came to arrest him.

Mary helped Benji off with his coat and beanie and told him to stand by the fire. "This will never do," she said. "It's too cold, and we need to get you out of these wet clothes."

Benji's hands traveled to his head. "I lost my hat."

Alfie didn't even want to think about how many spatulas they'd get for a lost hat. He frowned. Mamm had never used the spatula on them, not once. But today, for sure and certain, she'd pull the biggest spatula from the drawer and give it to Alfie and Benji but good.

Mary propped her hands on her hips and looked toward the road. "Lord willing, the police will be here soon to take you home. Both of you need to get in a nice, warm bath. The longer you're in those wet clothes, the more likely hypothermia will set in."

Alfie didn't know what hypothermia was, but it sounded like a dread disease. Mamm would probably give him the spatula if he brought home a dread disease.

Mary eyed Alfie. "It looks like you're counting something in your head."

Alfie sighed. "Spatulas."

Mary took off her coat and wrapped it around Benji's shoulders. "Get closer to the fire." She'd never looked so concerned or so upset, but Alfie didn't mind. Mary gave Alfie and Benji free doughnuts when she was worried about them. When Scilla Lambright kicked them out of the library, Mary tsk-tsked her tongue and gave them a free doughnut. When Perry Glick pinched Benji on the neck, Mary had given them both a free doughnut.

For sure and certain they'd get seven or eight free doughnuts for almost freezing to death. Alfie scrunched his lips together to keep them from trembling with cold. Benji would get more doughnuts than Alfie because Benji had almost drowned, but maybe he'd share the extras with his favorite *bruder*. It was only fair. But maybe it was Alfie who would get the extra doughnuts. Alfie had once again saved someone's life. That had to be worth three or four doughnuts right there.

It was the least Mary could do for Bienenstock's finest and bravest citizen.

Soup and Jerry made it to the fire. Jerry hooked his elbow around Benji's neck. "Are you okay, kid?"

Benji nodded, even though he was shivering violently. "S-S-Soup saved me. He didn't care about himself. He just ran right over and almost fell in."

Jerry propped a trembling hand on Soup's shoulder and stood staring at him for what seemed like an hour. Then he threw his arms around Soup and hugged the stuffing out of him. "Thank you," he growled, before bursting into tears. "Thank you, with all my heart. I'll never forget what you've done."

Soup buried his face in Jerry's shoulder and sobbed like a baby. "I'm sorry, brother. I'm so sorry."

"No," Jerry said, crying even louder than Soup. "I'm sorry for my bitterness, and I forgive you with all my heart."

It was a lovely, shivery, warm, and icy moment. They'd all either get frostbite or find their faith in humanity.

Chapter 6

Soup sat on the sofa on one side of Jerry while Mary sat on the other with a blanket around her shoulders and an unbounded joy in her heart. Jerry, handsome and determined and kind to a fault, held Mary's hand as if he'd never let it go. She didn't think she could love him any more than she did at this moment.

Soup leaned forward with his elbows propped on his knees. Jerry's other arm was tightly clamped around Soup's shoulders, lending Soup some of his own radiant warmth. Soup was still shivering, but he was smiling, and his countenance was full of light. All because Jerry had chosen forgiveness over the cold cup of bitterness.

Gotte had reunited two men who had been as close as *bruderen*.

Mary's eyes filled with tears.

The Jerry she knew and loved so well had come back to her at last.

Tintin had made a bed at Soup's feet, and the exhausted dog was fast asleep. It was indeed an extraordinary day because Rebecca never let Tintin in the house, and now he was lying on the rag rug with a blanket spread over him as if he was one of the family.

Mary smiled to herself. Their whole straggly, water-logged bunch had appeared on Rebecca's doorstep not fifteen minutes ago. No doubt

Rebecca had felt sorry for all of them, except for maybe Alfie and Benji who, according to Rebecca, had "brought this on yourselves, young men."

Rebecca carried a tray of mugs into the living room. She held out the tray to Soup and motioned for him to take a mug. "It's hot, but not scalding. The last thing anyone wants when they're near frozen to death is a burned tongue. And you look like you're frozen clear through."

Soup picked up a mug and smiled tentatively at Rebecca. "Thank you. That's very kind."

"It's the least I can do. You saved Benji and LaWayne, and I'm wonderful grateful. Those boys know better than to run out onto the ice like a pair of dodo birds, but as troublesome as they are, I would prefer if they at least made it to their twenty-first birthday. Then I can wash my hands of both of them."

Mary laughed, and she and Jerry each took a mug. Mary sipped slowly. It was deliciously warm and silky chocolate spiced with a hint of cinnamon. It had been the coldest day of her life, and the hot chocolate was the best thing she'd ever tasted.

As soon as Mary and the boys had arrived at Rebecca's, like a cattle driver, Rebecca had herded Alfie and Benji upstairs and drawn a bath for them. They were still up there, no doubt savoring the pleasantly warm water of the bathtub and trying to forget how cold they had been. It was a pretty *gute* guess they were also stalling because Mary suspected that as soon as they came downstairs freshly washed and sufficiently warmed, their *mater* would give them the lecture to end all lectures. They probably deserved it. Those boys had been reckless and disobedient, even if it was with the excuse of helping their fellow man. Lord willing, Benji would have no ill effects from falling in the icy water. Lord willing, none of them would catch cold or lose an extremity to frostbite.

The police had arrived at the pond within a few short minutes of Jerry and Soup pulling Tintin from the water. Jerry had smoothed things over with the police so they wouldn't arrest Soup. The nice officer had given Alfie and Benji, Mary, and Tintin a ride to the Petersheim's house in his police car, and Jerry and Soup had followed them home in the buggy.

Rebecca put the tray on the coffee table, picked up the last mug of hot chocolate, and sat down in the rocker. "So, Campbell, I understand you've been living in that cave down by the pond and my boys have been sneaking you Oreos and potato chips."

Soup lowered his eyes. "I didn't have anywhere else to go, ma'am. I was going to head south, but I needed to talk to Jerry first, and I couldn't get him to hear me out."

"I'm sorry," Jerry said, squeezing Mary's hand. Mary squeezed back reassuringly. Everyone had forgiven him. Everyone had forgiven everyone.

Soup shook his head. "I'm the one who's sorry. I don't deserve your forgiveness, but I wanted to explain. I lied to you about why I needed the money. My brother, Matt, was the one who owed Blade money." Soup closed his eyes as if it was too painful to look into the past. "It's my fault my brother got into drugs. It broke my mom's heart all over again. I was clean. I was getting better, but Matt was just digging himself deeper and deeper. Blade threatened to kill him, and I just couldn't let that happen. You were my best friend, my only friend, and I was too scared to tell you the truth. I thought you'd refuse to help my brother. That night you got stabbed, Blade got to me first." He cradled his head in his hands. "His boys knocked me out and left me for dead in an alley. I guess they realized I wasn't a source of income for them anymore, and they didn't want me to pull Matt out with me. I woke up the next morning in jail, and I didn't know what had happened to you until I got out six weeks later."

Jerry's expression was saturated with pain. "I should have let you explain. I thought you'd set me up."

"I didn't abandon you. I never would have let you face Blade on your own. After I got out of jail, I went to the hospital to see you, but you'd already been discharged. At the halfway house, they told me you'd been fired and you'd gone back to your hometown. As soon as I earned the money, I followed you here." Soup reached into his pocket and pulled out a plastic bag full of cash. "I already sent Pastor Andrea three hundred dollars and a letter explaining what happened. Here's your four hundred dollars, though I know it can't begin to make up for all your pain and suffering."

Jerry wrapped his fingers around the plastic bag, his eyes pooling with tears. "It is enough. It is more than enough." He lowered his head, and Mary could feel his body shake as silent sobs wracked his body.

Soup wrapped his arms around Jerry and gave him a bracing hug. "I love you, man. I'm sorry I singlehandedly destroyed your faith in humanity."

"I love you too," Jerry said. And all was right with the world.

"Isn't it humidity?" Benji stood on the threshold between the kitchen and the living room in dry, clean clothes, his hair damp and ruffled and his head tilted to one side in puzzlement.

Rebecca sprang to her feet and practically tackled Benji with a hug. "Can you feel all your toes? How are your toes?"

Benji made a face as if he was trying to concentrate on his toes while his *mamm* smothered him with affection. "They're okay, but my legs are itchy."

"Well, for goodness' sake, go get some lotion, young man. You'd think you don't have a brain in your head. And tell Alfie it's time to get out of the tub."

Benji ran up the stairs and was soon back with a bottle of lotion and Alfie. Alfie looked none the worse for the wear, but he was obviously reluctant to be anywhere near his *mamm*. Mary couldn't blame him. He and Benji had been very naughty, Benji could have died, and Rebecca's Doritos supply was probably quite low. Rebecca was a very unhappy *mater*.

Rebecca was obviously irritated at Alfie, but she gave him a hug anyway then gently pinched his earlobes between her thumbs and forefingers. "How are your ears. Can you feel your ears?"

Alfie grimaced, but he didn't shrink from Rebecca's attention. He probably thought it was wiser to let her fuss over him so as not to provoke her anger or remind her that he was in big trouble. "I can feel my ears, but my big toe is turning blue."

Her face full of concern, Rebecca squatted on her haunches and examined Alfie's bare feet. "Can you feel it?"

"*Jah*. I stubbed my toe yesterday. I think I'm going to lose my toenail."

Rebecca stood up straight and growled. "*Ach*, young man, don't give me a heart attack like that. I thought it was frostbite, but no son of mine is allowed to have less than ten toes."

"Okay, Mamm."

Benji sat down on the sofa next to Soup. "Are you okay? Can you feel all your toes?"

Soup grinned and mussed Benji's hair. "I can. I'm a little chilly, but I'm warmer than I've been for days."

"I lost my hat," Benji said, glancing at Rebecca as if waiting for her to react to the bad news.

Soup gave Benji's shoulder a squeeze. "Maybe you'll find it this summer when the ice melts."

Alfie's gaze connected with Benji's, and Benji nodded. "Mamm," Alfie said, "we were thinking."

Rebecca huffed out a breath. "Nae, you weren't. You disobeyed me and lied and stole my potato chips and Doritos. You broke three commandments in one day."

Benji nibbled on his bottom lip. "We stole the chips on Sunday, not today."

Rebecca's look made Benji shut his mouth tight. "That's four commandments, and stealing on the Sabbath is doubly wicked."

"But, Mamm," Alfie said. "We were helping our fellow man. Soup was starving, and we're supposed to feed the hungry. It's one of the Ten Commandments too."

Rebecca folded her arms across her chest. "Believe you me, there is nothing in the Ten Commandments about food."

"I'm sorry I ate your food, Mrs. Petersheim," Soup said.

Rebecca swatted away his apology. "As far as I know, Campbell, you didn't break a single commandment today. No need to feel bad for eating food that was given to you freely."

Benji bent over and petted Tintin, who was still asleep. "Soup deserves all the potato chips in the world. He saved my life."

Alfie lifted his chin. "I helped. The mayor said I am one of Bienenstock's finest and bravest citizens." Mary smiled to herself. Rebecca wasn't impressed. Alfie cleared his throat and tried again. "Like I said, me and Benji were thinking. It's really cold out there, and Soup deserves a warm bed and dinner every night. And you're the best cook in the world, Mamm. Soup would think he'd died and gone to heaven if he tasted your fried chicken."

Rebecca didn't seem fooled by Alfie's flattery, but she did train her gaze on Soup when Alfie mentioned the warm bed. "No one should sleep outside in Wisconsin in the winter."

"Like I said, me and Benji was thinking that the cookie tour starts tomorrow, and we're all out of peanut butter, and you need someone to help you make peanut butter. Jerry is too busy, but Soup doesn't have nothing to do. He could be your assistant and then you'd have plenty of peanut butter to sell when people come to our house for a cookie."

"Not just anyone can make peanut butter, young man," Rebecca protested, but Mary could tell she was already giving Alfie's idea serious consideration. "You have to have a food handler's permit and know how to work the peanut grinder."

Soup looked at his hands. "I don't want to put pressure on you either way, but I do have a food handler's permit. I worked in the kitchen at the halfway house in Green Bay. I'd be happy to help you make peanut butter. But I need to take a shower first."

Alfie nodded enthusiastically. "It wouldn't be hard to teach him how to use the grinder. Austin learned how, and he's *dumm*. How hard can it be?"

Rebecca peered at Alfie through half-lidded eyes. "Don't talk about your *bruder* that way, young man. Austin is my best peanut butter maker."

Jerry placed a hand on Soup's shoulder. "I don't want to overstep my bounds because I am also a guest in your home, Rebecca, but Soup could sleep in my room on the floor if you say it's okay."

Soup's eyes filled with tears, and his Adam's apple bobbed up and down. "I...that's really nice of you."

"I don't mind," Rebecca said. "The thought of you sleeping in that cave is indecent. What kind of Christian would I be if I let that go on any longer? I should have put a stop to it days ago, then Benji wouldn't have fallen through the ice."

Alfie was a little too smug. "*Jah*, Mamm. When you look at it that way, this whole thing was your fault."

Rebecca's glare probably singed Alfie's hair. "Don't try to blame your sins on someone else, Alfie Petersheim. You're this close to getting nothing but cooked carrots and cabbage to eat for the rest of your life."

Alfie shut his mouth, hung his head, and sat next to Tintin on the floor.

Rebecca realized she'd been too hard on him. She clucked her tongue and handed both boys a mug from her tray. "Now, have some hot chocolate. It will warm your insides and keep you from getting frostbite. Just remember, I made it for you because I love you more than life itself, and if you ever put yourselves in danger like that again, I'll give you the spatula."

Alfie looked up at his *mater*. "You're not going to give us the spatula tonight?"

"Of course not. I'm too glad you're alive and unfrozen to give you a spanking, and I need my spatula to make cookies." Rebecca sat down and sighed. "It's almost six o'clock. Benaiah will be back from Andrew's shop any minute. With all this excitement, my dinner plans have been completely waylaid, but we could have grilled cheese sandwiches. That would be easy and nutritious. Benaiah could help Mammi and Dawdi to bed, and the twins could do the dishes. I bet we'd have time to make three dozen jars before bedtime."

Alfie's mouth fell open. "We did the dishes last night."

"And you'll do them every night for the rest of your life. No son of mine is going to break four commandments and get away with it."

Mary almost laughed out loud. Rebecca couldn't be tenderhearted for long.

Chapter 7

Mary handed the box to the Englisch woman. "I hope you have a Merry Christmas," she said.

The woman took the cookies and smiled as she eyed the little bow Mary had tied on top of the box. "Oh, I will. My daughter and her family are coming in from Florida tomorrow. They like a white Christmas yet. And they'll love these mint chocolate chip cookies. They're everything I love about Christmas in one bite."

Mary and Jerry had been at the store since seven this morning, along with Hannah, Austin, Mary's *bruder* James, and Mary's *mamm*. They'd made another twelve dozen cookies because they'd nearly sold out of everything they had in the first two days of the Christmas cookie tour. Austin and Hannah were ecstatic. Yesterday was the most profitable day they'd ever had at the store, and today looked to be even bigger. Customers had bought quilts and furniture, cheese, produce, and jelly. And cookies, dozens and dozens of cookies.

James and Mary's *mamm* stood at a table near the stairs checking punch passes and handing out cookie tour cookies. Mary and Jerry were behind the bakery counter boxing bread, sweet rolls, and seven different kinds of cookies for eager Christmas customers, including the cute Englisch woman who'd just gotten two dozen mint chocolate chip cookies.

The woman crinkled her nose when she smiled. "Do you ever share your recipes?"

"Of course," Mary said. She pulled the recipe card for mint chocolate chip cookies from her apron pocket. "Do you want a pencil and paper to copy it down?"

The woman laughed and shook her head. "Ope! I guess I have to be realistic. I'll never make them myself. I'll just come here whenever I need a cookie fix."

Mary giggled. "For sure and certain. I'm glad you like them."

"I don't like them. I *love* them. I'm telling all my friends to get on over here. It's the last day of the cookie tour, isn't it?"

Mary nodded. "We close at 6:00 tonight."

The woman looked at her watch. "Seven more hours. You've got a long day ahead."

Mary was so happy, she thought her smile might fly off her face. "We're having so much fun, we hardly notice the time pass."

The woman got in line at the cash register where Austin was ringing up purchases as quickly as he could. Jerry sidled next to Mary, and though he didn't touch her, she could feel the warmth of his presence radiate clear to her heart. "It's really a test of my extraordinary willpower not to take you in my arms right here and kiss you," he murmured.

Mary's heart fluttered like a hundred moths around a bright golden flame as her eyes met his. She loved the deep timbre of Jerry's voice and the rich, warm light in his eyes. She had so much love in her heart for this wounded, strong, tender man who wanted so badly to change the world, his desire a constant ache in his gut and a throbbing in his heart. Lord willing, Jerry would find happiness and purpose and peace without thinking he had to chase it. With all her heart, Mary hoped she was the answer Jerry had been searching for. He was her everything, and she couldn't bear the thought of ever being separated again.

Jerry nudged his arm against hers. "You know I'm never going to leave you," he said, his voice soft and captivating.

Mary took a shallow, hopeful breath. "Are…you sure?"

"I've decided that Gotte doesn't need me to change the world as much as He wants my heart and my willing hands. I will do my best, love with all my heart, and leave the results to Gotte. From now on, I'm going to trust His plan. He is in control, and I never was. He will bring about miracles in His own time and His own way."

Mary found his hand and gave it a squeeze. "You've come a long way in a few days."

His smile lit up the entire room. "As Benji would say, I've found my faith in humidity again."

She giggled. "I've never had faith in humidity. Maybe I need to consult Alfie and Benji." She thought she might fly to the moon when he smiled back at her. "You deserve to be happy, Jerry. Gotte wants us all to be happy. I can tell because He sends us miracles every day. Whether it's a pink sunrise or a field of glistening snow or birdsong out my window, they're all signs of Gotte's love. Gotte wants to bless and preserve us every day. Happiness is our birthright."

Jerry glanced toward the front of the store, took Mary's hand, and pulled her a few feet back closer to the oven. It wasn't exactly more private, but when he looked at her, it seemed like they were the only two people in the room. "Mary, what I said before, about not wanting to marry you or have children. I wasn't myself. I was bitter and disheartened. Can you forgive me? This isn't the ideal place, but I can't stand one more minute of suspense. Will you marry me? Are you willing to settle for a man who failed at changing the world?"

Mary couldn't let him believe he was a failure. "You haven't failed at anything. You changed Soup's world. For sure and certain there are a handful of people in Mexico who bless your name. And I don't wonder but Pastor Andrea thinks you're remarkable."

"Even though she fired me?"

"Even though." Mary's eyes blurred with tears. "You've changed my world, and that means the world to me. Of course I'll marry you. I've been waiting for three years for you to ask."

He caught his breath as if she'd surprised him. "Now I can die a very happy man. I'll never want for anything else in my entire life."

"Excuse me. I'd like to buy some cookies." A tall Englisch man stood at the bakery counter, eyeing Mary and Jerry in amusement.

Mary felt her face grow warm. There would be plenty of time to stare into Jerry's eyes and savor his love after the cookie tour. "Of course. How many and what kind?"

Mary and Jerry worked side-by-side and filled five more orders before there was a short lull in customers. The front door opened, and Alfie and Benji Petersheim exploded into the store. It was the way they entered every place they went. Mary's heart filled to overflowing. These two troublemakers had once again brought Mary and Jerry together. They would get free cookies for life, as long as their *mater* approved.

The boys marched right up to the bakery counter. "We're here to help," Alfie announced as if he and Benji had come in the nick of time to save the day.

Both Mary and Jerry came out from behind the counter. "We're *froh* you're here," Jerry said. "As you can see, we're swamped. You can grab a broom and sweep the store. We haven't had time to tidy up."

Alfie's face fell. "We don't want to clean. We want to be your cookie tasters."

Benji puckered his face like a prune. "*Nae*, Alfie. Mamm said we needed to help, not eat cookies."

Mary cocked an eyebrow. "Your *mamm* doesn't need your help at home? I don't wonder but you've got lots of people at your house for the cookie tour."

Benji made another pruney face. "She says we're underfoot. I don't even know what that means, but she made it sound bad, like we needed to get out of there right quick. She said you would need our help more than she does."

Mary's lips twitched upward. Rebecca was a sly one. Mary had to give her credit for knowing her limits with her incorrigible sons. "Has she sold a lot of peanut butter this morning?"

Alfie took off his coat and mittens. "*Jah*. She and Soup and Dat were up at six this morning making peanut butter, then Mamm made about a thousand cookies, and then Englischers started coming."

"We helped," Benji said. "We ate breakfast with Dawdi and Mammi."

Alfie scratched his nose. "I poured the milk."

"Then we helped Dawdi tie his shoes, and we washed the breakfast dishes and Mamm's cookie sheets."

Alfie held up his fingers. "Five cookie sheets."

Jerry folded his arms and leaned his back against the counter. "I have some *gute* news for you boys. My parents have invited me to move back home so you boys will get your own room back. Isn't that *wunderbarr*?"

Warmth spread through Mary's chest. Another miracle. Jerry's parents had been so hurt when he'd left that they told him never to come home. Gotte had softened their hearts.

Alfie deflated like a leaky tire. "That's nice, Jerry, but Mamm has invited Soup to stay for as long as he wants. She says he's a stranger, and we gotta take him in."

Benji poked Alfie with his elbow. "But we like Soup, so we don't mind sleeping in the cellar."

Alfie sighed as if he was the most put-upon boy in the whole world. "I guess. But why doesn't Soup sleep in the cellar? He's used to being in the cold."

Four more customers paraded into the store, and Jerry gasped. "What is she doing here?"

His eyes were trained on a dark-haired, dark-eyed woman, wiry and petite. She couldn't have been more than five feet tall, but she seemed to command the whole room, as if she were someone very important. Her confidence wasn't arrogance as much as it was purpose, as if she was doing exactly what she was supposed to be doing in exactly the right place and time. Despite being small, she looked tough, like she could take on a whole room of criminals and not flinch, sort of like Rebecca Petersheim. But there was also a light in her eyes that hinted at great compassion and great kindness.

She gazed around the room until she caught sight of Jerry then marched toward him. "Well, Jerry, it took a minute to track you down, but I'm nothing if not persistent." She had a barely-discernable accent, but Mary didn't know enough about language to guess what kind of accent it was.

Jerry, obviously surprised to see her, stiffened beside Mary and stuttered on a reply. "Pastor...Andrea. I didn't think...what are you doing here?"

She looked at him as if he were crazy. "What do you think? I didn't come all this way for the Christmas cookie tour, though it is a charming idea and seems to be quite successful, judging from how full the parking lot is." She held out her hand to Mary. "You must be Mary Yutzy. Jerry told me all about you." She shook Alfie's hand then reached out to Benji. "And who are you, handsome boys?"

"I'm Alfie, and this is my brother Benji. We're preteens."

Pastor Andrea acted impressed. "Preteens? I bet that means you're very helpful to your mom, and you're old enough and smart enough to stay out of trouble."

"Something like that," Jerry mumbled.

Pastor Andrea snapped her gaze back to Jerry. "So a few weeks ago I got a letter from Soup with three hundred dollars enclosed with an explanation and a groveling apology. He said I'd been too hard on you, and I had to agree. I regretted firing you about five minutes after I'd done it."

Jerry hung his head. "I deserved it. I broke the rules."

Pastor Andrea scoffed. "What are any of us but incurable rule breakers? I believe in Jesus, Jerry. He loves broken people because there's nothing He'd rather do than fix us. The question is, do you believe He can fix you?"

Jerry lifted his head and looked into Pastor Andrea's eyes. "Yes. I believe that with all my heart."

"Then all is forgiven, and we've all learned some very valuable lessons along the way. The greatest lesson I learned is that I should never fire my most valuable asset in the heat of the moment. So I'm offering you a job."

Mary's heart sank. Pastor Andrea wanted Jerry to come back? Would Jerry go? And where did that leave Mary? Her mouth dried out as if she'd taken a bite of sand.

Jerry didn't hesitate for a moment. "I love what you're doing in New York, but I don't have the heart to leave my family and my life here in Bienenstock."

Amish Christmas Cookie Tour

"Maybe it was God's will that I fire you, because I've come to believe that He wants you here."

"In Bienenstock?"

Pastor Andrea put her arms around Benji and Alfie, including them in the conversation without saying a word. It was one of the most profoundly kind gestures Mary had ever seen. "There's a farm for sale about three miles from here that our ministry wants to buy and turn into a group home for five or six men. We'd eventually want it to become self-sustaining with income from farming and livestock." She motioned toward Mary. "We want you and your lovely wife to run it, with Soup's help."

"I'm...I'm not his wife," Mary stuttered, her heart thumping against her ribcage.

Jerry gave her a brilliant smile. "Not yet."

"We're also planning to hire an equine therapist to work with the residents. We think it has huge potential to change lives." Mary looked at Jerry. "What's an equine therapist?"

Pastor Andrea jumped in. "Someone who knows how to use horses to help people overcome addiction and mental health issues. It's something that can't be done in New York City."

Jerry's eyes filled with doubt, but there was also something else in his expression that Mary could only describe as unbounded hope. "You want me to run it?"

Pastor Andrea smiled, obviously sensing Jerry's excitement. "There's lots of details to work out, but you're perfect for the job, and you have more compassion and determination than anyone I know."

"But I broke so many rules. I'm not worthy of your trust."

Pastor Andrea scoffed. "Of course you're worthy. We are all worthy. The only thing God asks of us is to share and expand his goodness and to love as much as we can. And you've got that love in spades."

Jerry's gaze connected with Mary's. "I...don't know. It would only be possible if I could still be baptized and marry Mary, and I would need to talk to the bishop. But all of this is only if Mary says yes."

Pastor Andrea eyed Mary, her face full of curiosity and love. Real, sincere, accepting love. "What do you say, Mary? It would seem everything hinges on you."

Jerry nodded and took Mary's hand. "It always has, even though I've never told you."

Mary's heart nearly exploded with happiness. "I truly believe this is what Gotte wants. He gave you the deep longing to help others, but He also sent you to this time and this place and this community. I would never expect you to abandon the plan Gotte has for your life, even for me." Mary motioned toward Pastor Andrea. "If you want to do this, there is nothing I'd want more."

Jerry whooped so loudly that everyone in the store turned their eyes on him. He picked Mary right up off the floor and twirled her around in unbounded glee. She held on tight and held her breath. She was flying after all. "I want to do this," Jerry said.

He set her on the floor, and she smoothed her hands down her apron and checked that her *kapp* was still securely in place. "Let's finish the cookies first."

Jerry slumped his shoulders in mock dejection. "We probably should, though I want to be married to you more than I ever wanted anything in my life."

Benji's face lit up like a campfire. "Are you getting married?"

Jerry placed a hand on Benji's shoulder. "We are."

"So you've found your faith in humidity?"

Jerry laughed. Mary loved the sound of it. "*Jah*," he said, "it's all because of you and Alfie and your stubborn determination to do the right thing."

Pastor Andrea cocked an eyebrow. "You two are responsible for getting Mary and Jerry together?"

"Yeah," Benji said, "but we had to set a few fires to do it."

Pastor Andrea laughed. "That's remarkable. I must hear the story sometime. What good boys you must be."

Alfie made a face. "It would really help us if you would come to our house, buy two jars of peanut butter, and tell our *mamm* how great we are. Maybe she'll listen to you. Two of Bienenstock's finest citizens shouldn't be sleeping in the cellar."

Petersheim Brothers Peanut Butter Bars

For the bars

1 cup butter, softened

1 cup sugar

1 cup brown sugar

2 eggs

2/3 cup peanut butter

1 tsp. vanilla

1 tsp. baking soda

½ tsp. salt

2 cups white flour

2 cups quick oats

For the topping

1 ¼ cups semi-sweet chocolate
   chips

½ cup powdered sugar, sifted

¼ cup peanut butter

2-4 Tbsp. evaporated milk

Preheat oven to 350 degrees. Cream together butter, sugar, and brown sugar. Blend in eggs, 2/3 cup peanut butter, vanilla, baking soda, and salt. Stir in flour and quick oats. Spread mixture in greased jelly roll pan. Bake at 350 for 20-25 minutes. Remove from oven and immediately sprinkle with chocolate chips. Let stand 5 minutes. Combine powdered sugar, ¼ cup peanut butter, evaporated milk. Mix well. With a spoon, spread the melted chocolate chips evenly over the bars. Dribble with the powdered sugar mixture. Cool and cut into bars.

Doggone
Cookie Disaster

Rachel J. Good

USA Today bestselling author **Rachel J. Good** writes life-changing, heart-tugging novels of faith, hope, and forgiveness. She grew up near Lancaster County, Pennsylvania, the setting for her Amish novels. Striving to be as authentic as possible, she spends time with her Amish friends, doing chores on their farms and attending family events.

Rachel is the author of several award-winning Amish series in print or forthcoming, including the bestselling *Love & Promises, Amish Sisters & Friends, Unexpected Amish Blessings, Surprised by Love, Amish Detective Benuel Miller,* and two books in the *Hearts of Amish Country.* In addition, she has written more than two dozen anthology stories and novellas along with the *Amish Quilts Coloring Books.* She enjoys meeting readers and speaking at events across the country about Amish life and traditions. Please visit her online at:

Website:

http://www.racheljgood.com

Facebook:

www.facebook.com/people/Rachel-J-Good/100009699285059

Goodreads:

www.goodreads.com/author/show/14661177.Rachel_J_Good

Pintrest:

www.pinterest.com/racheljgood1/

Amazon:

www.amazon.com/Rachel-J-Good/e/B019DWF4FG

Bookbub:

www.bookbub.com/authors/rachel-j-good

Instagram:

www.instagram.com/rachelj.good

Rachel Good's Hitching Post on Facebook:

www.facebook.com/groups/196506777789849/

You can sign up for her newsletter at: http://bit.ly/1qwci4Q

Rachel's Amish Novels

Love & Promises Series

Amish Teacher's Gift

Amish Midwife's Secret

Amish Widow's Rescue

Sisters & Friends Series

Change of Heart

Buried Secrets

Gift from Above

Big-City Amish

Hearts of Amish Country Series

Secret Identity

Hearts Reunited

Unexpected Amish Blessings Series

His Unexpected Amish Twins

His Pretend Amish Bride

His Accidental Amish Family

Surprised by Love Series

Unexpected Amish Proposal

Unexpected Amish Courtship

Unexpected Amish Christmas

An Amish Marriage of Convenience

Her Pretend Amish Boyfriend

Dating an Amish Flirt

Missing Her Amish Boyfriend

Novellas

Amish Twin Trouble

Amish Wedding Day Revenge

Missing Amish Daughter

Amish Christmas Treasure

Anthologies

Springs of Love

Love's Thankful Heart

Plain Everyday Heroes

Love's Christmas Blessings

Love's Truest Hope

Summer of Suspense

Amish Christmas Twins

Amish Christmas Miracles

More Amish Christmas Miracles

Christmas at the Amish Bake Shop

Amish Christmas Kinner

Amish Spring Romance

Amish Across America

Nonfiction

Amish Quilts Coloring Book

Prayerful Author Journey

Chapter 1

Whew! Only two hours to go. Priscilla Miller sank onto one of the folding chairs in her basement-turned-catering-kitchen and studied her list. She'd been working nonstop for days to scrub every nook and cranny of her house and bake hundreds of cookies.

She cast a critical eye over the tables lining the perimeter of the room, displaying precisely placed platters heaped with cookies. Floor-to-ceiling display units stocked with canned goods and crafts for sale stood on each side of the double entry doors, and a nearby counter held flyers advertising her new catering business. Sample bags of cookies with recipes attached lay artfully arranged beside them. The center of the room held round tables with seating for eight.

Even by her own exacting standards, everything looked perfect.

Wait! Was that tablecloth hanging lower than the one on the adjoining table?

Priscilla hopped up, lifted the poinsettia centerpiece, and smoothed the green cloth up higher. She stepped back and cast a critical eye over her adjustment. Much better.

Nothing to do now but wait until the Lancaster Amish Christmas Cookie Tour bus pulled into her driveway to drop off her first group of guests. She inhaled the bracing scent of pine garlands draped over windowsills. The Christmas-y smell should have lifted her spirits and filled her with peace and anticipation.

But Priscilla couldn't relax. Would the *Englisch* visitors appreciate the low-key decorations of her plain and simple lifestyle? Would they like her cookies? Would they be interested in her talk about life in the Amish community?

A deep unease ran beneath all those anxieties. What if she didn't get enough customers to keep her business running and pay for *Mamm's* cancer treatments?

As these questions squirreled through her mind, Pricilla's nerves twanged. Work was the best antidote to worry. But what could she do to stay busy?

Baking cookies always soothed her, and she had cookie dough chilling in the refrigerator for tomorrow. Maybe she could slide a tray or two into the oven before everyone arrived. The aroma of freshly baked cookies would greet her arriving visitors.

After she slid the trays into the oven, Priscilla scurried upstairs to do another last-minute check. She moved from room to room, aligning the quilted wall hanging a smidgen, tweaking the crocheted blanket draped on the rocking chair, wiping a speck of dust from a windowsill.

Her business cell phone chimed in her pocket. Was the tour company calling about a delay?

To her surprise, her sister's shaky voice greeted her. "Pris, I'm so sorry. All of us have the flu."

"What?" Priscilla's voice rose in a screech. She couldn't believe this. "None of you can come to help?"

"*Neh.* I'm sor—" Her sister gagged, and the line went dead.

Priscilla shook the phone. *Impossible.* What could she do? It was too late to cancel the tour.

She sank into the rocker, not even caring she was mussing the afghan she'd just straightened.

Her four sisters and *Mamm* were supposed to help serve cookies, fill mugs with hot chocolate, lead tour groups around the house, take catering orders, and sell cookies, crafts, and canned goods. How could Priscilla possibly do all that alone? She'd planned to circulate among the guests, introducing herself to the visitors, answering questions, and—

Maybe her cousins could help. She dialed her uncle's woodshop. The phone rang and rang. When the answering machine kicked on, Priscilla blurted out, "I need help."

Guilt flooded over her. Here she was, worrying about herself and her business when her family was sick.

She gulped back her plea for the cookie tour. "This is Priscilla. *Mamm* and my sisters all have the flu. *Daed* may need help with the little ones."

After she hung up, she dropped her head into her hands. *Lord, please take care of everyone in my family, and show me what to do.*

All her careful planning and preparation had been for naught. God had a plan and purpose in this, but Priscilla had no idea what it might be.

Acrid smoke choked her.

Ach! The cookies!

The battery-powered fire alarm went off.

Priscilla dashed downstairs and yanked open the oven door. A choking cloud of smoke curled up from the charred cookies and clogged her throat. She held the tray to one side as she rushed for the back doors. Using one elbow, she shoved the panic bar on one of the glass doors.

A gust of frigid air whooshed around her, and she shivered. Last night's dusting of snow had turned to slush. She slipped and slid to the garbage bins on the side of the house, then scraped the cookies into a metal can with a tight-fitting lid.

When she entered the smoke-filled kitchen, tears stung her eyes. She propped both doors wide and fanned the burning smell toward the outdoors. Freezing air wafted in, but the odor lingered.

I tried so hard to do everything right, to make sure everything was perfect. What am I going to do, Lord?

Chapter 2

Loud incessant buzzing startled Zeke Esh awake. He leaped off the bed and stared around, disoriented. His battery-powered clock flashed six-twenty. Why was he fully clothed?

Before he could figure it out, a blur in the blackness bashed into him, knocking him back onto the bed. What was going on?

A wet tongue slurped across his face.

One mystery solved.

His recently adopted rescue puppy—if a ninety-pound, five-month-old Great Dane could be called a puppy—had jumped up to show his affection.

"Here, Blue," Zeke held out a hand to pet his dog, and the rest of Zeke's day came rushing back.

He'd been up all night and most of the day fighting to contain a major fire in the woods along with several other stations in the area. A few fire-fighters had stayed for hours afterwards to wet things down and prevent embers from endangering nearby houses. As one of the single men, he'd volunteered for that duty. After he got home, he'd showered and flopped on the bed to rest. He must have fallen asleep. And staying here at *Onkel* Les's house while his *onkel* was in rehab had disoriented Zeke.

The shrill whine still split the air. That's what had woken him. A fire alarm. All Zeke's senses jumped to alert.

It came from next door. He raced downstairs and grabbed the kitchen fire extinguisher. Blue wove in and out between Zeke's feet, tripping him up.

"Stay," Zeke commanded before he pulled the back door open.

Blue squatted on his haunches.

Smiling, Zeke patted the puppy's head. "Good boy." Maybe this lively ball of energy was finally learning some commands.

He tugged open the back door and dashed onto the porch. Before the screen door slammed shut behind him, a ninety-pound weight bowled him over. Zeke tumbled down the two steps of the porch. Right into a puddle.

He caught himself with one hand and twisted sideways to keep the fire extinguisher from smashing into the ground. But slush soaked his knees and pant legs.

He pushed himself to his feet, dripping with frigid muddy water.

"*Neh*, Blue," Zeke yelled as he chased the escaping dog.

Blue seemed to think they were playing a game. He darted left and right, evading capture. Zeke stopped abruptly.

Smoke billowed from the neighbor's basement windows and doors. What if she was inside? He had to alert her to the danger. She needed to get out.

Zeke changed directions and charged toward the house. The woman had moved in two weeks ago, but he hadn't met her yet. Nothing like breaking through a new neighbor's doors or windows to rescue her.

Barking wildly, Blue bounded off after a squirrel. That should keep the puppy busy for a while. Zeke prayed Blue would stay in the patch of woods behind the houses.

To his surprise, both of his neighbor's back doors were propped open. He sprinted inside, extinguisher at the ready.

Clang! Metal rang against metal.

Oof! His pretty, young neighbor groaned as the extinguisher clashed into the heavy urn she was carrying. She staggered back. The lid clattered to the floor. Hot chocolate splashed over the top and onto the floor.

Zeke jumped aside before the liquid burned him. "*Ach!* I'm so sorry." His free hand shot out to steady her. An unexpected tingle ran up his arm. He'd never touched such soft skin. He let go so quickly she wobbled, but soon regained her balance.

Eyes wide and uncertain, she stared from him to the chocolate puddle on the pristine white linoleum.

"I, um . . ." He gestured with his chin to the extinguisher. "I came to put out the fire."

"What fire? I only burned some cookies." Her teeth clamped down on her full pink lower lip. A lip that made him wish—

Zeke tugged his gaze from that temptation and met her eyes again. She seemed to be fighting back tears.

Had he hurt her?

"Are you all right?" he asked in alarm. "Let me help you with that." He started to reach for the urn, then realized he still held the extinguisher. He set it down and held out his hands.

"I can do it." Priscilla angled her body away from him, causing more liquid to dribble over the sides and onto her shoes.

Zeke had no doubt she could handle it. Judging from the pristine room with everything laid out so beautifully, she was one talented *maedel*. But he wanted to help. "It's the least I can do after causing this accident."

"Well . . ."

As she hesitated, he stepped sideways, took a firm hold on the urn, and gently pried it from her arms, trying not to admire the gracefulness of her wrists and hands.

Good heavens! What was going on with him? He'd always kept his attention away from women to focus on work. Ever since Daed had died, Zeke had worked two or three jobs to make ends meet, and he'd volunteered at the fire station. He'd been saving for years to open his own business. Until then, he intended to steer clear of romantic attachments. The last thing he needed was to fall for anyone.

His neighbor stared at him like a little bird, her head cocked to one side, looking so adorable, he almost changed his mind about not courting. *Almost.*

He caught himself in time. But heat flushed up his neck and burned his cheeks. "Sorry. I was thinking—" Zeke snapped his mouth shut before he revealed what had been on his mind. He didn't even know this *maedel's* name.

From the way her lips curled into a semi-smile, she must have guessed what he'd been thinking.

"I'm Zeke," he offered. "And you're . . .?"

"Priscilla." Her clipped answer showed she didn't share his flights of fantasy.

Not that he blamed her. His attempt at rescue had been a major fail.

He sighed. "Where do you want me to put this?" He held the heavy urn while she appraised him. Despite her sharp tone, he couldn't help hoping she liked what she saw.

Her mouth twisted. "I'll need to clean it off before you set it on the buffet table."

"Good idea." To keep his mind off the graceful sway of her dress, he studied the room as she headed for the sink. A professional kitchen with gleaming propane appliances filled the large space to the left of the stairs. A small alcove to the right held a small woodstove that hadn't been lit. The rest of the room held tables, all beautifully decorated with green cloths and pots of poinsettias wrapped in shiny gold paper. But the full trays of cookies caught his eye.

"Those cookies look delicious. You're having company?"

Wringing out the cloth in nervous hands, Priscilla answered tightly, "I'm expecting the Christmas Cookie tour bus to arrive in a little over an hour, but now. . ."

She didn't have to finish her sentence. He got the point. He'd messed up her clean room, and now she'd have to fix it.

"It's my fault. I thought your house was on fire."

When she turned, the tension in her eyes and lips added to his guilt. "*Jah*, well, with all the smoke, I can see why. I don't know how I'll get the smell out before everyone arrives." Moisture shimmered in her eyes. "I worked so hard to make everything perfect."

She didn't add, *And you ruined it all*, but Zeke's conscience blamed him.

"I'll stay and help you clean up."

Her teeth caught her lower lip again. "You don't have to."

He most certainly did. He'd been responsible for this mess.

She gestured toward the urn with the damp dishcloth. It dawned on Zeke that the wet side faced his shirt. He turned it so she could clean it.

"*Ach!* Your shirt."

"No worries. It'll match my knees."

A small giggle erupted. Zeke laughed with her. He must look a sight.

"What happened?" she asked, as she painstakingly wiped the urn.

"My dog knocked me off the porch and into a slush puddle." That reminded him. Where was his puppy?

Lord, please give me a sign that Blue's safe.

Zeke tamped down his worry to concentrate on helping his neighbor. "Now, where do you want this?"

She pointed to a table that held mugs, and Zeke toted the urn to that spot. After he set it down, she rotated it first one way and then the other. Unlike him, she paid attention to the tiniest details.

"Where's your mop? I can clean up the spill while you fix that."

She shook her head. "No need. I'll do it."

Her tone indicated he couldn't be trusted to do it right. Zeke wanted to prove that he could. He spied a narrow door that might lead to a broom closet. He crossed the room and opened it.

Jah, he'd been right. He'd never seen such a neat closet. Each tool hung from its own peg. She'd arranged cleaning supplies by category on shelves.

Zeke grabbed a mop and bucket. He'd filled the bucket and started mopping by the time she'd arranged the urn to her satisfaction.

She hurried across the room and stood, hands on hips, watching him. From the slight frown creasing her brow, she didn't approve of his technique. She held out her hand for the mop.

Reluctantly, he turned it over. She'd just finished swiping the spot when a loud *woof* resounded right outside the open door.

Blue! Danke, Gotte!

Before Zeke could dash to the door to collar his exuberant puppy, a tiny kitten skittered in, shivering and frightened. She scooted up the nearest shelves. Blue, his paws wet and muddy, burst through the door and attacked.

The shelving unit teetered. Glass jars flew in all directions, shattering around Blue. Blobs of raspberry jam slithered across the floor. Pickles and chow-chow oozed over broken glass.

"Stop!" Zeke shouted and lunged to snatch his puppy's collar.

Blue evaded Zeke's grasp, bumping the shelving so hard it tipped.

As the shelf wobbled, the kitten leaped to the nearest table.

Zeke grabbed for the metal posts to steady the unit before it crashed to the floor. Two more jars tumbled off. He ducked before they hit him. Peaches splashed his pants and shoes. Slices wriggled like worms as waves of juice flooded the linoleum.

When the shelf stopped rocking, Zeke whirled to find the desperate kitten leaping from table to table. Blue chased it, pawing each tablecloth, leaving muddy prints behind. Poinsettias tipped, spilling dirt across the tablecloths.

Skidding through the sea of slop, Zeke sprinted after them. "Blue, stop!"

The Great Dane ignored the command.

The cat scampered across the long tables. Blue jumped and snapped at it all along the way. Carefully stacked towers of cookies cascaded onto the floor. Blue's huge paws crushed them into crumbs.

Finally, Blue cornered the kitten beside the urn. Back arched, the tiny cat clawed at the puppy's nose. Yipping, Blue backed away.

As Zeke dove for the puppy's collar, the kitten seized the opportunity to escape. It streaked toward the stairs.

Ach, no! She'd destroy the upstairs too. Zeke couldn't believe the chaos Blue had unleashed.

Chapter 3

From the moment that tiny ball of fur scooted into Priscilla's house followed by a huge blue-gray monster, she'd been gulping back shrieks. Stunned, she'd stood motionless as an unbelievable scene flashed past her eyes. Shattered jars, overturned centerpieces, muddied tablecloths. This couldn't be real. It had to be a nightmare.

Please let me wake up, she begged.

She'd had terrible dreams like this before. Ones where everything spiraled out of control. She pinched her arm. *Ouch!* The sharp sting proved this was actually happening.

How would she ever clean up the disaster?

She pressed a hand over her mouth as tray after tray of cookies smashed to the floor. She had to do something, but what?

The cat hightailed it up the stairs. *Ach!* Would it destroy her nice clean rooms?

Zeke grabbed the dog's collar with two fingers. The dog whimpered and twisted away from her neighbor's tenuous hold.

"Can you head him off?" he yelled as the enormous dog headed in her direction.

Priscilla's mouth went dry. Dogs scared her to death. Even small ones. And he wanted her to capture this giant? What if it bit her?

"Stand in front of the stairs!" Zeke shouted. "Don't let him go up!" As if sensing her fears, he added, "Blue won't hurt you. He's friendly."

Still, she hesitated. She'd been badly bitten once. She wouldn't make that mistake again.

"Priscilla, please?"

His gentle plea touched her. As much as she longed to respond, instinct took over. She sidestepped the dog, letting it barrel past.

Zeke shot her a disappointed glance before charging after the animals, and Priscilla regretted her inaction.

In shock, she stared around the room that had been beautifully decorated only a few minutes before. Now everything was in shambles. She'd never be able to set it right before the tour bus arrived. What was she going to do?

***

Zeke galloped up the stairs two at a time. He had to stop Blue's destruction. The thought of the wreckage downstairs sickened him.

What would Priscilla do now that everything she'd so carefully prepared for visitors had been ruined? How could he make it right?

He couldn't think about that yet. Not until he captured his runaway dog.

The kitten, with Blue trailing close behind, had knocked picture frames crooked, upset a battery-powered lamp with a pretty glass shade, clawed holes in an afghan, and left paw prints across a tan couch. Blue's muddy prints grew fainter as he chased the kitten across the shiny hardwood floor and onto the oval rag rug. His tail whipped back and forth, sweeping the few carefully placed knickknacks off the tables and into shards.

Amish Christmas Cookie Tour

The animals zipped down a narrow hallway and into a bedroom. Zeke slammed the door, trapping them inside. Then he slowly eased the door open an inch at a time so neither of them could escape. They paid no attention to him. Blue sank his teeth into the quilt and twisted it off the bed, trying to reach the kitten perched on the headboard.

Zeke slipped inside and shut the door. Pounced on Blue. Wrestled him to the ground. Got a firm hold on his collar. Marched him to the door.

The kitten jumped to the dresser. Blue tried to pull away. Zeke clamped down tighter. No way would he let go until Blue was back home. Zeke shut the door to keep the kitten in the room until he returned.

When he reached the bottom of the stairs, Priscilla dumped a dustpan full of broken glass into a large trash can.

"I'm so sorry. I'll take him home and come back to help."

"I don't think—"

Zeke couldn't blame her for not wanting his help, but he had to clean up this mess. She hadn't even seen the upstairs yet.

Her phone rang. She pulled it out of her pocket as Zeke guided Blue to the door.

A loud voice boomed out. "This is Ned Parker, bus driver for the cookie tour. We have a flat tire so we haven't gotten to our next stop. We'll be running about a half hour late for yours."

"I'm going to have to cancel—" She stared at her phone. "Hello? Ned?" She shook it. Redialed. "*Ach, no!* No answer. His phone went dead." She mumbled to herself. "I can't do this. I don't have cookies. I can never get this place clean enough."

"I don't want you to cancel because of me. I'll help you sweep and mop."

Priscilla's hollow laugh made the whole catastrophe worse. "Even if I get this place straightened. I have to throw out all the cookies. I can't serve the ones on the table. The cat walked over them. The health inspector . . ." Her voice trailed off, and she pressed a hand to her forehead.

When he thought back to what the room had looked like ten or fifteen minutes ago, his heart sank. How would she ever replace all the cookies, not to mention cleaning up this room? What had he done?

"I'm sorry Blue and I ruined the cookie tour for you." Zeke tightened his hold on the puppy's collar, but without the kitten to distract him, Blue had settled down. Or maybe he'd worn himself out.

"It's not just this." She waved a hand at the shambles. "My sisters and *Mamm* were supposed to handle sales and serving and tours. They have the flu."

Priscilla caught his sympathetic gaze and shrugged. "These things happen."

She sounded so defeated, Zeke's heart went out to her. After all her hard work, it seemed so unfair that she had to pay the price for his unruly puppy.

"If I can get ahold of the driver, I need to cancel." She turned away but not before he noticed a glimmer of tears in her eyes.

An idea flickered in Zeke's mind. "Wait before you do that. I'll be right back."

Zeke didn't trust Blue in the house. He'd already gotten into too much trouble both here and at Priscilla's, so Zeke put his puppy in the basement with food, water, toys, his favorite blanket, and a shoe Blue had chewed beyond recognition a few weeks ago. Blue sprawled out on the blanket, contentedly gnawing the shoe leather.

Knowing Blue, he wouldn't stay that quiet for long. At least he couldn't get into too much mischief down here. Zeke bounded up the stairs and secured the door. Blue had managed to open it before, and Zeke didn't want to come back to rooms that looked like Priscilla's.

Before heading to Priscilla's, Zeke made one phone call and changed his clothes. He wasn't exactly sure why, but he didn't want her to remember him as disheveled and coated in chocolate and mud. Plus, if the bus tour arrived, he should be presentable. He planned to do whatever he could to help.

Chapter 4

Priscilla stared as Zeke hurried out the door with Blue loping beside him. She forced her thoughts away from him. She'd learned how painful it could be to fall for a handsome man, no matter how kind and charming he appeared on the surface. She still had the scars on her heart to prove it.

Instead, she focused on the room. This devastation in no way compared to Henry's betrayal, but right now, it overwhelmed her. She'd lost all her cookies. The whole downstairs had been turned upside down, and judging from the crashes she'd heard upstairs—

She didn't want to think about that. With so much to clean, she'd be up until all hours tonight. And she'd never have time to bake all the cookies for tomorrow's buses. Mechanically, she swept up the shattered glass.

No way could she get all this *redded* up before the bus arrived, even if Zeke came back to help. Besides, he'd never meet her exacting standards. Few people did.

That thought brought Henry to mind. When he'd admitted to secretly seeing someone else after their five years of courting, Priscilla had been devastated. Then he'd twisted in the knife:

Mary accepts me the way I am. She doesn't always try to improve me like you do. If you don't relax and stop being a perfectionist, you'll never find anyone to date. Everyone is imperfect, including you.

That last line kept echoing through Priscilla's head. Henry had been right. She was so far from perfect that she agonized over it all the time. Her grandparents reminded her of that every day when she was growing up, no matter how hard she tried to be good and do everything right.

But shouldn't you always try to do your best? she'd longed to ask Henry. She'd never had the chance because he'd walked away before she could choke out any words.

Even now, with how hard she'd worked and how carefully she'd tried to do everything right for this cookie tour, she'd still ended up with an unsightly mess. If she hadn't baked that last batch of cookies . . .

Zeke had blamed himself, but it was all her fault. She hadn't paid attention to the time. She'd burned the cookies. She'd left the back door open. If she hadn't, none of this would have happened.

And now, she'd lose out on all the sales and future customers tonight. They'd probably take her off tomorrow's tour too. It would be a black mark on her reputation. Nobody would trust a caterer who canceled at the last minute.

Without business, how would she ever pay for *Mamm's* treatments? Not to mention her loans. She'd have to give up her catering business and move back home. And face Henry and Mary living next door.

Despite mopping up all the jam-pickles-peaches glop, Priscilla couldn't possibly fix all this damage and bake enough cookies for tonight's tour group. She reached into her pocket for her phone. When the bus driver didn't answer, she dialed the tour company. A tinny announcement informed her that the business was closed for the day and would reopen the next morning. She left messages in both places, hoping someone would get them.

Now what?

***

Zeke dashed across the yard, avoiding the slushy puddles, which were now icing over as the temperatures dropped. He burst through Priscilla's back doors for the second time that day, but this time, he paid attention to where he was going.

In his hands, he held two battery operated fans. "Maybe these will get the smell out." He set them up near the door to pull out any lingering fumes and odors.

"I don't think it matters. Plus, it's already freezing in here."

"*Jah*, that's for sure." The room had reached arctic temperatures, and she'd even donned her coat. He kept his on too.

"I can light the woodstove to warm things up. Once the fans have cleared the air, we can shut the doors, and the room will be toasty in no time."

"But—but—"

"And help is on the way."

"What?" She stared at him, confused and uncertain.

"You'll see." He wanted to surprise her. By the time he had the stove going, he hoped his rescue plan would be in place.

She'd already cleared away the broken jars and set to work on the cookie crumbs as he fetched the wood and started the fire. His guess about the timing had been exactly right.

A tap on the doorjamb startled both of them.

Priscilla gasped. "*Ach*, no! The tour bus has arrived. I called to cancel. I'm not ready for—"

Zeke hurried to the door. "It's all right, Priscilla. This is my *mamm*. And my sisters." He reeled off their names rapidly. "They came to help you get ready for the tour."

"But I—"

"You canceled?"

"I tried, but got no answer."

"We'll get everything ready, just in case they didn't get the message." *Mamm* smiled at Priscilla. "If they don't come tonight, you'll be ready for tomorrow."

"You don't have to do this. It's all my fault. I'll clean it up."

"From what I hear, my *sohn*'s dog created this mess. So, we should help him set things right."

Priscilla opened her mouth to protest, but *Mamm* turned to Zeke's sisters. "Why don't you girls start cleaning? Priscilla and I can bake."

"What?" Priscilla stared at her in disbelief

Mamm ignored her. "Let's get started." She put an arm around Priscilla and ushered her toward the kitchen.

Zeke smiled. *Mamm* had things well in hand. He headed off to help his sisters.

***

Priscilla gaped at Zeke's *mamm*. Everything had happened so quickly Priscilla hadn't had a chance to take it all in. Zeke's sisters each held cleaning supplies. Mops, brooms, and dustpans flew.

One sister removed a tipped poinsettia from the table and set it on the floor. "I'll just shake these out, dust them off, and flip them over. That way the paw prints won't show."

Priscilla cringed. She wanted to rush over and insist they launder the cloths. She couldn't believe anyone would even consider hiding dirt instead of washing it off. Before she could protest, Zeke's *mamm* pulled cookie sheets from a cupboard.

"Do you have your recipes?"

"They-they're on the cookie bags."

"Great. We can mix up some dough and get started."

The dull pressure in Priscilla's head escalated to a painful ache. Her eyes burned. Everything was moving too fast.

"Priscilla?" Zeke's *mamm* studied her with concern. "Are you all right?"

"I-I'm not sure."

"Let's get some cookies baked before the tour arrives. We'll need butter." She pulled open the refrigerator. "Oh, my, it looks as if you have plenty of dough already made up."

"*Jah*," Priscilla wished her brain would function. "That's for tomorrow."

"Well, let's use it now, and then we can all help you whip up more for tomorrow."

In seconds, Priscilla had joined Zeke's *mamm*—had he said her name was Irene?—in rolling out and cutting sugar cookies. Priscilla wished she'd made drop sugar cookies instead. They'd go much faster. But Irene proved to be a whiz with a rolling pin, and soon they'd filled trays and slid them into both of Priscilla's ovens.

"Martha," Irene called, "can you take some of this dough to your house and bake it?" She handed her daughter the huge container of chocolate chip cookie dough. "Split it with Faith. She can take it next door to bake it."

Two of Zeke's sisters disappeared out the door with the container after reading Priscilla's instructions on the sample bags near the door—the only table the dog and kitten hadn't destroyed.

Zeke sniffed the air. "Anyone still smell smoke?"

"Just from the woodstove," one sister answered.

"*Gut*. I'll close the doors and get rid of these fans."

Priscilla glanced over. The cookie tables had been cleared, and the cloths flipped so they appeared clean. Only she and Zeke's family knew what lay underneath—cat and dog hairs, filthy paw prints, and ground-in soil from the poinsettias.

Even the round tables looked almost presentable. Some of the table-cloths hung slightly askew, but Priscilla didn't have time to fix them. She squeezed her eyes shut and tried not to mind. But she did.

Irene set a hand on Priscilla's shoulder. "You know, dear. God can turn even the worst mistakes around for His glory. Why don't you relax and trust Him to work miracles?"

Although Irene was right, Priscilla couldn't relax. She gritted her teeth and forced her hands to keep moving while nagging thoughts ran through her brain. *You shouldn't leave dirty cloths on the tables. The girls probably didn't sweep and mop the floor well enough. You should go over their work to be sure they picked up every last crumb. Making these cookies now won't allow them to cool long enough to ice. The upstairs has to be in total disarray.*

Priscilla sucked in a breath. *The kitten.* Zeke had cornered his dog, but she hadn't seen the cat since.

"What's the matter?" Irene looked over at Priscilla with concern.

"I don't know where the kitten is."

Irene's brow knitted. Then her face cleared. "You mean the kitten Blue chased?"

Zeke must have told his *mamm* the story.

When Priscilla nodded, Irene called to Zeke. "Where's the little kitty?"

"*Ach,* I should have checked on her." He leaned the mop against the wall and dashed upstairs.

Priscilla prayed everything upstairs hadn't been clawed to pieces.

Chapter 5

Zeke couldn't believe he'd forgotten about the cat. She could have done all kinds of damage. Why hadn't he taken care of that right away?

Only one answer came to mind. Priscilla had distracted him. He'd tried to keep his mind on cleaning, but he'd angled himself so he could watch her and *Mamm* baking. No matter how many times he told himself he couldn't date right now, his thoughts stayed focused on Priscilla.

He mentally shook himself. He had no time for this. After he reached the living room, he scanned for a sign of the kitten. The room still held the scratches, paw prints, and breakage, but nothing else seemed to be damaged.

Zeke headed down the hall, peeking into each room, marveling at the neatness and prettiness of each one. Priscilla certainly was an exceptional housekeeper. He reached the bedroom to find the kitten curled up on the quilt on the floor.

He tiptoed to the staircase and called down, "The kitten's curled up sleeping. You don't want me to turn her out into the cold, do you? I'd take her home but with Blue—"

"Doesn't she belong to someone?"

"I doubt it. She's so scrawny, she's probably one of the litter of Yoder's barn cats."

"Why don't you leave her there?" *Mamm* suggested. "We can find a home for her later."

Zeke shut the bedroom door and headed back downstairs, where his youngest sister, Lena, had finished the cleaning.

"Anything else we need to do?" she asked him.

"Just the upstairs."

"I'll take care of that." His sister mounted the stairs. "Maybe you could help with the baking." She gave him a teasing grin.

"*Jah*, I can do that."

He turned toward the kitchen. The slight frown lines marring Priscilla's pretty face bothered him. He'd been the one to put them there. He yearned to make her smile.

"Do you have any dough I could take next door? I can bake a few batches."

Priscilla's eyebrows shot up. She gave him the same look she had when he'd tried to mop up the cocoa. Obviously, she doubted he could do it.

"I do most of my own cooking," he assured her. "Well, except when *Mamm* makes things for me."

His mother laughed. "Don't worry, Priscilla. You can trust him. Didn't I see more drop cookie dough in the refrigerator?"

Priscilla's frown deepened. "*Jah*, I do have orange-oatmeal-raisin dough in there, but—"

"Great. I'll grab the bowl and a recipe." Before she could object, he whisked the dough from the refrigerator and left with a sample bag. All he had to do was to plop blobs of dough on cookie sheets and time them. How hard could that be?

***

Fifteen minutes later, Zeke reappeared carrying the first batch of—of—

Priscilla tried hard to think of a kind way to describe the well-browned, ragged lumps of all different shapes and sizes. She squeezed her eyes shut for a moment, hoping when she opened them, lovely, evenly shaped circles would greet her eyes.

Unfortunately, that didn't happen.

He stood there proudly, holding out his offering. "Timed perfectly. Oh, and they're delicious." A sheepish look crossed his face. "Some of them fell apart, so I sampled them. No point in letting them go to waste."

"Of course not." She tried to say it graciously without a sarcastic bite. She must not have succeeded.

His face fell. "I know they don't look as good as yours. I saw how nice yours were earlier."

What could she say? He'd gone out of his way to help, and here she was—acting churlish and ungrateful.

Irene stood silently nearby, watching their interaction. That made Priscilla doubly guilty. After all Irene's family had done . . .

"*Danke*. Could you put them on the table?" Maybe they could pile other cookies on top, and the guests wouldn't eat down far enough for them to show.

Zeke crossed the room and set the chipped stoneware plate on the table.

"If you put them on a platter, you can take your plate back home with you."

Please, please, please.

He picked up his plate. "I'll head back to make more."

"Wait." Priscilla opened a drawer and pulled out a cookie scoop. "If you use this, it'll make the cookies even. And I take the cookies out just before they get brown on the top. They still cook a bit when they come out, but it keeps them moist."

Zeke laughed. "I'll probably never be an expert like you, but thanks for the tips."

Priscilla's cheeks heated. She'd sounded so bossy and critical. Exactly what Henry accused her of. Unlike Henry, Zeke seemed unruffled by it. Still, she needed to curb her need to have everything perfect.

Her phone buzzed in her pocket. She pulled it out. The bus driver.

"We'll be loading everyone into the bus in about fifteen minutes, so we'll be at your place in half an hour. You're the last stop, so people may stay a bit longer there."

Without giving her time to respond, he hung up.

Should she call him back and tell him not to come? Anxiety clawed at her insides.

Irene turned to her. "Did I hear him say they'd be here in thirty minutes?"

Priscilla nodded.

"Do you think you'll have enough cookies?" Irene stared at the cookies cooling on the racks.

Zeke stopped in the doorway. "Don't worry. I'll stick more pans in the oven and let Martha and Faith know to bring their batches over. We can all keep baking, even after the tour bus arrives."

Priscilla tried not to flinch. She'd never imagined she'd be doing a tour without enough cookies to serve, let alone cookies that weren't perfectly baked or shaped. All her hard work and attention to detail . . .

Irene put an arm around Priscilla's shoulders. "I can see this is hard for you, but Zeke's right. Don't worry. People will enjoy themselves even if everything isn't perfect."

Priscilla swallowed the lump that formed in her throat at that gentle reassurance. Her grandparents never would have agreed with it, but Priscilla had no choice tonight but accept that she'd fall far short of their expectations. And hers.

"People may appreciate things looking lovely, but more than anything," Irene said, "they'll remember how you treat them."

Her wisdom jabbed at Priscilla's conscience. She often fussed more over unimportant details than over making sure others were happy. Maybe God had planned this so she'd have to change her focus.

She and Irene had finished two more batches of cookies in each oven when Zeke entered with a platter of cookies. To her surprise, they didn't look too bad. Or maybe she was examining them without her usual critical eye.

Irene chuckled. "You did good, *sohn.*" As he carried them to a serving table, she whispered to Priscilla, "How they taste is more important than how they look."

"I know." And she did. "But they actually look pretty *gut.*"

"I'm glad you think so." Irene's eyes twinkled.

Zeke turned, giving Priscilla an appraising glance. She squirmed. For some reason, she really cared what he thought and hoped he liked what he saw.

"Martha and Faith are on their way. They got a few neighbors to help. We don't have much time now, so maybe you want to change your apron and—"

Ach! Priscilla didn't want to hear any more. She darted upstairs before he could hurt her feelings more.

As she passed through the living room, she missed several of her favorite knick-knacks. She'd placed them precisely, which made their glaring absence even more noticeable. And though the room appeared tidy, the afghan hung crookedly over the rocker. The lamp sat off-center on the table, and her pillows cross-stitched with Bible verses had been tossed on the couch rather than meticulously placed. She had no time to fix them.

She yanked open her bedroom door and stopped abruptly. A kitten lay curled up on her quilt. Normally, she would have worried over cat hairs on the fabric, but Irene's comments had made an impression. Priscilla sympathized with the tiny kitten.

"Poor baby. You must be tired after that dog chased you."

Instead of changing her clothes, she rushed to the kitchen and poured a bowl of milk. Then she filled a plastic pan with some of the extra potting soil she'd used for the poinsettias. Even if she didn't have time to change her clothes, she wanted to be sure the kitten stayed comfortable. That was more important than her looking perfect.

With the litter box and food in place, Priscilla changed her apron. She'd just smoothed her hair and repined her *kapp*, when wheels crunched in the gravel driveway. She ran downstairs to greet the guests.

"Priscilla?" Zeke's soft voice stopped her headlong rush. He leaned close. "I didn't mean to embarrass you. It's just that you seem to like everything just right, so I thought—"

"That I wouldn't want to greet visitors while I was so untidy." She finished his sentence. *Jah*, he'd guessed correctly. But did she come off as so persnickety that even someone she'd just met could tell?

"You looked fine to me," he continued, "but I worried you wouldn't think so."

Warmth rushed through her. He thought she looked fine? Her pulse sped up even more than it already had. *Neh*, she reminded herself. *You fell for a handsome, charming man before. Don't make the same mistake again.*

"I, um, need to see to the visitors." She broke away, trying desperately to concentrate on smiling at the stream of *Englischers* descending the bus steps.

A blast of icy air hit her as the first guests opened the double glass doors and filed in.

"*Gut'n Owed,*" she greeted each one. "*Danke* for coming."

A young mother of two school-aged daughters leaned over to whisper to them, "She just said *good evening* and *thank you.*" She beamed. "I've read those words in Amish novels." Then she blushed. "I'm sorry. Good evening to you too. And we're glad to be here. Thank you for having us."

"I'm glad you're here." And Priscilla genuinely meant it.

As people milled about the room, she took stock of everything. She tried to tamp down her dismay at how things looked.

Instead of her carefully stacked heaps, the trays held sparse, slapdash displays of cookies on mismatched serving plates, Zeke's sisters must have arrived while she was upstairs. All of them wore flour-coated aprons except Lena, who was graciously offering tours of the upstairs. Priscilla hoped nobody had cat allergies.

Irene, her *kapp* askew and wisps of gray hair escaping, was acting as backup cashier between keeping Priscilla's ovens going nonstop. Zeke, who must have changed his mud- and hot-chocolate-stained clothes earlier, now had smears of cookie dough on the sides of his black broadfall pants, and flour dust on his shirt and hair.

That made her long to brush it off. She reined in her thoughts.

He bent and pulled two cookie sheets out of the oven while his *mamm* totaled up several purchases.

Priscilla hurried over. "I can do that."

Zeke waved her away. "I've got it. You need to talk to your customers." He stuck two trays of cut-out cookies into the oven and set the timer.

His mother must have prepared them while Priscilla had been upstairs. Deftly, he slid the baked Christmas trees onto the cooling racks. He seemed to know what he was doing. They wouldn't be iced, but at least she had a few more cookies to put out.

"Once you've finished, you might want to check your clothes and, um, your hair."

He glanced down at himself. "I need to clean up, huh? Guess that's not good for your business."

Priscilla wished she'd kept her mouth shut. Better to ignore a little flour and cookie dough than to hurt his feelings. She nibbled on her lower lip. Why hadn't she kept her mouth shut?

Chapter 6

"Excuse me?" A redhead with way too much makeup touched Priscilla's arm. "Could you hold up this quilt so I can see the whole thing?"

Priscilla lifted the quilt as high as she could, but even standing on her toes, she couldn't display all of it.

A deep voice startled her. "Let me get that." Strong male hands reached over her to take the top edge.

Zeke stood so close behind her that the warmth of his chest heated her back, setting her blood flaming. She ducked under his arms, desperate to escape the strange sensations flooding through her.

But she missed his closeness. All she wanted to do was to move nearer rather than farther away. Instead, she stood mesmerized by his broad back and rippling muscles as he extended his arms over his head and spread them wide.

"Does that help?" he asked the *Englischer*.

"Yes." The woman studied the design, stepped back, and examined it from a distance. Then she moved in and fingered the fabric and the stitching. "I think I'll take it. Could you fold it up and leave it by the counter for me? I'll pay for everything when I leave."

"Of course." Zeke gave her a friendly smile.

A smile Priscilla wished he'd directed at her. "Here, let me get the lower edge." She focused on the soft lavenders and spring greens of the Star of Bethlehem pattern rather than the man across from her as she stretched out the quilt.

"Very beautiful."

Zeke's admiring gaze moved from the fabric in his hands to her. He must mean the quilt, but the way his eyes locked on hers, she had to wonder. Her cheeks burned.

His eyes mesmerized her so much as they folded the quilt, she didn't notice the timer ding. Irene, taking money from a customer, called to them, jarring Priscilla from her daze.

By the time she turned, an *Englischer* was slipping the cookies from the oven.

"*Ach!*" Priscilla dashed across the room to the kitchen. "I'm so sorry. I should have been here to do this." She reached for the cookie sheet, but the woman waved her away.

"No worries, dear. I'm happy to help. You and your husband were staring at each other with such love in your eyes. I didn't want to interrupt."

A blaze began in Priscilla's chest and splashed across her face. "We're not— He's not—" She couldn't bring herself to admit Zeke was only a stranger she'd met a few hours ago. This woman would think Priscilla was wanton.

The woman chuckled. "Nothing to be embarrassed about. It does my heart good to see young love. My husband once gazed at me with the same adoration."

Adoration? Is that what it looked like to everyone here? *Ach!*

The woman slid the cookies onto the cooling racks. "Enjoy it while you have him, dear. My darling Harold went to be with the Lord five years ago. It's left a gaping hole behind, but I thank God for the time we had together."

"I'm sorry. It sounds like he was a wonderful husband." Priscilla didn't know what to say. Telling this sweet old lady the truth—she wasn't married and likely never would be—seemed cruel.

"And like your man, he loved to help me in the kitchen. I think common interests in a marriage are the glue to keep you together. And faith in God, of course."

"Of course." Priscilla doubted she and Zeke had common interests. He'd only helped her out because of guilt. If his dog hadn't upset her room and tromped on her cookies, he most likely wouldn't be baking.

Zeke hurried over. "Why don't I take those to the serving table?" He sidled past Priscilla, who stood there helplessly, watching the elderly woman shovel the last cookie off the tray.

She beamed at him. "I was just telling your wife what a sweet couple you are. And we agreed that having God at the center of your marriage is the most important requirement."

His Adam's apple bobbed up and down. "You—you did?"

Ach! Why hadn't she corrected the lady when she first made the mistake?

***

The cooling rack tipped and almost slid from Zeke's hands. Priscilla told this woman they were married? He righted the rack before any cookies slipped off. The last thing he needed was to break any of them. He'd done enough damage already.

He wanted to catch Priscilla's eye to verify that, but if he did, he might end up drowning in her eyes again. If this lady hadn't stepped in, these cookies would have gone up in smoke.

A heavyset woman leaning on a cane tottered over. "Grace, how did you get to bake cookies in the Amish oven? May I have a turn?" She turned pleading eyes to Priscilla, whose eyes widened in astonishment.

Zeke hid a smile. Poor Priscilla! She liked to do everything perfectly. How would she handle an *Englischer* baking in her kitchen?

To his surprise, Priscilla smiled and answered graciously, "Certainly."

But from the tiny twitch in her jaw, this was hard for her. It made him admire her even more.

A young teen girl with a nose ring and tattoos approached. "If she gets to bake, can I do it too?"

Priscilla blinked. "I guess so."

Next thing they knew, a long line had formed. Most of the guests wanted to try their hand at baking in an Amish oven.

Zeke wanted to help, but first, he had to put these cookies on the table. When he returned, he caught Priscilla's eye. "I could take some people next door," he suggested.

Priscilla's eyes widened. "I guess so."

"Ooo, take me." A woman with unnaturally long eyelashes and overly pink cheeks clutched his arm.

They divided the line. The woman who'd grabbed his arm earlier stayed by his side as they crossed the lawn, her excitement bubbling over. "I can't believe I'm going to get to see inside two Amish houses."

After they entered, Zeke rolled the lamp from the living room into the kitchen. "Welcome to my *Onkel* Les's house. We'll be baking orange oatmeal drop cookies." He held up the cookie scoop.

Aaaroooo! came from the basement drowning out the rest of his speech.

"Sorry, that's my puppy. He needs to go for another walk."

"*Aww.* Can we see him?"

"He's quite a handful." Besides, Zeke didn't need Blue getting loose again. "If you don't mind waiting, I'll take him out."

A woman elbowed her way to the front of the crowd. "I can take care of things here until you get back." She reached for the cookie scoop. "Everybody line up, and we can take turns. If we each drop two cookies, we'll all have a turn."

The only positive thing about *Onkel* Les being in rehab was he wasn't here tonight. He'd be overwhelmed by a bevy of *Englisch* ladies cooking in his kitchen.

"How does an Amish stove work?" the self-designated leader asked.

"It's run by propane," Zeke explained, "so it's like a gas stove."

"Propane? I thought you used wood stoves."

"Some Amish do, but most use propane, at least in Lancaster County."

"Oh, we didn't get to see the ovens in use on the rest of the cookie tour. Everyone already had their cookies baked and set out."

Zeke sighed to himself. Priscilla would have too, if it hadn't been for him and Blue. Although he wished she'd had the perfect tour she deserved, maybe her customers were having more fun. He hoped that would make up for his terrible debacle.

By now, Blue was clawing and snuffling at the basement door.

"I have to go." Zeke opened the door a crack and stuck his hand through to get a firm grip on his puppy's collar before he slipped through the gap. "Everyone, this is Blue. I'll be right back."

Voices around the room chirped: "Oh, how adorable!" "He's so huge, he can't possibly be a puppy." "What an unusual color." "He does look blue." "What a darling doggy."

When Zeke returned, the cookies were in the oven, and women were milling around, peeking into cupboards and downstairs rooms.

Zeke sighed in relief that his sisters had recently held a cleaning day for Les. His *onkel's* house might not be as pristine as Priscilla's, but it was passably neat.

After the timer dinged, Zeke scooped the cookies off the sheets to the ladies' delight. Once the cookies had cooled for a few minutes, they each ate one and stacked the rest on a plate.

Then, they all traipsed back to Priscilla's kitchen, where the other group was munching on the cookies they'd baked. The two groups exchanged platters.

The bus driver finished one last cookie and announced it was time to go. They'd stayed much longer than their allotted time.

As people scrambled to make their final purchases and pick up their cookie samples with the recipes, Zeke drew in a long breath. He was exhausted. He'd had only three hours of sleep over the past two days. Of course, he couldn't leave before helping Priscilla clean up, but he couldn't wait to fall into bed tonight.

***

Priscilla couldn't help noticing how tired Zeke appeared. The chatter and all the work must have worn him out. She could sympathize. At least he could go home as soon as everyone left, but she'd be up most of the night cleaning and baking for tomorrow's tour groups.

She fluttered around, totaling up sales and scheduling catering jobs. When she glanced up, she was stunned to see all the dishes washed and her kitchen sparkling.

An elderly *Englischer* hobbled over to Priscilla and patted her arm. "I've gone on many of these tours, and they're always so well-orchestrated. Everything prepared and in its proper place."

Priscilla winced inwardly. Hers would have been too. "I'm sorry."

"Not at all. It's wonderful to see how a real Amish family lives. You all do such a wonderful job of getting along. A real example for some of today's dysfunctional families."

"But we're not . . ." She'd been about to admit they weren't her family, but Zeke's family had done everything her own family would have done despite being complete strangers a few hours ago.

Before she could explain, another group of ladies standing nearby pressed closer.

"I totally agree," one said. "This has been the best visit so far. I always feel so intimidated when a house is spotless. Yours feels so homey."

"That's for sure," another agreed.

A blonde woman with a blinking Christmas tree sweater and bright red nails smiled at Zeke, who was helping tote purchases to the bus. "It's so nice your husband helps with the business, even the baking. I wish mine would."

Her friend, dressed in reindeer antlers, chimed in, "I didn't know Amish husbands did that."

Priscilla opened her mouth to explain that Zeke wasn't her husband. A sudden pang shot through her at the thought he never would be.

But a grandmotherly woman clutching a quilt and two jars of jam interrupted them. "Can I buy these? By the way, all your cookies were delicious."

A chorus of yeses followed that remark, and several of the women booked Christmas catering events or ordered cookie trays for their holiday parties.

Priscilla relaxed a little. Maybe this hadn't been a total disaster.

Chapter 7

Once all the guests had boarded the bus, Priscilla blew out a long breath. *Danke*, Lord. She never could have done this without all the help from Zeke and his family. These complete strangers had pitched in to salvage what could have been a total fiasco.

She turned to Irene and Zeke, her eyes prickling with tears. "I can't thank you enough for all you did tonight."

"We were happy to." Irene beamed at her. "Now what can we do to help get ready for tomorrow."

"You don't have to do that," Priscilla protested.

Someone banged on the door, startling her. Priscilla hoped it wasn't another customer. She spun around to find Martha and Faith smiling at her through the glass. They'd been back and forth all evening bringing the cookies they'd made, so they must have used all the dough she'd given them. Yet, Faith held two huge containers of cookies, and Martha balanced Priscilla's large bowl filled with dough.

Martha bustled in. "I'll put this in the refrigerator in case you need it tomorrow. We made extra batches of your chocolate chip cookies."

While they deposited everything in the kitchen, Priscilla blinked back the tears that had been threatening to fall. How kind and giving this family was.

Irene closed the money box and headed for the sink to wash her hands. "What do you want us to do now?"

"*Danke*, but you've done enough."

"Nonsense. The girls and I can stay for another hour or two. Let us help."

Priscilla shook her head. She couldn't impose on them any more than she already had.

Irene set her hands on her hips. "I know you think you have to do everything yourself so it'll be perfect. But didn't you find out tonight how much fun it could be when others work alongside you?"

"*Jah.*" Priscilla couldn't deny that. Despite the dropped blobs of dough trampled on the kitchen floor, the flour dusting counters and clothing, and the crumbs scattered everywhere, everyone seemed to have fun. And she had too.

***

Zeke smiled at Priscilla's bemused expression. It warmed his heart to hear she'd enjoyed herself. He'd been worried she might think his family was too careless and casual. He'd seen how she'd winced when they flipped the tablecloths upside down. And how she'd tried so hard not to show her dismay at his first batch of misshapen cookies.

If only they could help her get back to the beautiful layout she'd had before Blue's romp through the house. They should at least try.

He turned to Lena. "Maybe you could collect all the tablecloths and wash them."

When his sister headed off to get them, Priscilla turned to him with surprised, but grateful, eyes. He'd guessed right. That had really bothered her.

"I'll wash all the tabletops." He gathered soapy water and rags while Martha and Faith pulled out the broom and mop.

Irene put an arm around Priscilla's shoulders. "Why don't you and I make more dough and cookies?"

Zeke had chosen a job that allowed him to face Priscilla, and he took full advantage of it. Her face had softened as the night went on, and the tension in her jaw had relaxed. Those changes had made her even more beautiful. Now her eyes, overflowing with gratitude, sparkled, making her irresistible.

He'd been drawn to her from the moment he met her, though he couldn't figure out why. *Jah*, she was lovely, but his feelings ran deeper than physical attraction. And touching her soft skin accidentally had started an ache deep inside that turned to longing. A longing for a wife and family. He wondered if she had a boyfriend, or worse yet, a fiancé. Surely, as charming as she was, she was already taken.

Martha elbowed him. "You've been rubbing that same spot on the table for so long you might have worn a hole in it."

Zeke tore his attention from Priscilla. Under his sister's watchful eye, he cleaned the rest of the tabletop vigorously without looking up once.

She giggled softly. "That's hard for you, isn't it?"

"What is?"

"Keeping your eyes on the cleaning."

Had it been that obvious?

Martha smiled. "Thought I'd never see you interested in a girl. It would be nice to see you courting."

"Not until all you girls are married." Even as he parroted the reason he'd always used to avoid dating, Zeke realized it was a flimsy excuse. Truth was, he'd never found anyone he wanted to ask out. Not until now.

"I'll leave you to your daydreams." She scooted off with a knowing smile.

If his attraction had been so obvious to Martha, maybe Priscilla had noticed too. His face burned at the thought. Suppose she had no interest in him? Besides, they'd only just met. He couldn't ask her out after spending a few hours with her. They'd need time to get to know each other, but he had no idea how to do that. Once he'd finished helping her tonight, he'd have no reason to come calling.

And after all the havoc he'd caused, he wouldn't blame her for wanting to stay as far away from him as possible. But when she'd met his eyes while they'd folded that quilt earlier. . .

***

After Lena finished laundering the tablecloths, she rubbed her eyes. "I need some sleep. We have to get up at five for work at the farmer's market."

Priscilla sucked in a breath. "Do you all work there?"

Lena nodded. "Well, all except Zeke. We have a stand at the Green Valley Farmers Market."

Guilty about keeping them so late, Priscilla raised her voice so everyone could hear her. "*Danke* for all you've done, but you need to go home so you'll be ready for work in the morning." Despite everyone's protests, she insisted and shooed them out the door.

"I don't have to go," Zeke said quietly as the rest of his family left.

"That's all right. I can do it myself." Even though, she was pretty sure she couldn't.

"You planning to have your visitors bake cookies again?" His tone held a teasing note.

"If I have to."

"I'm staying until everything's done."

The look he gave her made Priscilla's heart skip a beat. She turned away to hide her reaction.

"Besides," he said, "I'm used to staying up nights."

That made her spin around. "You are?"

"I work third shift at the MXL factory repairing their manufacturing equipment. Plus, I'm a volunteer firefighter, so I can get called out any time."

"I see." She tried to act casual, but now that they were alone together, her pulse responded to his nearness. "Why don't I make more oatmeal cookie dough, and you can bake that." Better to have him next door than here beside her.

***

Zeke hid his disappointment. Her suggestion sounded like a brush-off. She didn't want to spend time together. He determined to make the most of the time it took to mix the dough to find out more about her.

As she pulled out ingredients, he asked what he could do to help. "Can you get the largest bowl in there?" She pointed to a nearby cupboard.

He retrieved the bowl, racking his brains for a way to start the conversation. "So, what made you move to this area?"

Her back went rigid. For a moment, he thought she wasn't going to answer.

"I, um, saw this house had a walk-out basement and a large parking area—just what I needed for a catering business."

"Do you like living here?"

Her little trill of laughter did strange things to his insides. Zeke swallowed hard.

"I've only been here a week. I expect I'll like it."

He'd wished he'd come over to welcome her when she'd arrived, but he'd gone straight from his all-night shifts at MXL to Beechy's Cabinet Shop to help them catch up on Christmas orders. Then he ate a quick dinner and slept a few hours before heading back to the factory.

"Where did you move from?" he asked.

Again, she appeared reluctant to answer his question. Maybe she just didn't want to talk to him. After all, he hadn't made a good impression on her from the moment they'd met. Now, he kept firing questions at her.

Zeke sighed. Could he do anything more to ensure she'd never want to see him again?

Priscilla picked up on his sigh. "Are you all right? You don't have to do this." She mashed white and brown sugar together with butter in the large bowl.

"I'm happy to do it. Besides, I owe you for the disaster I caused."

"Don't feel you have to make it up to me. I forgive you."

"You do?" Zeke wished he could stuff the words back inside. It sounded like he doubted she'd be capable of forgiveness.

"Of course."

"I didn't mean I didn't believe you. It's just that I wouldn't blame you for being upset."

"I'm not upset anymore." She broke an egg into the bowl and confessed, "I panicked at first because it's hard for me to make mistakes."

"You didn't. Blue and I did."

She beat in the next egg so hard he wondered if she was remembering everything Blue had done, but her response, when it came, sounded mild. "I don't hold it against you. Dogs will be dogs. And I could have helped you catch Blue if I wasn't so scared of dogs."

Oh, great. He'd terrorized her too. No wonder she'd stood motionless. Add that to his list of errors. "I wish I'd known. I'm sorry Blue frightened you. He's so big and lively."

"I survived." Her attempt at a smile trembled.

"*Jah*, you did. You also survived all his destruction and had a good cookie tour. People really seemed to like it."

"They did. Even when they baked their own cookies."

"Especially the baking. Maybe you should have some events where people come to cook." He loved the way her hands measured each ingredient so deftly and then stirred it in. Everyone would enjoy watching the whole process.

She hesitated. "I don't know. There's no way to tell how things will turn out."

"Sometimes that's the fun of it." Zeke grinned, but Priscilla looked almost sick.

"It's hard for you to be spontaneous?" he asked gently.

"Suppose something went wrong?"

Zeke shrugged. "Then you just laugh and do what you can to fix it. Like you did tonight."

"That wasn't me. If you and your family hadn't helped, I'd have canceled everything."

"Think of all the fun you'd have missed out on."

His comment made her smile. "And all the business. I got a long list of catering events. If I'd called off the tour, I'd be here worrying if I'd have to close my company."

Her company? What about her family? She'd mentioned them earlier. They were sick or something and couldn't show up to help. So, she wasn't alone in the world. What had made her move away from her family to live on her own?

He'd asked too many questions already. She hadn't asked any back. Maybe she was tired. Or not interested. Or maybe she thought he was prying.

Gently, she folded in oats and raisins. "There you go. It's all ready."

The relief in her voice made him wonder if she couldn't wait to get rid of him.

***

Whew! Two batches of cookie dough finished. She turned to hand Zeke the bowl. "I really appreciate this."

The huge amount of dough she'd given him should last for a while. Once he left, she could relax. While she started on the sugar cookies, he stood there studying her. Why didn't he go?

"Do you need something else?"

From the way he jumped at her question, his mind had been elsewhere.

He blinked. "What? Oh, um, *neh.*" He headed for the door. "I'll see you later."

"*Danke* for doing this. And if you get tired, please stop."

"Don't worry. You can count on me. I'll see it through."

After the door swung shut behind him, his words echoed in her head. *You can count on me. I'll see it through.* That brought a Bible verse to mind: *He that is faithful in that which is least is faithful also in much.*

The way he'd stuck with her all evening—cleaning up after the dog, baking cookies, waiting on customers, opening his home to the *Englischers*—all proved he could be trusted with little things.

Unlike Henry, who hadn't always been trustworthy in fixing small mistakes before his big betrayal, Zeke seemed dependable in not only admitting his faults but also in dealing with them. What about big things, though? Like being honest and faithful. Was there a way to tell a man's character? How he'd react under pressure or when tempted?

Priscilla pulled herself up short. She had no business even letting her mind wander in that direction. Never again would she get involved in a relationship. Once had been enough for a lifetime.

Chapter 8

As the night wore on and they both grew more exhausted, rather than getting punchy and irritable, Priscilla grew softer and her defenses lowered, making her even more appealing. Zeke had a hard time tearing himself away after he brought over each new batch of cookies. Only the timer ticking on his oven made him hurry back. He didn't want to mess up anything more.

During their brief conversations, Zeke learned more about her. The more he discovered, the more his heart ached for her. She didn't only feel compelled to make everything spotless for her guests, she also judged everything she did and thought by the same impossible standards.

After a little probing, she admitted, "My grandparents quoted this verse in Matthew to me all the time: *'Be ye therefore perfect, even as your Father which is in heaven is perfect.'*"

Jah, the Bible did say that, and Zeke admired her for working so hard to reach that goal. "I agree we should always try for that, but nobody's perfect except God."

Her lovely forehead crinkled. Zeke tamped down the urge to reach out and smooth away her distress.

She looked close to tears. "That's true, but it doesn't mean we shouldn't try."

From the tension in her face, she'd set herself an impossible-to-attain aim. "You put a lot of pressure on yourself, don't you?" he asked.

"I have to. As the oldest in my family, my grandparents insisted it was my duty to be an example. If the little ones did anything wrong, I got in trouble too."

"That doesn't seem fair."

Priscilla shrugged. "To them it was, and of course, I did things wrong."

"It's hard enough trying to do the right thing yourself, let alone taking the blame for someone else's sins."

"*Dawdi* pointed to the Scriptures say that no one should put a stumbling block in his brother's way." Priscilla's mouth lifted in a wry smile. "*Mammi* made sure I understood it applied to sisters too."

Heavyhearted, Zeke rushed home to take out more cookies. What a great burden Priscilla carried. That verse came from God's Word, but did it mean she should be punished if someone else stumbled?

That was the first question he asked her when he returned.

She had a ready answer. "*Mammi* and *Dawdi* had a quote for why I got in trouble for my sisters' misbehavior: *It were better for him that a millstone was hanged about his neck, and he cast into the sea, than that he should offend one of these little ones.*"

"How old were you when they told you that?"

"I'd just turned six. My five-year-old sister had stolen two lollipops at the market. *Mammi* marched us both back to the stand and handed the candy back. She scolded us in front of Nick, the man at the candy counter, and she paid for the candy, even though she'd returned it. When we got home, *Dawdi* made sure neither Beth nor I could sit down at the supper table that night."

Zeke's chest tightened. Amish parents were strict about correcting misbehavior, but it sounded as if her family was way too harsh. And why had Priscilla been punished when she was innocent? His throat closed too much to even ask, but after she unbottled this childhood pain, she kept talking.

"After supper, *Dawdi* read me that Bible verse and made sure I understood what a millstone was. I was terrified the next time my sisters did something wrong, he'd knot that stone around my neck and toss me into the pond behind our house."

"*Ach*, Priscilla!"

She continued on as if she hadn't heard him. "I often had nightmares and woke up choking, clutching at my neck, clawing to untie the rope holding the millstone."

Fear pooled in her eyes, and Zeke longed to pull her close and hold her until the frightening memories had passed.

"I still have those scary dreams from time to time." Her hollow laugh revealed she harbored much of that childhood dread.

This time, when Zeke sprinted back to his oven, guilt filled him at the thought of how painful it must have been for her to face the overturned room and his sisters' well-meaning—but sloppy—flipping of tablecloths and their casual dumping of cookies in untidy stacks.

He prayed Priscilla didn't have the millstone dream tonight because of him, Blue, and his family. If only he could help her erase those awful memories.

***

Priscilla had never told anyone about her childhood. She couldn't believe she'd shared her innermost secrets. And with a man. A man she'd only met today. What must he think of her?

At first, she'd bristled under his questioning. He was only being friendly, but sooner or later, she'd worried he'd probe her sore spots. When she was young, she'd erected a wall to hide her imperfections and inadequacy. And since then, she'd always tried hard not to get close to anyone.

Somehow, he'd gotten through her defenses. He'd made her feel so comfortable. Too comfortable. She needed to be on her guard when he returned.

She baked drop cookies while she waited for the sugar cookie dough to chill. Then she switched to rolling out that dough. This time, when Zeke stopped in, he carried cookies and a black book. *A Bible?*

After he deposited the cookies into one of her large plastic storage containers, he flipped the Bible open to a place he'd bookmarked. "I know you've read this before, but—"

Priscilla stared down at Luke chapter seventeen. The first two verses were the ones she'd quoted about the millstone. She'd heard them so often she had them memorized. They hit her like a sledgehammer. She squinched up her eyes until the words blurred while she tried to block out the old pain.

Zeke's kind and gentle voice came to her from a distance. "I didn't mean to hurt you. I wanted you to look at what comes right after that."

With gritted teeth, Priscilla opened her eyes, ready for more condemnation. When she skimmed verses three and four, though, they focused on forgiveness. Zeke pointed to the fourth verse— the famous passage about forgiving a brother seventy times seven.

She nodded. She'd heard those verses many times before.

"Why do you think these verses come right after the millstone? Maybe God wants us to pay more attention to forgiveness than to punishment."

Priscilla let his words sink in. Her grandparents hadn't focused much on forgiving her after the mistakes and sins. They spent more time harping on her shortcomings and bringing them up frequently to remind her of recent and past misbehavior.

Zeke paused to let her consider that before continuing, "It says if someone repents, you should forgive them. Right?"

"Of course. We're taught how important that is, and we say it in the Lord's Prayer." Even as a tiny child, she'd been required to ask forgiveness. And to forgive others.

"You repented when you did something wrong." He stated it as a fact, rather than a question.

He'd never know how much she appreciated his belief in her. "I did, but—"

Pictures of *Dawdi's* stern face and *Mammi's* suspicious glances floated before her eyes. They always acted as if they doubted her sincerity when she asked for forgiveness. Their nods in response to her request appeared dutiful.

"But?" he prompted.

"I never really felt forgiven. And deep down, I knew they'd add it to the long list of faults they'd bring up later."

"That's too bad. Even if we, as humans, forgive imperfectly, it's comforting to know God is merciful and forgives completely. If we've repented, all those past sins have been cast into the depths of the sea."

Zeke's compassionate words almost did her in. Luckily, the bell dinged for the cookies. She rushed for the oven.

She'd almost shed tears earlier around his family. If she spent more time with him, she might turn into a waterworks. *Unbelievable.* She never, ever cried.

Priscila kept her back to him, so if a drop or two fell, he wouldn't see it.

***

"I need to get back home to get my oven." Zeke's timer would go off two minutes after hers. He hated to leave now when she seemed so close to a breakthrough.

Before he shut the door, he called over his shoulder, "Remember, everything on your grandparents' list is gone—as far as the East is from the West."

Once he got home, he prayed for her as he took out the cookies. Holding high standards was *gut*, but berating herself every time she fell short was not. And being unable to believe in or experience forgiveness led to a lifetime of pain and regret.

Priscilla seemed chained to the past and that held her back from enjoying life. She'd seemed to have fun tonight once she'd relaxed a little, but he'd love to see her truly believe she was forgiven.

Lord, please use Your Word to heal her.

Although Zeke rushed to plop balls of dough onto the cookie sheets, he made sure each ball was uniform. He was proud of the cookies cooling on the rack. They all appeared even, with nicely rounded edges. He hoped they'd meet Priscilla's expectations.

When he returned, Priscilla had clammed up, and she kept her back to him. Had she had enough of his prying? Did she think he was too preachy? Perhaps he shouldn't have criticized her grandparents.

Then, he noticed her lower lip trembling as she turned to get more sugar cookie dough from the refrigerator. Had she been crying? Maybe he should stay quiet and let God work in her heart.

***

When the door closed behind Zeke, Priscilla whirled around. Had he thought she was shutting him out? Didn't want to talk to him?

Despite the pain of the old memories he'd brought up, she enjoyed his company and missed him now that he was gone. She didn't know how to let him know she'd like him to stay but wanted to stick to casual conversation.

Zeke popped in and out all night with batches of oatmeal cookies. After he ran out of dough, he stayed to help her cut out sugar cookies and took extra trays to his oven to bake them. She loved working side by side, but her throat had closed, blocking off her words.

He didn't seem to mind. Most of the time, he stayed silent. A few times, he chatted about his family, and she nodded or made *um-hum* sounds to let him know she was listening.

Once in a while, they bumped elbows, and Priscilla sucked in a silent breath at the tingles that ran through her arm. When Zeke moved farther away to avoid accidentally touching her, she couldn't help being disappointed.

"Priscilla?" Zeke's voice stirred her from her reverie.

Her *jah* came out choked.

"I hope I didn't offend you or make you feel bad."

Inwardly, she berated herself for hurting him. She had to let him know she wasn't upset with him. Through strangled vocal cords, she managed to say, "*Neh*, you made me think."

After everything else she'd confessed, she may as well be honest. "I never talked to anyone about my childhood before." She pressed her hand to her throat. "My words are stuck here."

Zeke's caring smile only made the lump in her throat increase.

"It's all right. Sometimes working together in silence is nice. If you aren't feeling angry at each other."

"*Ach*, no."

He laughed. "I didn't mean you. I meant if two people—not us—were holding grudges. You know, like a married couple. . ." A blush spread across his face, and he added hastily, "Or a brother and sister. Or two friends or—"

She cut him off. His discomfort loosened her tongue. "I understand what you meant."

"*Gut*." He changed the subject. "How many more batches do you have to make?"

"No more tonight. I'll mix up dough and put it in the refrigerator. Then I'll get up early and bake some more. Eight buses are scheduled tomorrow."

"Eight? Tonight you had only one. How will they all fit in?"

"They won't all come at once. Each bus usually stays fifteen to twenty minutes before it moves on to the next stop. I'm not the final house on the tour this time."

"Oh, that's why they stayed so long tonight. So, what time will you get your first visitors?"

"Nine."

"I'll be over at eight."

"You don't have to do that."

As soon as she said it, she regretted it. She enjoyed his company, and she'd need some help. To her delight, Zeke insisted he wanted to come. But how would two of them handle eight busloads?

Chapter 9

Priscilla crawled into bed at three in the morning and set her alarm for five-thirty. She'd never stayed up this late before in her life. She wondered how Zeke managed working third shift.

When the alarm rang, she batted it off and rolled over to go back to sleep. A tiny mewl startled her awake. *The kitten.* She'd been so tired last night she'd forgotten all about it. Had she hurt it?

She fumbled for the DeWalt light hanging on her bedpost. Before she could flick it on, needlelike claws kneaded her arm through the sheet. *Ouch!*

The kitty must be defending its territory. Priscilla reached out and stroked the soft fuzz ball to reassure the kitten she was safe. "I had no intention of hurting you, little one, but you didn't know that."

A sudden realization struck Priscilla. "You're just like me. Swiping out at people so you don't get hurt." Her thoughts went back to Zeke's probing questions last night. At first, she'd reacted to him in the same prickly way the kitten had to her.

What did kittens do when they were afraid or cornered? Swipe out, scratch people, or run and hide.

"We're more alike than you know." Priscilla rubbed behind the kitten's ears. "Sometimes I scratch back too. Most often, though I run away or hide." She'd also done that last night. First, being sharp and giving short answers. Then after Zeke had gotten through her defenses and she'd spilled secrets about her childhood, she'd gotten scared, hidden deep inside herself, and avoided talking to him.

Zeke had seemed unfazed by her sharp comments or her silence. He'd been unfailingly kind and understanding. He seemed to have a totally different take on life. He and his family saw mistakes as a way to learn and a chance to practice forgiveness. She doubted she'd ever be able to accept her own errors that way.

Priscilla couldn't help wondering if once Zeke had paid her back for his dog's mishap, she'd scare him off. Whenever she'd gotten too critical with Henry, he snapped back, and they ended up in a tiff. They'd both spent a lot of time apologizing and forgiving each other. Maybe her cat-like, claws-out reactions should have been a clue she wasn't cut out for marriage—not just with Henry, but with anyone.

That thought depressed her as she dressed hastily, but neatly and hurried downstairs to do more baking. She wanted everything to be perfect before Zeke arrived.

Her stomach churned at the word *perfect*. Yesterday, she'd done that, and look what had happened. Even more disturbing, Zeke's comments and Scripture verses came back to her. All her life, she'd accepted everything her grandparents said as true about her. But Zeke had suggested they'd been too harsh. Had they?

Priscilla refused to think ill of her family or her upbringing. She pushed away the questions. But fighting the nagging doubts proved difficult. If she let them in, they might alter how she looked at her childhood and her whole life.

***

When Zeke knocked on the door, Priscilla turned to greet him with a wide, welcoming smile that immediately dimmed. That disheartened him, but he focused on her first reaction. The one before her strict inner rules warned her not to act too friendly. Deep down, she must be as glad to see him. His heart sang with that thought.

"What's this?" she asked, pointing to the large bags in his arms.

"Thought you might need some cat food, litter, and toys."

Her brow creased into a frown. "You didn't need to do that."

"I wanted to. If you don't like accepting gifts"—he had a strong feeling she didn't—"think of them as my presents for the kitty."

Zeke waited as her face flickered through multiple emotions before settling on gratitude.

"The kitty thanks you," she said at last.

He smiled. "I'm glad. Why don't I go and set up this litter box? Where do you want to store the food and litter?"

Her face screwed into a worried expression. She probably needed to figure out the ideal place.

"What about the broom closet?" He motioned over the bags with his chin.

"*Neh*, I don't know if the inspector would approve of that. I'm not allowed to have pets down here."

Ach! Blue and the kitten had run wild through here yesterday. Could she have lost her license?

When Zeke was growing up, his *mamm* had never let them have pets in the house because she baked for the market stand, so he'd been grateful to be staying at his *onkel's* house when he'd rescued Blue. Zeke had never dreamed he'd put Priscilla's business at risk. They'd cleared away most traces of the animals before any visitors arrived. Suppose someone had arrived during the chaos?

Luckily, no one had, and Zeke vowed to do everything right today so he didn't cause her any more trouble.

"Could you put them in the upstairs kitchen pantry?"

Priscilla's question startled Zeke from his musings.

"Sure." He headed up the stairs and opened the door. Faint meows came from a room down the hall. "Should I feed the kitten?"

She gasped. "I was so worried about getting everything ready, I forgot about her."

"Don't beat yourself up," he said gently. "You're not used to having a pet."

***

Priscilla couldn't believe she'd done this. "I should have taken care of her first thing. I don't know how I could have forgotten. I—"

"Priscilla!" Zeke's sharp command sliced through the air. "You made a mistake. Mistakes happen. Forgive yourself."

Forgive myself? How could she do that when she was filled with so much guilt?

As if he'd read her mind, Zeke said, "Do you believe God can forgive?"

"Of course."

"Then ask for and accept His forgiveness."

When he put it like that, feeding the kitten seemed rather a small thing to bother God about, but He cared about every sparrow.

Dear Lord, I'm sorry I spent more time worried about impressing visitors than in caring for one of Your creatures. Please forgive me.

By the time she lifted her head, Zeke had closed the basement door. Overhead, two metal bowls clattered to the floor. Then pellets clinked into a bowl. A loud, joyful meow warmed Priscilla's heart.

If only she could be around Zeke all the time, she'd become more accepting of herself and others. And he inspired her by his cheerful attitude. Even his steps on the floor above seemed upbeat and happy. She'd like to be more like that instead of always fretting.

When he came back down with a smile stretching across his face, he brightened the room. "What do you want me to do?" He glanced around. "Looks like everything is beautiful, and those cookies smell delicious. Must be *wunderbar* to be in this buttery- and sugar-scented air all the time."

Priscilla had never paid much attention, but now that he'd mentioned it, she drew in a deep breath and let pleasure flow through her. "You're so *gut* for me."

The second she said it, she cringed. She'd made a terrible mistake. What would he think of her? "I mean—" She fumbled for words to explain away her slip of the tongue.

***

Her words thrilled Zeke, but he held up a hand. As much as he loved her spontaneous compliment, he'd done nothing to deserve it. And he told her so.

Quickly, he moved on to something else. "*Mamm* and my younger sisters have to work at the market today, but my three older sisters will be here soon to help with customers. They can bake too, if you run low on cookies."

Priscilla's eyes widened. "You didn't have to do that."

"I saw how busy you were last night. You and I can't do it alone, and my sisters are happy to assist."

"I can't believe this. Your family doesn't even know me. I want to pay all of them for their time."

Zeke shook his head. "They're not doing it for pay."

Priscilla didn't have time to argue with him because Lydia tapped at the door. Zeke let her in, along with Emma, Sarah, and three of their daughters, who were sixteen, thirteen, and eleven. He introduced all of them to Priscilla.

"My brother Abe and his wife are watching the younger children, but the older girls wanted to help," Lydia said. "I hope that's all right."

"That would be great." Priscilla stared at them as if overwhelmed.

"Everything looks so lovely," Sarah exclaimed. "When we were younger, we did some Christmas Cookie Tours, so we were excited when Zeke asked us about coming here today."

Emma's appreciative gaze took in the room. "Just tell us what to do."

"If you have more cookies to bake, we could do that," Sarah offered.

"You can take the dough over to *Onkel* Les's house if you need more ovens." Zeke had scrubbed the kitchen after last night's baking but left out all the baking supplies.

A short while later, Sarah took two of the girls to her house with batches of orange oatmeal dough, and Lydia and her oldest daughter went to *Mamm's* kitchen to bake chocolate chip cookies.

They all returned with containers of cookies just before the first bus pulled in. A whirlwind of tourists whooshed through the room, selecting items to buy, taking tours through the house, and sampling cookies. Soon after they left, another group arrived.

Things were flowing along well, but the cookies were disappearing quickly. Lydia and Priscilla returned to baking.

"I need to walk Blue," Zeke told Priscilla, but I'll be back as soon as I can.

He headed to the house, and remembering Priscilla's comment about no pets in the kitchen, he took Blue out the basement door and kept a firm hand on his puppy's leash.

***

Priscilla missed Zeke's uplifting smile and deep bass voice after he left to walk the dog. As the next busload filed in, she tensed and kept a sharp watch on the door. Suppose Blue got loose again and slipped inside?

Vivid pictures of the dog gallivanting through the room leaving paw prints everywhere, jumping up on people, crushing cookies, and—

Those alarming images vanished because a totally different nightmare appeared.

Chapter 10

Ach, no! It couldn't be. Priscilla's eyes had to be playing tricks on her. She rubbed them, but nothing changed. What were those two doing here?

Most of her guests were *Englisch* women, some with children and husbands, who wanted to see Amish houses or buy cookies and crafts. Very few Mennonites and Amish families came. Why would a young Amish couple come on this tour?

The timer dinged. Grateful for an excuse to turn away, Priscilla bent and removed the trays from the oven. She inhaled deeply. Zeke was right. That buttery, sugary smell was delightful. And calming.

"Those smell *gut.*"

Priscilla recognized the girl's voice. *"Danke."* She forced out the word as she slid cookies off the sheet without turning around.

"You always did make delicious cookies." The reedy tenor grated on Priscilla's nerves. So did the fake-sounding compliment. When had he ever said anything positive about her cooking?

She pretended not to hear as she hurriedly scraped the snowmen off the second cookie sheet and onto a cooling rack. Maybe if she ignored them, they'd go away.

But distress and anger tightened her shoulders and her jaw. Why had he come here? To taunt her? To rub in his happiness with someone else?

Henry had never been interested in going on any of the Amish bus tours to cities around the state that Priscilla had wanted to try, no matter how much she'd begged. He'd refused to even board the school buses that transported people a few miles to mud sales. He'd claimed he couldn't stand being cooped up in a bus with other people, and besides, buses gave off terrible fumes that made him sick.

Now he was riding around the countryside on a tourist bus to Amish houses? Whose idea was this? Mary's? If so, she had more influence over Henry than Priscilla ever did. The thought stabbed through her. *Maybe he never cared about me.*

"Aren't you going to say hello?"

"Hello," she forced out as she reached for the third cookie sheet.

Lydia's oldest daughter came racing into the house with a container of chocolate chip cookies. "Where did you want me to put these?" She had to edge around Henry to reach Priscilla.

The teenager's closeness blocked Henry and Mary from Priscilla's peripheral vision. She tried to act natural as she scanned the tables.

"Looks like we need more cookies near the urn. And could you check to see if we have enough hot chocolate?"

The girl gave Priscilla a sweet smile that eased some of her tension. "Sure, and I'll make more if we need it."

"That would be great. *Danke.*"

"Since when do you trust anyone help you? Especially a *youngie?*" The sarcasm in Henry's voice bit into Priscilla.

"I've changed," she said lightly. As she lifted the last few cookies off the sheet, she realized it was true. She'd lightened up a little since Zeke had come into her life.

Jah, deep down, she still worried that the teen wouldn't make the hot chocolate recipe correctly, but she'd learned to let some of that pressure go.

"I'll say."

Was there a note of admiration in his voice? Priscilla whirled to face him.

Mary gasped. "Priscilla Miller?" She rounded on Henry. "I wondered why you were talking to her like you knew her." She planted her hands on her hips. "I didn't know she'd moved out here. Did you know Priscilla's house was on the tour?"

"Maybe." Henry waved a hand toward Emma's daughter, who was gathering a small group for a tour of the house. "Why don't you go with them to see the upstairs?"

Mary tossed her head. "I'm not an *Englischer*. I don't need an Amish house tour."

"Well, I have some unfinished business with Priscilla, so I'd appreciate some privacy."

"What?" Mary practically screeched. "We're engaged. Your business should be my business too."

"Not this. Go on the tour. I'll tell you about it later."

Dragging her feet and looking back over her shoulder, Mary headed toward the group gathering by the steps.

A knot formed in Priscilla's stomach. Henry's attitude toward Mary reminded Priscilla of the way he used to treat her. Memories of her grandparents' scoldings and punishments drifted through her mind. Had she accepted Henry's treatment because she was used to her family's disapproval? After her talk with Zeke yesterday, she saw clearly that her unwillingness to accept God's forgiveness had made her assume she deserved constant blame and criticism.

That knowledge gave her the courage to face Henry. She'd always reacted to his ultimatums like her frightened kitten—by scratching or fleeing. But Henry no longer had a hold over her. She wouldn't let him intimidate her.

"I'm surprised to see you here, Henry. I thought you disliked bus tours." Although it pained her, she added, "You must care for Mary a lot to agree to come."

Henry blinked a few times, obviously unused to Priscilla speaking her mind like this. Then he squared his shoulders. "It was my idea."

"You wanted to come on this tour?"

"Not exactly." He shuffled his feet. "I wanted to talk to you."

"You could have stopped by."

"I wasn't sure if you'd open the door if you saw it was me."

She might not have wanted to, but she couldn't be that rude. So instead, he cornered her in a place where she had no choice but to stay and be polite.

Sarah came bustling over with an empty platter. "Is everything all right?" She scrutinized Henry, then Priscilla.

"Everything's fine," Henry assured her. "My girlfriend and I are just working out a disagreement."

Priscilla stared at him open-mouthed.

"I see." Sarah flashed him a sympathetic smile. "I'll just take these cookies and get out of your way." She collected the cooling cookies and scooted off.

Fists clenched by her side, Priscilla struggled for words. "Your—your girlfriend?"

Henry had the grace to look embarrassed. "*Jah, vell,* that's what I came to talk to you about. I'd like to get back together." He took a step forward.

She took two steps back. "You came with your fiancée to ask *me* about dating again?"

"More than just dating. I want to marry you."

***

Whistling, Zeke strode across the lawn after walking Blue, happier than he'd ever been in his life. For the first time, he'd met a woman he'd like to court. A woman he hoped might want to share his future.

He pulled open the door to Priscilla's basement and made a beeline toward her kitchen. He'd almost reached her when noticed a man standing close to her. The man's words ricocheted into Zeke's heart like bullets ripping holes into him. Five words. Five bullets. Five gaping holes.

I want to marry you.

That sentence echoed over and over in Zeke's ears. He'd hoped to say those very words to Priscilla someday. Instead, someone else had said them to her first.

Thoughts flashed through his mind: *Get out of here before she notices you. Don't let her see how you feel about her.*

Slowly and cautiously, he backed to the door, blocking out any sounds from that part of the room. He couldn't bear to hear her reply.

He made it to the parking lot and turned to jog across the yard, then stopped. He needed to be alone to wrestle with his feelings. But where could he go? Emma and her daughter were baking in Les's kitchen. Zeke started for the woods.

"Zeke?" his sister Sarah called.

He didn't want to talk to anyone or let his family know the depths of his disappointment. His dreams had just crashed and shattered.

Sarah caught up to him and touched his elbow. "I'm sorry."

"For what?" His voice came out as a croak.

"You know." She waved back toward the house.

What had she seen? What had she guessed? Of all his sisters, Sarah had always been the sweetest, the kindest, the most understanding. The family peacemaker, she felt others' pain as if it were her own.

"I can tell you like Priscilla and—"

"Was it that obvious?" Zeke's face flamed. Who else had figured it out? Had Priscilla known?

"Don't worry. Priscilla doesn't have any idea, and I don't think anyone else was paying much attention."

Zeke's breath leaked out, leaving him drained and flat. At least he hadn't made a fool of himself in front of Priscilla. As long as she didn't suspect, he could wish her well in her relationship and keep his heartache to himself.

"I heard more of their conversation. Do you want to know?"

Not really. What he'd heard had been devastating enough. But he nodded.

"At first, I thought that guy was bothering her because she didn't look happy to see him. I went over to ask if she needed help."

"He said he and his girlfriend were working out a disagreement, so I left them alone." Sarah paused. "I guess they're dating."

"They must have worked out their problem because when I came in, he asked her to marry him," Zeke said bitterly.

"Ach, Zeke, I'm sorry. It's too bad things didn't work out for you. All of us really like Priscilla."

Zeke nodded. *So do I.*

***

Marry him? Shell-shocked, Priscilla stared at Henry. He'd come here with his fiancée. "You're already engaged."

"It was a mistake."

A mistake? If Henry had asked Priscilla about getting back together soon after the two of them had broken up, she'd probably have been grateful and eagerly agreed, despite him leaving her for Mary. Now that she'd spent time around Zeke, she could clearly see Henry's unfaithfulness and his manipulation.

Who brought the girlfriend they planned to break up with on a trip to propose to someone else? The cruelty of that took Priscilla's breath away.

"If you really mean that, why didn't you break up with Mary first?"

"I—I, um . . ." Henry looked everywhere except at Priscilla.

"You were waiting to see if I said *jah?* If I don't, you'll marry Mary?"

Henry turned belligerent. "That's none of your business."

"I think it is. If you truly loved me, you'd never have come here with Mary."

"That's not true. Besides, I couldn't come on a cookie tour alone."

"So you're using her?"

He bristled. "*Neh*, I'm not. You've changed, Priscilla." He studied her up and down. "You used to be prickly, but now you're—you're . . ." He seemed at a loss for words.

"Honest?" she suggested.

Henry shook his head. "Mean."

Chapter 11

The driver called out a final warning to board the tour bus, and Priscilla released a sigh of relief.

Mary, her eyes blazing, grabbed Henry's arm. "We have to go."

Although Priscilla had once resented Mary, now she pitied Henry's new girlfriend.

Henry planted his feet and resisted her tugging. "So, what do you say, Priscilla?"

"*Neh*, never."

His *hochmut* didn't accept that answer. "You don't mean that."

"I most certainly do." Priscilla faced Mary. "Be sure to ask your *fiancé* what we talked about." She rather doubted Henry would tell the truth, and she wished she could warn Mary before Henry broke her heart.

***

Zeke stayed outside for a while after Sarah went back in. Hidden in the shadows of the trees, he watched the tour group board the bus. His stomach twisted as the Amishman emerged from the door. Zeke had only seen the back of him, but he recognized the cocky posture and blue shirt. Only one other Amish man had come on the trip, an older man with a bent back and green shirt, so this had to be Priscilla's boyfriend.

A girl clutched at his coat sleeve, dragging him toward the bus. She must be his sister. They didn't resemble each other, but they both had dark hair and eyes. The man continued to gaze through the glass doors at Priscilla.

Zeke didn't blame him. He wanted to do the same, but now that he knew the truth, he tore his gaze away.

After the bus pulled away, his sisters and nieces rushed around taking batter to be baked. The cookie platters looked low. He should probably help bake.

Lord, give me the strength to help her even when my heart is breaking.

He sucked in a calming breath, straightened his spine, and strode into her basement. Priscilla shot a radiant smile in his direction. For a moment, he forgot all about her boyfriend and responded with one of his own.

Then he sobered. He'd never seen her this happy. It must be because she'd made up with her boyfriend—*neh*, her fiancé—if she'd agreed to marry him. If she hadn't, she wouldn't be this sunny.

If Zeke planned to propose, he'd never have done it during a public tour when Priscilla was so stressed and had so much work to get done. Surely, her boyfriend could have found a more appropriate time and place.

But who am I to criticize? I'll never get a chance to propose. Only one woman had ever stirred these feelings in him. Now that he couldn't have her, he'd never marry.

***

Priscilla's heart jumped when Zeke walked through the door. She wished he hadn't taken so long to walk the dog. Maybe he could have saved her from Henry's proposal.

She prayed Henry would accept her answer. He never liked being told *neh*. It made him even more determined. She hoped having a backup bride would be enough.

In her relief at Zeke's return and Henry's departure, Priscilla's happiness overflowed, adding a spring to her step and an irrepressible smile to her face. Most of her joy stemmed from the freedom that came from accepting God's forgiveness. She caught herself humming under her breath as she floated around the kitchen.

"What do you want me to do?" Zeke asked.

"Why don't you cut out the cookies while I roll out dough?" She wanted Zeke beside her to drive away any thoughts of Henry. Also, talking to Zeke made time fly because he always chose interesting topics for conversations. She particularly loved his use of Scripture verses to deepen her faith.

It dawned on Priscilla that she and Henry rarely discussed spiritual things. She wanted a husband who focused all his thoughts and decisions on God's Word. Why had she never noticed Henry's self-absorption and disinterest in discussing sermons or Bible passages?

"Is something wrong?" Zeke studied her with concern.

Not now that you're here. Priscilla smoothed out the frown that had wrinkled her brow at the thought of Henry. She pushed all memories of him from her mind. They belonged in the past. She didn't want to spoil even a second of her time around Zeke with worries about a man she'd banished from her life. Her attention belonged completely to Zeke.

She beamed at him. "I'm so glad you're here. I love spending time with you." She regretted her exuberance when Zeke appeared taken aback.

"You know," Zeke said, "we'll get more cookies made if I take some dough and a few cookie cutters over to my kitchen."

"If that's what you want." Had she scared him off by acting overly enthusiastic?

Priscilla tried not to let her disappointment show as she transferred some dough from the refrigerator into a bowl and handed it to him. "*Danke* for helping."

"I'm happy to." His polite response lacked the usual twinkle in his eyes.

She missed that and his upbeat attitude. He took the bowl, careful not to touch her fingers. She should be glad, but her spirits plummeted. He almost seemed to be avoiding her.

"I'll get these back to you before the next bus arrives." A brief semi-smile flickered across his lips before he turned his back.

Maybe staying up so late had caught up with him and caused him to droop. She hoped that's all it was. As far as she could remember, she hadn't said or done anything to hurt his feelings—at least not since early in their conversation last night when she'd been *murrish* and standoff-ish. But they'd moved past that, and she'd relaxed enough to be honest and share her childhood. Things had flowed well after that.

Zeke welcomed her confidences and invited more. What did she know about him, though? Suppose he had a girlfriend? Or even a fiancée? Maybe, in the light of day, he'd realized their closeness and sharing had been inappropriate. Now, he was pulling back. As much as it hurt, she had to accept it. She respected him for setting limits. His future wife could trust him.

Priscilla tamped down the small voice that whispered *If only I could be that wife.*

She had no hope of that. After the fiasco with Henry along with Zeke's coolness, she'd learned her lesson. Marriage wasn't for her. She smashed the rolling pin onto the dough and rolled furiously.

"Whoa." Emma's daughter laughed. "Who made you so mad? *Onkel* Zeke?"

"*Neh*, he's been nothing but kind." Priscilla didn't want anyone to think ill of Zeke, not after he'd been so helpful and supportive.

"Was it that handsome man who was talking to you in the kitchen?"

Ach! How many people had been watching their conversation? Priscilla had been so engrossed in trying to fend him off, she hadn't thought about all the visitors. She shook her head.

Beating the cookie dough like that could make the cookies tough. She rolled more gently. "I'm mostly upset at myself."

That was the truth. She'd gotten entangled in a relationship with Henry because she feared being an *alt maedel*. And she must have done something to cause a rift with Henry. Why else would he have left her for Mary?

"I know that feeling," Emma's daughter said. "I feel like I'm always making mistakes."

"Me too," Priscilla admitted.

"My *mamm* made some big mistakes when she was a *youngie*. If *Daed* hadn't been such a forgiving, accepting man, *Mamm* might never have married."

"I see." Priscilla wasn't so sure Emma's mother would appreciate her sharing family secrets.

"I worry because I have a rebellious heart just like *Mamm*. Maybe nobody will want to court me."

Priscilla had the same concerns, but she wanted to encourage this young teen. She had no doubt He had a husband planned for this sweet, honest, and open *youngie.* "We have to trust God for that."

So, why couldn't she trust Him for a future partner for herself?

***

Zeke had been reluctant to tear himself away from Priscilla, but he had to be honorable. He had no business being attracted to another man's future wife. The less time he spent around her, the better. He also hoped staying busy would keep his imagination from wandering.

By Monday, he'd be back at both his jobs, which would limit his musing, but tomorrow, being an off-Sunday would be rough. He was supposed to have this weekend off from the fire station unless he got called in for a major fire, but maybe after the cookie tour ended, he'd offer to take someone's place.

Who was he kidding? Even if he spent every waking hour working, he'd never overcome this heartache.

Chapter 12

When Priscilla woke on Sunday morning, she smiled and stretched. The kitten nestled beside her, filling her with a sense of peace and contentment. She ran her fingers over the fuzzy softness and delighted in the kitty's rumbling purr.

Yesterday had gone well—except for the small blot of Henry's appearance. Priscilla pushed that from her mind. The cookie tour had run smoothly, and she'd added quite a few names to her list of catering events. She'd also sold most of her crafts and canned goods. The business was off to a good start, and she'd made friends with Zeke's sisters.

And Zeke . . . Just thinking about him sent a wriggle of happiness through Priscilla. He'd gotten a little standoffish toward the end of the day, but she hoped it stemmed from exhaustion. He'd had only a few hours of sleep. She couldn't believe he'd stayed until almost three in the morning to help with the baking and then returned to assist with all the busloads of visitors. What a kind and giving heart he had.

She was looking forward to getting to know him better. Maybe even . . .

Once again, she stopped her thoughts, her fantasies. First of all, she didn't know if he had a girlfriend. Second, if he didn't, why would he be interested in her? And third, hadn't she decided yesterday that she wasn't marriage material?

Following that depressing conclusion, she slipped out of bed without disturbing the kitty. After she washed and dressed, she called her cousin to check on her family, who were all still sick. Barbie insisted they didn't want Priscilla to come and risk getting the flu, not when she had holiday catering jobs this week. That meant Priscilla would spend this off-Sunday alone. Unless . . .

Loud battering on the catering kitchen door startled her. Zeke? She wrenched open the door to the basement and raced downstairs to answer. Partway across the room, she skidded to a stop.

Neh!

With an impatient look, Henry motioned for her to open the door. She hesitated. His expression darkened.

He rattled the knob. "Hurry up, Priscilla."

She opened the door a tiny crack. "What are you doing here, Henry?"

"Let me in. It's freezing out here." He shivered to emphasize his words.

Although she felt sorry for him, she wasn't about to give in. Once he came inside, she knew how persistent he'd be.

"I told Mary about us."

That wheedling tone had always gotten on Priscilla's nerves. Now it made her wonder what she ever saw in him. Henry discarded women like used tissues. Suppose she agreed to get back with him—not that she would, of course—but how soon would he get rid of her for a better opportunity?

"Come on, Pris. I did what you asked."

Henry's use of her nickname grated on her. He was acting like she owed him something for doing the right thing.

"Now you need to keep your part of the bargain."

"My part? I didn't agree to anything."

Something brushed Priscilla's ankles, and she jumped, accidentally letting the door open a little wider.

Henry took advantage of it to muscle it farther. Then he stopped in surprise. "A cat? You have a kitten?"

Ach, the kitten. She must have left the door open at the top of the stairs. *No pets in the kitchen. What if the food inspector found out?*

And she didn't want the kitty to go out in the cold. She, who'd never wanted a pet, had become attached to this little ball of fur. Priscilla tried to pull the door closed, but Henry jerked it open even more.

"I need to go. I have to take the kitten upstairs."

"Do that. I can't believe you have a cat. You know I'm allergic."

"Then it's best you don't come in."

"I can't believe you're treating me like this after I gave up my relationship with Mary for you."

"I'm sorry you did that because we're not getting back together."

"You can't mean that. What's gotten into you, Priscilla?"

"I've changed." In so many ways, thanks to Zeke. And to God's work in her heart.

Henry frowned. "I can see that." He didn't sound happy about it.

"We're not right for each other anymore." Even as she said the words, Priscilla could feel the truth of that statement in her whole body. "I don't think we ever were."

Harry jiggled the door, but Priscilla leaned forward, putting her entire weight into keeping it closed.

"Why are you being so stubborn?"

Ignoring his question, she spoke firmly, "You need to go. I have things to do." Getting the kitten out of her catering kitchen was her first priority.

He glared at her indignantly. "More important than spending time with me?"

Much more important.

"Don't provoke me, Priscilla."

The exasperation in his words warned her Henry was on the verge of losing his temper. If he did, things could get ugly.

***

Zeke had slept later than usual and dressed halfheartedly. Only Blue's yipping and dancing to go out inspired Zeke to get moving. All his dreams last night had been of Priscilla—walking together, laughing together, holding hands. Yet, each time he woke, reality smacked him in the face. She belonged to someone else.

After hurrying to the basement where Blue had spent the night, Zeke clipped on the leash and pushed down the lock on the retractable handle to keep Blue close as they headed outside. Zeke had no desire to end up in a puddle again today.

When they crunched onto the frozen grass, he released the lock and gave Blue more freedom. The dog romped ahead of him, bounding and sniffing across the lawn.

Raised voices attracted Zeke's attention. A man stood in the doorway of Priscilla's basement, yanking at the door, his profile contorted in anger. She seemed to be trying to prevent him from entering.

Tugging on Blue's leash, Zeke sprinted over to protect her. When he neared, he slowed. Not an intruder, but her boyfriend. She might not want Zeke to interfere. But Blue didn't get the message to stop.

The Great Dane hurtled forward and leapt playfully at the man holding the door handle, knocking him off his feet. As he tumbled backwards, he dragged the door with him, jerking Priscilla off balance.

Zeke jumped forward to catch her before she nosedived onto the ground. In his haste to save her, he dropped the leash. Barking joyfully, Blue shot past Priscilla and into the kitchen, chasing a tiny streak of fur.

Not again! Helpless to follow his puppy, Zeke glanced down at Priscilla to apologize, and all words fled. He still had his arms around her, pressing her close to his chest. She glanced up at him, and their eyes met. And held. At the gratitude on her face, his heart escalated into a furious staccato. Her appreciation seemed to be for far more than just preventing her from falling. Could it be?

A growl behind Zeke alerted him to Priscilla's boyfriend struggling to his feet. What was Zeke doing holding another man's girl? What was he doing staring into her eyes like a drowning man? For that matter, what was he doing touching any woman?

The man leapt toward Zeke. "What do you think you're doing?"

Zeke let go and jumped back, his arms up in an *I'm-sorry* gesture.

At the abrupt lack of support, Priscilla wobbled but clutched at the doorjamb for balance. "Henry!"

Her sharp command stopped her boyfriend before he snagged Zeke by the suspenders.

Priscilla glared at him. "What do *you* think you're doing?"

The crisp, no-nonsense echo of her question pointed up Henry's out-of-bounds behavior. Anger warred with shame on his face. Anger won.

"Who is this? And what's he doing here hugging you?"

"Not that it's any of your business, but this is my friend Zeke." Her eyes narrowed. "He saved me from falling when you yanked me off my feet."

"That wasn't my fault. His monster dog slammed into me."

"Speaking of dogs," Zeke said, brushing past Priscilla, "I'd better corral Blue. You know what happened last time."

"Last time?" Henry yelped.

Priscilla rushed after Zeke. "*Jah*, let me help you."

"What about me?" Henry called after her.

"Stay there. Your allergies, remember?"

With a huff, Henry stared after them.

Zeke breathed more easily for two reasons. First of all, he didn't want to be around Priscilla's boyfriend. And second, Blue's tail had dislodged several things from tables and shelves, but none had broken. Maybe that wasn't actually a victory. It might be because Blue had shattered everything breakable before.

Following the trail of wet paw prints and frantic barking to Priscilla's bedroom, Zeke laughed. The kitten had scooted under the bed, but Blue's snout had gotten stuck. The puppy pulled back, emitted a series of frustrated yips, then poked his nose under again. Priscilla reached the doorway and giggled.

Zeke clamped a hand on Blue's collar and pulled him out. With a tight grip on the leash, Zeke retracted it until Blue stood right beside him. Then, he flicked the lock into place. "Stay, boy," he directed, not that Blue would heed his command.

Priscilla knelt beside the bed and held out a hand. "Here, kitty, kitty."

"You haven't named her yet?"

She stared up at him with a surprised expression. "I guess I should." She nibbled her lip.

Every time she did that, Zeke longed to kiss that sweet mouth. *Neh*, what was he thinking? He hoped his desire didn't show in his eyes.

Priscilla's eyes swam with tears. "I never had a pet. My grandparents wouldn't allow it."

"They lived with you?"

"*Jah*, we moved in with them after *Daed* died when I was five. They took care of us while *Mamm* worked."

Zeke had assumed her grandparents had visited or lived in the *dawdi haus*, but she'd been around them all day. Remembering the stories she'd told, his heart broke for her. "I'm sorry."

She nodded. "It wasn't easy." She ducked her head and looked under the bed. "Here, Blessing." She wriggled her fingers until the kitten came to her. Cradling it in her arms, she stood. "I've had a lot of blessings in the past few days. Her name will remind me to count them."

An appreciative smile lit her face. Was she including him among those blessings? Her glistening eyes seemed to answer that question. Sparks zinged between them.

Blue woofed and strained toward the kitten. Priscilla held the kitten out of his reach.

"Maybe they could make friends," Zeke suggested.

Priscilla appeared skeptical, but when Zeke asked her to bring Blessing closer, she complied. She lowered the kitten toward Blue, but it hissed and clawed at her arm. Priscilla kept petting Blessing until the kitten quieted. Then she tried again.

Blue sniffed at the ball of fur. Blessing swiped out at the Great Dane's nose. He yowled and backed away. After a few more sniffs, swipes, yelps, and retreats, the two touched noses.

"I think they'll be all right if you set Blessing down," Zeke suggested.

Hesitantly, Priscilla lowered the kitten to the floor. Blessing wove in and out, rubbing against Blue's legs. Blue stared at her, entranced.

The same way I look at Priscilla, Zeke admitted to himself. He had to get that under control before they went downstairs where her boyfriend waited.

Zeke's jaw clenched. He disliked Henry's treatment of the woman he'd proposed to yesterday. Sarah had said the two of them were settling an argument yesterday. Had they already had another one?

Maybe it was none of his business, but Zeke longed to protect her from abuse, especially after hearing about how her grandparents treated her. "Do you and your boyfriend fight like this often?"

"He's not my boyfriend." The words hissed out from behind clenched teeth.

"Your fiancé," he corrected himself.

"Henry is not my fiancé and never has been."

Hearing that, Zeke's spirits soared. But reason quickly asserted itself. She might feel that way now because she was upset, but when she cooled down, she'd change her mind. "I know you're angry with him, but—

"He broke up with me months ago. Now he doesn't believe I don't want to get back together."

Zeke didn't blame Henry for wanting to get back together, but how could he have broken up with her in the first place? "That must have hurt."

"It did. But now that I've met—" She reddened, clamped her lips together, and turned her face away.

Her words hit Zeke like a punch to the gut. She'd found someone else. But one thing was clear. She wanted to get rid of the man downstairs. He'd help her do that. Henry didn't deserve her.

"Priscilla," Henry bellowed. "What are you two doing up there?"

"Come on." Zeke put a supportive arm around her shoulder to turn her toward the door, but he dropped it when tingling surged through him. Not only shouldn't he be touching a woman, he definitely shouldn't be touching *this* woman. She'd just admitted she cared for someone else.

Chapter 13

Priscilla closed her eyes as Zeke supported her. If only they could stay here like this forever. When she'd fallen into his arms earlier, her heart had gone wild. She'd resisted the urge to twine her arms around his neck and pull him closer.

No wonder the *Ordnung* forbids touching.

"We'd better get down there." She forced away her longing for Zeke's embrace and hurried to the basement stairs.

Zeke followed close behind, still holding Blue's leash.

"We'll have to leave these two upstairs." She waved at Blue and Blessing.

"Oh, right. Henry's allergies."

"*Neh*," she corrected, "I don't want to lose my catering license."

Ach, he'd forgotten about that. She could get in trouble because of Blue.

"I'll put them in the bedroom. I think they'll be all right together for a while."

Priscilla waited until Zeke joined her at the top of the stairs. She didn't want to face Henry alone.

As they walked down together, Henry demanded, "What were you two doing up there so long?"

"Calming our pets." Priscilla tried to sound casual. Good thing he didn't know what else had happened.

***

Zeke hid a smile. They'd done more than settle their pets down. Then he sobered. None of that should have occurred. Priscilla cared for someone else. Right now, though, he needed to help her by sending Henry on his way and ensuring he didn't return.

Hand outstretched, Zeke crossed the room. "It's been nice meeting you. I'm Zeke." He shook Henry's hand, then motioned to the exit. "Why don't I walk you out to your buggy?"

"But—but I just arrived. I drove all the way from Honey Brook. And I haven't talked to my fiancée yet."

Priscilla waved to the door. "You told me you had."

After the momentary confusion on Zeke's face cleared, his lips twisted. "I meant you."

"Me? Your fiancée? I've never been that." Priscilla's strangled words made Zeke even more determined to get this man out of her house.

She recovered enough to throw a jab. "You must be mixing me up with Mary. Remember the fiancée you brought here yesterday?"

Zeke couldn't believe it. Henry asked Priscilla to marry him while he was engaged to someone else?

The stubborn set of Henry's jaw revealed he wasn't about to leave until he had his say. "I told you that's over."

"That's good." Priscilla looked relieved. "I worried about Mary."

"You promised you'd marry me if I broke up with her."

"That's not what I said at all. And you know it."

Maybe Zeke should have stayed around yesterday. He might have kept Henry from bothering Priscilla. Zeke wanted her to be happy, even if it was with someone else. He hoped the man she'd fallen for was kinder and more honorable than this one.

"Sorry you've come so far, Henry, but Priscilla and I need to get going. We're having dinner with my family."

Priscilla's eyes widened, but Henry's gaze stayed fastened on Zeke. "You? And her?" He waved in Priscilla's direction. "Didn't take you long to find someone else to date," he said bitterly.

"It's not surprising. Priscilla is a beautiful woman with a charming personality and a good heart. Any man would be privileged to date her."

Henry spluttered. Off to his right, Priscilla's eyes glittered with tears.

"Let me walk you to the door, so Priscilla can lock up." Zeke ushered Henry to the exit. "Dinner's at noon, and my extended family will be there, so we should leave."

His mother, who didn't know Priscilla had a boyfriend, had suggested inviting her to dinner sometime. He hoped *Mamm* wouldn't mind a surprise visitor.

And Zeke didn't know if Priscilla normally locked her doors. Many Amish families around here didn't, but he hoped she'd take his hint and do it today. He'd hate for her to come back and find Henry waiting inside her house.

***

Zeke's compliments left Priscilla floating, her spirit lighter than air. She'd been embarrassed about spilling her feelings for him when they were upstairs, but it seemed he felt the same way. He'd come over to invite her to his family dinner.

Even better, he'd sent Henry away and made sure her annoying ex-boyfriend, who was now slinking across the parking lot like a scolded puppy, would never come back. Priscilla couldn't be happier.

Before Henry reached his buggy, he whirled around. "Hey, I remember seeing you." He shook a finger at Zeke. "You brought in cookies yesterday," Henry smirked at Priscilla. "That guy doesn't love you. He only wants to take over your business."

A light dawned for Priscilla. "You wanted to run my business?" Had Henry come to check out her house and business yesterday? Now the sudden marriage proposal made sense. And he had no right to insult Zeke. She snapped, "Zeke is too honorable for that."

When Henry's jab didn't land, he changed tactics. "Once I report you to the health inspector, neither of you will have the business."

Priscilla cringed inside. Would they close her down for the animals running through it twice? She couldn't afford to lose her income. If she did, she couldn't afford to pay for *Mamm's* treatments.

Zeke straightened to his full height. "Priscilla's kitchen is spotless. The inspector won't find any violations."

The flicker of fear in Henry's eyes showed Zeke's taller, more muscled physique intimidated him. But Henry used his usual weapons—sarcasm and cruelty. "I'm sure Priscilla's not allowed to have other people baking for her in unapproved kitchens."

Priscilla bit back a gasp. She hadn't even thought about that.

But Zeke remained unfazed. "For your information, all my sisters have licensed kitchens for home-based baking. My family runs a baked-goods stand at the farmer's market."

She stared at him in astonishment. No wonder his sisters had done such a wonderful job of cookie-making.

"Told you he wanted your business," Henry taunted.

"You're wrong." Zeke smiled. "If anything, we'd be happy to buy her cookies if she has any time to make them with all the catering jobs she has scheduled. And we'll all work with her for free if she needs help with serving at events."

Henry opened his mouth as if to say something, then snapped it shut, and climbed into his buggy.

As he drove away, Priscilla turned to Zeke. "*Danke* for getting rid of him. And I do want to pay your sisters."

Zeke waved away her offer. "Nobody in my family will accept money for helping you." He headed back toward her kitchen. "I'd better take Blue for a walk. Then I'll help you clean up the paw prints in case Henry really does call the inspector."

"You don't have to do that."

"I want to."

His smile lit her whole body on fire. Could her heart get any fuller?

***

Priscilla had cleaned up all traces of Blue's visit by the time Zeke returned. He should have done it himself. After all, his dog had—once again—made the mess. At least she wasn't expecting company this time, but still . . .

The smile that blossomed on her face when she saw him set his pulse thrumming. If only it had a deeper meaning than friendship.

He swallowed hard. "Shall we go?"

Her long lashes fluttered before she gazed into his eyes. "Lead the way."

His heartbeat matched his pulse. "I-It's not far if we cut through the woods." He pointed to the path at the end of his *onkel's* yard.

Crystallized blades of grass crackled underfoot as they crossed the lawn. Zeke tried to distract himself from the soft swish of her skirt, the sway of her hand so close to his. He could reach out and clasp her soft fingers and . . .

Stop it, Zeke! That's not allowed. Besides, she's interested in someone else. Think of something different. Anything at all. Anything but her appealing smile . . . the gorgeous depths of her eyes . . . the sweet curve of her lips . . .

To end the temptation, he started nattering. "My oldest sisters, Lydia and Emma, live in Upper Dauphin County, but they and their families are visiting for the Christmas holidays. Sarah lives next door to *Mamm*."

"So, your sisters used this path when they baked the cookies last night? I wondered how far they went."

"Not far at all."

After they entered the woods, the path narrowed. Trees crowded in on each side. Every time his arm brushed hers, sparks shot through him. He couldn't wait to get to the hustle and bustle of his family. Between everyone chattering and the children's antics, he wouldn't have to force himself to think of things to say. He could just stare at Priscilla wordlessly. That probably wasn't a great idea either, but being around her had turned his brain to mush.

Zeke released a pent-up breath when they exited the woods. He pointed out Sarah's house and led Priscilla to the back door of *Mamm's*. They were soon swept into his family's joking and laughter. His sisters swarmed around to welcome her, and Zeke introduced Priscilla to the rest of his family.

Off to one side, Sarah raised an eyebrow and beckoned for Zeke to follow her into the mudroom behind the kitchen. Once they were alone among the barn boots and winter gear, she asked, "What's going on? I thought you said Priscilla was engaged."

He sighed. "It's a long story." He gave Sarah a brief account of the morning's encounter with Henry.

Sarah beamed. "*Wunderbar!* You have a chance."

"*Neh,* she told me she's met someone else."

"I'm sorry. She seems like the right *maedel* for you."

"*Jah,* she'd be perfect."

"But why did you invite her here for dinner?"

"I had to get her away from that Henry, and the only excuse I could come up with was having dinner here. I felt sorry for her, and—"

Sarah was wriggling her brows frantically. "Hi, Priscilla."

Ach, no! Zeke dreaded turning around. Had Priscilla heard? In trying to hide his true feelings from Sarah, he'd made it sound as if asking Priscilla for the meal had been a chore. He hadn't meant to insult or hurt her.

***

Priscilla's stomach dropped. Sarah's overly cheerful greeting hadn't covered up Zeke's comment.

Trying to sound natural, Priscilla pushed out words, but they came out cold and wooden. "Your *mamm* asked me to call you for dinner."

With a brilliant smile, Sarah took Priscilla's arm and turned her toward the kitchen. "We're so glad you've come to eat with us today. My sisters and I all enjoyed meeting you last night."

Numbness spread through Priscilla. Sarah's statement hadn't included Zeke. Had that been intentional?

Zeke had only invited her to the meal because he pitied her. He wanted to help her over her failed romance the same way he'd helped her with the cookies. He'd also run to her aid with a fire extinguisher. Assisting people in need came naturally to him.

She pasted on a smile and pretended she'd come for the company. With all the banter and laughter, she enjoyed herself, but sadness and disappointment lurked below the surface. The beautiful future she'd imagined with Zeke crashed down, smashing into a million shards.

Chapter 14

After the meal, Zeke stood in the shadow of the doorway while his younger nieces and nephew begged Priscilla to play Uno with them. Her lovely bell-like laughter sliced through him as he pictured another man enjoying her charms. And when she offered to hold his brother Abe's baby, an even sharper shaft pierced him. How beautiful she'd be as a mother. The intense pain caused him to turn away.

Sarah laid a hand on his shoulder. "Have you prayed about this?"

Zeke shook his head. He should have done that. But what should he ask? It wouldn't be right to request that she break up with someone else.

Lord, you know my intense longing for Priscilla, but first of all, I pray for her happiness. Help me accept the husband You have planned for her. And please show me Your will for my future.

When Zeke lifted his head, his heart remained heavy, but his spirit had lightened. He'd trust God to lead him in the right path.

"Time for naps," Sarah announced, swooping in to take the infant from Priscilla's arms.

Priscilla let go with obvious reluctance. Then she stood and brushed off her apron. "I should go. Thank you all for having me today."

Amid a chorus of *dankes*, goodbyes, and compliments, Zeke stepped forward. "I'll walk you back."

A doubtful look crossed her face. "You don't have to worry about me. I'll be fine."

"I, um, had something I wanted to say." He needed to apologize but didn't want to do it in front of everyone.

Again, she hesitated. And when she nibbled her lip the way she did while deciding, Zeke almost changed his mind about accompanying her. He wasn't sure he could keep his mind on the conversation. Still, he had to let her know he hadn't invited her out of pity.

Lord, please help me say the right thing.

When she nodded, he rejoiced, and they headed for the door together. A brisk wind hit them in the face as they stepped outside, whipping Zeke's first words away. He cleared his throat and tried again as they entered the woods.

"Priscilla, you might have heard what I said to Sarah."

The tightening of Priscilla's jaw revealed she had.

"I didn't ask you to come here out of pity. Dinner was the first idea that popped into my head to get rid of Henry."

"I see."

Her stiff answer made Zeke more determined to make things right. "But I really wanted you to come. I like you—your company."

Priscilla's eyes widened at his slip up. But she lowered her lashes as he quickly corrected his mistake.

He didn't want her to get the wrong idea. "I hope we can stay friends."

She nodded but kept her gaze on the ground.

As they exited the trees, loud buzzing assaulted his ears.

A smoke alarm.

Frantic barks came from Les's house. Wisps of smoke curled out the back door.

Zeke dashed toward Les's, but Priscilla ran toward her own house. Had the fire frightened her? Zeke didn't have time to calm her. He had to put out the flames before they destroyed the house.

He yanked open the back door to a room filled with smoke. His eyes watered as he searched for the source. Holding a hand over his mouth and nose, he headed for the oven.

A corner of a dishtowel lay smoldering on the stove. He grabbed tongs and tossed the burning cloth into the sink. Then, he wrenched on the faucet.

Water gushed over the blaze. The flames died with a sizzle, releasing an even larger cloud of gray smoke. Coughing and choking, he hurried to the door and fanned it back and forth to disperse the haze.

How had that cloth caught fire? He hurried over and checked the oven, which was scorching hot, and set on bake.

He couldn't believe it. As a firefighter, he was always super cautious about hazards and double-checked the stove every night before bed. Yesterday, though, he'd been so upset about Priscilla marrying another man, he'd not only forgotten to turn off the oven after the last batch of cookies, he'd never done his nightly check.

And he always kept flammable things away from the stove, but he'd tossed that cloth on the counter as he'd headed upstairs. He must have missed. One corner of the cotton towel had been draped over the hot stove since last night.

If he'd fixed breakfast this morning, he would have noticed it. But he'd taken Blue out the basement door instead of the kitchen, and then he'd been sidetracked by protecting Priscilla from Henry.

After they'd gotten rid of her ex-boyfriend, Zeke had walked Blue, let him in downstairs, and rushed back to meet Priscilla to take her to his *mamm's* for dinner. If they hadn't arrived home right then, his *onkel's* house might have gone up in flames.

As the alarm quieted to intermittent chirps, Priscilla burst into the room, the nozzle of her fire extinguisher at the ready. What a picture she made!

His heart burned within. She hadn't run away from the fire. She'd wanted to help him. He longed to have her fierceness and determination beside him to fight the fires of life.

She glanced around the room. "Where's the fire?"

Sheepishly, he pointed to the soggy, charred dishtowel. "I left the oven on and the towel nearby." Before she could say anything, he added, "I know. I know. A firefighter should be aware of hazards. Usually, I am, but . . ."

Zeke's face flushed with heat. He couldn't tell her why he'd been distracted.

Priscilla's lips curved up into an alluring smile. "Nice to know you're not perfect."

"Perfect? Me? I'm far from it."

"You seem like you are. You came to help a stranger, you have the answers for everything, and you—"

Despite wanting to hear more compliments from her lips, he cut her off. "I hope I didn't come off like a know-it-all."

"*Neh*, what you said helped a lot. It made me realize that no matter what I do I can never be perfect, but God forgives us and loves us as we are. Your words even helped me forgive my grandparents."

"That wasn't me. It was God."

Priscilla nodded. "*Jah*, but you opened my eyes to it."

"I'm glad I could help." Zeke averted his gaze from her glowing face. If he didn't, he might say something he'd regret.

Blue was still barking up a storm in the basement.

"I'd better let the dog out." To lighten the mood, he teased, "Thank you for coming to the rescue. At least you didn't crash into me with your fire extinguisher."

She giggled. "That turned into quite a mess. But it turned out all right in the end, thanks to you."

"I made so much extra work for you, though."

"You helped to clean it up. And if you hadn't asked your family to come to assist with serving and baking, I'd never have been able to handle the crowds."

"You'd have managed. Maybe you'd have let the visitors make cookies sooner."

"I doubt it. If you hadn't been there, I wouldn't have gotten so, um…" Her cheeks blossomed in a lovely shade of rose. "I-I'm not blaming you," she murmured so quietly he barely heard.

His neck and face rivaled the still-steaming dishtowel. Had she been as engrossed in him as he'd been in here?

Blue whined and scratched at the basement door. Zeke broke their gaze and lifted the leash from a peg in the hallway. Blue woofed and threw himself against the door. Zeke had to attach the leash to the puppy's collar quickly before Blue burst out.

The dog banged his body into the wood so hard the door rattled.

"Better step out of the way," Zeke warned Priscilla.

She flattened herself against the sink as he undid the lock and latches. Then he pressed his whole body against the door to prevent Blue's escape as he reached in and felt for the collar. When the metal hook clicked into place, Zeke released a pent-up breath and eased the door open against Blue's frantic pushes.

But Zeke was unprepared for Blue's final desperate body-slam. It knocked Zeke backward, and Blue exploded from captivity.

Zeke flailed to keep his balance and lost his grip on the leash. Blue bounded out the open door.

Priscilla set down the fire extinguisher and swooped for the flopping leash. The black plastic handle flew up and clipped her chin. Still, she managed to trap it with both hands.

Blue dragged her out the door.

"Push down on the button," Zeke yelled. He regained his balance and sprinted after them.

When he caught up, he wrapped his arms around Priscilla and fumbled for the button to halt Blue's headlong flight. Zeke cupped his hands around hers and both of them dug in their heels to bring Blue to a screeching stop.

With a soft release of air, Priscilla sank back against Zeke's chest. The blood thundering in his ears had nothing to do with the running he'd just done. The leash tautened as Blue romped at the end of it, drawing them even closer together, filling him with yearning to hold her like this forever.

***

Priscilla's eyes stung at the tender way Zeke held her. His hands covered hers gently, but firmly. And his strong arms encircled her in a cocoon of safety and strength. If only . . .

"Priscilla?" His voice, soft and breathy by her ear, stirred a deep longing in her soul.

She shivered. "*J-jah?*"

"We should move apart." He sounded as reluctant as she felt. "Can you stand?"

Her face flamed. She'd collapsed against him. If anyone saw them . . .

"Sorry," she whispered. Her apology wasn't entirely honest. She didn't regret being in his arms even if she should. But she couldn't ruin his reputation in the neighborhood or the *g'may*.

She eased herself away from his chest, and he lifted his warm hands one at a time so she could free hers. Quickly, she slid them into the depths of her coat pocket, hoping the memory of his touch would linger. She still remained inside the circle of his arms. She'd have to duck under them to get out.

When she semi-turned, Blue raced around both of them, tangling them in the leash. As the puppy made another circuit, the lead tripped Priscilla, and she fell face-first into Zeke's chest.

His arm tightened around her, holding her close, while Blue ran in a ring, getting nearer and nearer as the leash wrapped around their legs, binding them together. Then Blue flopped into a heap by Zeke's feet, panting.

"I'm sorry about that." Zeke sounded breathless.

Priscilla wasn't. She'd be happy to stay here with Zeke's heart hammering in her ear—matching the syncopated rhythm of hers. How she wished he felt the same way about her as she did about him.

But he stepped over the leather strap around their ankles. Then he bent and carefully untangled the leash from hers. She supported herself on his shoulder as he freed her from each loop. When the last one had been undone, she reluctantly let go.

He stood, only inches from her. Her breath caught in her throat as their eyes met.

"Zeke?" His name came out in a breathy whisper.

***

His choked question echoed hers. "Priscilla?"

Was it possible? Could he trust what he read in her gaze?

She said she'd met someone else. He stumbled back a few steps. But the message her eyes flashed seemed to be for him.

Lord, is she the right one? Please show me—

Before he could finish his prayer and ask for a sign from God, Blue bumped the back of Zeke's legs, nudging him forward again. Then the puppy settled back on the ground.

Blue never lay still like this unless he was sleeping. That must be a sign. So was the eager expression on Priscilla's face.

Zeke started again, this time with more confidence. "Priscilla, the real reason I asked you to dinner is because"—he drew in a breath—"I like you and want to spend time getting to know you."

"Really?" She stared at him as if dazed.

"When we were upstairs at your house, you said you'd met another man. If you're dating someone else—"

She cut him off. "I'm not." Her cheeks rosy, she lowered her lashes. "I-I meant you."

It took a moment to sink in. *She's interested in me?* Then, his spirit burst into the Hallelujah chorus.

***

Could it be? Zeke liked her and wanted to spend time together?

He answered her unspoken question. "Want to come on a walk with me?"

"I'd love to."

Zeke jiggled the leash, and Blue leapt to his feet. "Maybe I should have asked you for a jog," Zeke called over his shoulder as Blue pulled him away.

A joyful laugh spilled from Priscilla's lips as she chased after them. She had a feeling their life together would always be fast-paced. After all, look at their courtship. But as far as she was concerned, God's timing was always perfect. And so was the man he'd chosen for her. And when things weren't perfect, they depended on forgiveness.

Sugar Cookies

2 ½ c. flour

¾ tsp. baking powder

½ tsp. salt

1 c. sugar

1 c. butter

2 eggs

2 tsp. vanilla

Preheat oven to 350°F. Cream butter and sugar together until smooth. Beat in eggs one at a time, then stir in vanilla. Next, combine dry ingredients. Beat them into the butter mixture. Form the dough into two or three flattened rounds. Wrap them in plastic wrap and chill for at least two hours, or better yet, overnight. Roll out on a well-floured surface to about 1/3" thick. Cut out with cookie cutters. Bake for about 10 mins. For soft cookies, take them out when they are barely set and not yet brown. Wait a minute or two before transferring them to a cooling rack.

Makes about 3 dozen cookies.

To Decorate

Brush tops of cookies with milk and add sprinkles before baking, or let the baked cookies cool and ice them.

Icing

4 c. powdered sugar

3 tbsp. milk (add a little more if needed)

2 tbsp. corn syrup

½ tsp. vanilla

food coloring

Orange Oatmeal Cookies

1 c. softened butter

1 c. brown sugar

½ c. white sugar

2 eggs

1 ½ tsp. vanilla extract

1 tbsp. grated orange zest

1 tsp. orange extract

1 ½ c. all-purpose flour

1 tsp. baking soda

3 c. rolled oats

1 c. raisins

Preheat oven to 350 degrees F (175 degrees C). Cream butter and sugars until smooth. Beat in eggs one at a time, then stir in vanilla, orange zest, and orange extract. Combine flour and baking soda. Stir into the butter mixture. Add oats and raisins. Drop by rounded tablespoonfuls onto greased cookie sheet. Bake for about 10-11 mins. For softer cookies, remove from oven before they brown. Wait a minute or two before transferring them to a cooling rack.

Makes 4 dozen cookies.

Icing

Melt 8 oz. white chocolate. Stir in 1 tsp. shortening to thin it. Drizzle stripes of icing over the cookies.

The Cookie Thief

Mindy Steele

To Cathy and the Golden Girls who know how to find the best adventures.
To Tiffany, for taking the time to help me paint a picture.

Bestselling and award-winning author Mindy Steele is a welcomed addition to the Amish genre. Not only are her novels uplifting, they touch all the senses. Her storyteller heart shines within her pages. Research for her, is just a fence jump away, and her research aims to accurately portray the Amish way of life. Her relationship with the Amish credits her ability to understand boundaries, and customs, giving her readers an inside view of the Plain life. Mindy and her husband, Mike, have been blessed with five grown children, ten great-grandchildren, and many wonderful neighbors.

Find out more about Mindy

Website:

wordpress.com/view/mindysteele.com

Facebook:

www.facebook.com/mindy.h.steele

Instagram:

www.instagram.com/msteelem07/

Goodreads:

www.goodreads.com/author/show/14181261.Mindy_Steele

Amazon:

amazon.com/author/mindysteele

Twitter:

twitter.com/mindysteele7

Mindy's Books

Millers Creek Amish Series

To Catch A Hummingbird
The Butterfly Box
Cicada Season
Ladybug Landing

Heart of the Amish series

The Flower Quilter

Romantic Suspense
Mountain Protectors Series

Bones on the Mountain
Breaking McKinley's Curse
Deadly Sanctuary

Standalones

An Amish Flower Farm
His Amish Wife's Hidden Past
Christmas Grace

Stories

A Brookhaven Christmas (Christmas Cookies Mysteries)

Chapter 1

Joel Wickey left the town chamber meeting with the local Amish bishops feeling mighty proud of himself this morning. *Mamm* would tell him to wipe that smirk off his face. That pride was a sin, but then she would give him one of her signature grins for being a part of something as important as this.

"You did well, Joel," his *onkel* and *Bishop*, Simon Graber complimented, wrapping his steel gray scarf around his neck. "The money will indeed help all our schools."

Joel hoped that was so, but Bishop Miller was currently looking like he'd just eaten prunes for breakfast and the leftovers would be lunch. "Do you need a lift back to Cherry Grove?"

"*Nee*, we have a driver," his *onkel* replied.

Joel bid the men farewell and made his way to his buggy parked near the post office. Snow floated lazily about, adding to the inch that had fallen overnight. Appletop, his horse, was sniffing the air. He smacked his lips and tasted the white stuff. Joel would have laughed at the creature with extra human senses, if not for the eighty-year-old Bishop sitting in his buggy seat.

"Bishop Mast?" Joel puzzled why he wasn't with the other men.

"I reckon *naet* to ride around all day in a crowded car. The cold air is better for a man."

Joel wasn't sure he believed that considering the elder was merely a slip of flesh and bone, but who was he to question a bishop?

Joel climbed into the open buggy and released the brake. Working his way out of town, Joel blew into his cold hands as December air bit at his cheeks. Still, his smile stretched his cheeks muscles until they hurt as he considered what he had accomplished today. The Chamber board members were always working on new ways to raise money for charity, from festivals and bake sales, to auctions and fairs.

This year the Sheriff wanted to include the Amish communities. Corbin Mitchell had become a good friend, especially after Joel's arrest three years ago. He knew Joel wasn't guilty, but agreed setting an example to his younger brother Alan was worth the embarrassment. The sheriff was always working to help both *Englisch* and Amish spread out living within the W shaped county map.

This year's charity proceeds were to be split between the local women's shelter and the Amish school fund. Six schools would benefit if Joel could convince others to partake, because although all the local bishops nodded ahead the agreement, Joel was the one doing all the work. He didn't mind. It was a privilege to see it all come together for the good of so many.

The Christmas Cookie Tour was gonna be a success. He'd heard all about how well they did up north in Ohio, and as far away as Pennsylvania. Having local *Englisch* businesses to participate, now that was just sprinkles on the cookie. Joel's idea had been welcomed with praise.

"You have taken on a chore with this cookie business and the *Englischers*," The bishop finally spoke.

A blustery cold wind snapped at his hat. Joel pushed it down firmer over his dark hair as he brought the buggy to a halt next to one of the only three traffic lights in town. Streets were empty at this early hour, a working community more than a shopping one, but the candy cane striped light poles and flood of lights and greenery were a welcome to the season, even for a Plain man.

"*Jah*, but the schools will benefit."

The bishop grunted, his pointed chin lifting slightly. "But you must get others to accept this."

Joel was aware it would be a task considering their very faith taught them to be separate from the world, but in business, few seemed to enforce the matter. Not everyone would be open to thoughts of working with the *Englisch*. Joel suspected the bishop sitting next to him, was one.

Veering out of town, he aimed for the tall hills and curvy lanes of Walnut Ridge and considered the list in his head. Six local *Englisch* businesses had quickly volunteered to be part of the self-guided tour.

The Apple Store at Browning's Orchard had volunteered. Famous for their homemade apple cider, candied apples, and heritage, it was a great place for folks to visit and already drew in many during the harvesting season. They offered to give tours of their cider room which had been built, according to Maggie Browning, 'Before any of you pups were even born.'

The sheriff agreed to open his office, giving a historical account of the jail and the old courthouse in hopes someone else would do all the baking. Joel could bake when necessary, but with all his duties and helping to run the family's Bulk Foods Store, he hoped someone else would gladly help bake cookies to spread out amongst anyone lacking in the skill.

Brenda from the Covered Bridge Museum had been very vocal about selling ornaments and handing out bridge location maps and the history of the area, but admitted she was a terrible baker as well. Yes, he would have to find someone to help with much of the baking. He added that to the top of his mental list of duties.

There was Vicky Maddox, the local woman had turned her farm into a pet sanctuary. Everything from chickens to alpacas and depended mostly on the charity of visitors to keep the little pet farm thriving. Her idea of handing out cookies shaped like horses, goats, and cats Joel thought clever.

Charlotte Newsom happily raised her hand, even when her husband Glen grunted at adding another chore to the already filled season at the local tree farm. Joel knew them both well enough, having worked his younger years there, to know Glen would sell used shoes if Charlotte asked him to.

Many seemed surprised when Helen Cole showed up. The local bookstore owner had never attended a meeting before according to a few whispers, yet happily volunteered to serve hot cocoa and cookies and sell items from a few local vendors.

Joel's parents would be happy to help. Verna Wickey was the most giving woman Joel knew, and his mother would happily offer a tour of the Amish schoolhouse and sell Amish goods too. It was all coming together. Once he collected a few Amish shops willing to join the cause. Joel glanced over to the bishop, his frown embedded tightly and eyes roaming the landscape. Joel had his heart set on matching venues. It was only fair considering the Amish schools were benefiting with half the money raised on tickets for the tours. He let Appletop have his head to maneuver the icy hill of Walnut Ridge and considered other Amish shops possibly willing to participate.

"I reckon you plan on baking too," The bishop lifted a bushy brow.

"If need be," Joel leaned towards him. "I was raised by a fine baker." He winked and smiled. This bishop didn't appreciate a smile when he saw one.

"We will stop at the creamery," the bishop ordered. Joel nodded and tried not to note the way his wiry thin beard flapped with the breeze. It was Joel's belly that demanded his attention currently. The unsettled feeling, empty, and swirling at the mere mention of the creamery.

The Amish creamery would be a great place to start. It was no secret that the owner was born *Englisch*, married and raised a family, before becoming a widow, falling in love and becoming Amish. For a time it had been all the gossip, but between Abram's cabinet-making, and Elli's beloved goats and connections with two very different worlds, Schwartz Creamy had flourished.

"Abram's *fraa* can handle such a cause as this," he said with a lilt of objection in his voice. "But you will need help getting more folks to be willing to take part."

Joel wrinkled his brow. He could handle convincing others to agree to bake a few cookies and sell goods to tourists, couldn't he? Suddenly the bishop had him doubtful.

"I can handle finding at least five between the communities." Joel replied. He didn't mean to sound offended. This bishop didn't truly know him.

"Man should not work alone. He needs a helpmate. You are a *gut sohn* to your parents, but you should be married, Joel Wickey."

Joel let out a quiet sigh. Apparently all bishops had the same lecture to share to the unmarried. Joel should be, but things hadn't worked out as he once hoped they would.

Joel always knew what he wanted to do with his life. He loved working at his family's bulk food store and as eldest *sohn*, would one day inherit the family store when the time came for his folks to retire. Unlike most of his *freinden*, he had taken his baptism instead of stretching out his rumspringa, or running around time. Already two of Joel's *freinden* had left Cherry Grove to seek work up north and Alan Beechy had gone and bought a car, much to his father's heartbreak.

His own *Mamm* had been hopeful that after his baptism he would marry. *Daed* thought him picky, but Joel was the least picky person he knew. Joel wanted the right woman, not just any woman, and he knew just who she was. If only he hadn't ruined his chance two years ago.

"You will ask Rachel Yoder to help you."

Joel snapped his head towards the bishop. Surely the elder didn't read thoughts. "Rachel Yoder," Joel replied, having promised himself to put that young mistake behind him.

"She knows everyone about and can bake a fine peanut butter blossom."

The bishop's gray eyes warmed. Joel tried not to swallow his tongue. Not only was Bishop Mast capable of tenderness, but out of all the *helpmates* the bishop thought to suggest, he'd chosen her. Rachel Yoder made his palms sweaty and his heart jackrabbit jump. And she worked at the Schwartz Creamery sitting just a few miles ahead of them. Joel squirmed on the seat. Surely the stern bishop wasn't...

"I won't trouble her with such a chore." *Because she would certainly be troubled if she had to spend more than five minutes with me. Do I have to do this? He's not even my bishop.*

"It is our duty to help others. You need the help. She's a worthy *maedel*, and will do so happily."

Joel just stared at his elder. Clearly he didn't know his *sohn's* former girlfriend like he thought he did. And with that thought, came the memory.

Joel recalled his first attempt to catch Rachel's eye. A total bluster. It had been spring, and like a new rose, she stood out amongst all the daisies and petunias at the large youth gathering of all the neighboring communities. She was poised and elegant, and Joel was instantly smitten. She was a book cover from a faraway era to a boy of nineteen. She was three years younger, but turned his heart over in his chest like a new penny flipped to seek heads. Joel's landed on tails. Perhaps he shouldn't have sat by admiring her. Patience was a virtue unless you were a young boy love-struck in a room full of other love-struck boys.

Before Joel gathered his wits to speak to her, she accepted a ride home from the bishop's son, Martin Mast. It was to Joel's heartbreak to hear they'd started courting. One hesitation on Joel's part had cost him waiting two years for his chance to get to know her.

Joel tried to be content in his work, stay in his community without thinking of the girl in the neighboring one. But then just as quick as Martin stepped in front of Joel's intentions, he was gone. His unexplainable leaving had kept all the tongue wagglers *verra* busy. When Joel learned Rachel was working at the creamery and was no longer courting the bishop's son, he made a point to visit with some lame excuse for selling cheese at his parent's store in hopes of seeing how she was doing. Yeah, he was smitten alright and the corner display of Schwartz Cheese at his parent's store proved it.

Until the day Joel found her minding the creamery alone, sobbing and broken-hearted. He offered a kind word, his heart ached to see her so miserable. Not willing to be hesitant this time, Joel in all his eagerness asked to court her right then and there.

It was not his best day.

Instead of accepting a man who would never leave her, Rachel nearly took his head off. Clearly her heart belonged to one man, and that wasn't him.

That was two years ago. Two years was plenty enough time to forget boys who didn't know a rose from a weed. At least Joel hoped that was so, because he wasn't about to decline the Bishop's request.

"Our Rachel is a *gut* woman. I worry for her. She no longer smiles." *Because your son broke her heart!* "Spending time with others, doing *gut*, is best, and…" he turned his gray eyes on Joel again, "you are just as *gut* as any to help her. Don't mess it up."

As he pulled into the Schwartz Creamy, Joel was no longer smiling.

Chapter 2

Rachel Yoder stepped out of the large walk-in cooler into a slightly warmer kitchen. Working for Schwartz Creamery was cold work, and required many layers. The full-time dairy required many hands to keep things running smoothly and Rachel was blessed to be a part of the middle process. Making cheese.

As head cheesemonger, or cheesemaker as Rachel preferred being called as it sounded much less disturbing, she had an important duty. The dairy sold butter, sour cream, and various soft and hard cheeses. She knew the creamery inside and out, with the exception of actually milking one of the thirty pesky goats owned by Elli Schwartz. Thankfully Elli loved her creatures and never in two years' time had asked anyone else to do the milking.

And it was a far stretch from baking all day and night. Having a family who owned a bakery but finding your passion making cheese had inspired a few bleak moments between her and her mother over the years. Rachel found that making cheese, just as sewing, came easy. Creating and experimenting with different herbs, textures, forging new flavors, gave a woman...purpose.

The process required patience and Rachel thought herself a scholar of patience. Two years waiting for her intended to return was proof of that. Elli said one should never put all her marbles in another's pocket, if they valued marbles that was. Rachel didn't own any marbles, but she did own a heart, and it was severely broken by the boy who tossed it to the wayside on his rush out of Walnut Ridge in search of deep blue water and freedom. Freedom from the very roots that created him.

Her happily-ever-after never came. So Rachel nursed her brokenness, making cheese.

She moved over the wooden floor of the main shop, knowing the creaks by heart, and set down her tray. She slipped off her heavy shawl and gloves. The wood stove in the center of the room was doing a fair job today against the wintry season outside.

While Hannah, the only other employee, and Elli worked on a special order, Rachel peered out the window of the shop. Overnight, snow had transformed Walnut Ridge into the start of a Christmas dream. Cedars hung heavy with the bearing weight. Birds stood out against the snowy backdrop, searching for seeds underneath the creamy, soft, white layers. Rachel loved this particular season. Everyone was always happier around Christmas, and snow always made her young heart smile.

"The ladies auxiliary said they will pay more if we wrap the baskets up ourselves," Elli informed them as she worked a sample of Schwartz products into over a dozen baskets along the stretched-out counter. Beside her were a large roll of clear wrapping and rolls of thick ribbon.

There was chevre, aged cheddar that Rachel was certain was going to impress, chocolate balls filled with cocoa and marshmallows, which was Hannah Glicks idea of Christmasy, and Rachel's newest invention of Schwartz ' Garlic Herbed Cheese Spread. Rachel abandoned her gawking to help and began by adding rounds of fresh goat-milk mozzarella sporting the Schwartz Creamery label. It wasn't as elastic as when she had tried it at home using Daisy, her family's milk cow, as her supplier, but it was good.

"It's a wonder if anyone will *kumm* out today" Hannah commented. Snow, albeit beautiful, made traveling this far up the mountain more a risk than pleasure. The hill of Walnut Ridge was straight up and down, and had been the reason for more accidents than not.

"Gives us more time to ready baskets," Elli grinned happily, never one to consider any moment spent was one wasted. "Did you two enjoy your day off?"

Rachel cringed at the question. She had spent her day making cinnamon and pecan rolls for her mother's shop despite Hannah's offer to go shopping.

"*Jah*, but not as much as our Rachel. Instead of shopping for winter underclothes, she abandoned me to bake all day." Hannah smirked teasingly and added two chocolate-dipped pretzel sticks rolled in broken candy cane pieces in the baskets next.

Rachel shot her a scowl. Hannah knew such would only encourage Elli to deliver another one of her speeches about living outside of habit. Elli was a stickler for one to make many friends, tasting new foods, and getting your feet wet every time it rained. Elli had strange thoughts.

"Is that so," Elli's disappointment was apparent. "You should spend more time with *freinden*, Rachel,"

"She's become a recluse."

That wasn't true. Hannah had a habit of speaking of one while she was standing in the same room. She was a terrible gossip.

"I go to gatherings," Rachel snapped defensively. "I *kumm* three days here, do I not?" Not exactly a homebody, she scoffed.

"You attend Sunday church," Hannah frowned. "That's not the gathering she means, and you missed *mei bruder*'s wedding." Hannah said, obviously still sore over Rachel's absence. "It's been two years Rachel. There, I said it."

Rachel heard the concern in her words. Two years and Rachel had still kept to herself, avoided weddings, and friends, and anything that resembled another chance of getting her heart hurt.

"I..." Words failed her.

"You should be courting," Elli boldly suggested. "Being alone isn't healthy for one so young."

Rachel cringed at the idea. She was no more interested in courting than she was in attending weddings where two more hearts joined and began their future together.

"Abrams' nephew is still single yet."

Rachel made a face. No one wanted to court her even if she considered such a foolish idea. Rachel wasn't blind to the fact most found her overly obedient. But good morals were often confused with stubbornness. *Nee*, no man in all of Walnut Ridge dared court the woman who displeased a bishop's son.

No one but...

The old memory crept in, one where she had attended her first youth gathering with all the neighboring communities. She had baked her *grossmammi's* favored sugar *kichlin*, because *grossmammi* said the way to a man's heart was a good *kichli*.

At sixteen, Rachel felt she was plenty old enough to find her future husband. A girl could never start too young caring about things such as her future. Then Joel Wickey, the most handsome boy in all of four communities, caught her staring. She'd only but a handful of times caught a peek of him, and suddenly he was looking at her. When he smiled her way and tipped his hat like a true gentleman, Rachel felt her nerves tingle until her whole body shivered.

He strolled over to the table and inspected the various delights. She remembered how long she held her breath, waiting to see if he approved. *Nine heartbeats.* Then she watched as he lifted her plate of *kichlin*, and took them inside. That had been the first time she discovered how fragile hearts could be. He obviously found her baking terrible so she decided right then that she would not take part in her family's bakery unless forced and save any future heartache.

He was the first hint that perhaps no matter how hard she tried at a chore, she simply wasn't good enough. Then Martin appeared, with his wide smile and mischievous water-blue eyes. A girl sometimes had to take what *Gott* was offering, and she learned her second lesson in womanhood. If he puts someone in your path, best to pay attention.

One buggy ride home and she was officially courting, and all her *freinden* were happy for her. Martin loved her *kichlin* and her smile. He had big thoughts, which often made her giggle. He had strong hands, which always made her feel privileged when he'd tried holding hers. All reasons why the day he left her had been so hard. She had cried like a *boppli* with a fresh Band-aid and Joel Wickey of all people found her at that very moment.

He thought to make it all better by offering up himself. Well, she didn't need his pity and lashed out at his bold offer. If he was so interested in her, then he would have said just as much before Martin did, she concluded. *Nee*, Joel Wickey, handsome or not, would not be the man she would consider after the way his choices had affected her life. He was probably courting anyway.

"I'm not interested in Abram's nephew. Not everyone gets what you and Abram have." She turned back to the job at hand, setting out the various cheeses for Elli to incorporate into the baskets.

"Nonsense," Elli replied. "*Gott's* timing can sometimes surprise us. We all deserve love and when it fails, a second chance. You will have a second chance," Elli winked. "This I know."

A second chance…at love.

Rachel took a long inhale. It would be wonderful, but no way could Elli know such a thing. Could she?

Rachel had spent two whole years unbinding her feelings for a man who could make promises one minute and disappear into the night the next. Elli always said the heart was strong, capable. Rachel hoped that was true, that her heart was strong and capable. The thought of having a family, of being half of a whole, was all she had ever wanted. Perhaps *Gott* would deliver an ounce of mercy on her.

"*Vell*, if *Gott* decides to send a second chance my way, I will consider it," she said stubbornly.

Gott must have disagreed on gifting that ounce of mercy as the creamery shop door opened, and in walked the last person she'd waste her new second chance on.

Joel locked eyes with her immediately. At sixteen he had been very slow to show an interest. *Or you had been too quick to give yours*, her heart spoke just as nausea took over her stomach.

Handsome. He looked so handsome in his long coat and black felt hat. He had certainly grown into those eyes, big and bold and brown like brownsugar frosting. Rachel shook off the dark thought. She once admired his confident stance, but learned it could easily be mistaken for cocky. Looks weren't everything, and he had only finally asked to court her out of pity. She had suffered enough sorrowful looks to be full of them. Joel thought courting him would simply make her broken heart suddenly heal. He was no better than Martin Mast was, toying with hearts like they did.

"Joel," Rachel sputtered out despite not being a sputterer. Not only was the man in her current thoughts right there, but he was with…her bishop. Warmth wormed its way up to the tips of her ears and a clutch of fear in her chest.

"Hello Rachel." Why did her name sound different coming from his lips, like something buttery and crisp on the top. She coolly brought the tray she had been carrying to her chest. He had no effect on her whatsoever. A woman's hands simply need not be empty nor idle, that was all.

Joel removed his hat revealing a dark head of tousled hair. Not one strand worked with the other. He was imperfect in all matters and yet, Rachel couldn't stop looking at him.

"*Willkum* Bishop. Joel. I hope Verna isn't out of herbed butter already. We're running a bit low, filling seasonal orders." Elli said, tying a red bow on another basket filled with Schwartz Creamery products.

"Joel has matters to discuss." The bishop said, looking at the ribbons with a deep-seated frown. Rachel had warned them the red was too fancy.

"I've *kumm* hoping you would join us this year for the town's charity." All eyes landed on Joel in mock confusion.

"The town's charity?" Hannah questioned with a lifted brow.

"A Christmas Cookie Tour." He stood taller and smiled, drawing out her curiosities.

"A cookie tour?" Rachel loved *kichlin*. Baking them, gifting them, eating them. Though she wouldn't tell the women that.

"*Jah*," he stepped further inside, and with each movement, closer to her and adding to her irritation. She would do well to keep her thoughts quiet.

"The sheriff has asked us to be part of this year's fundraiser," Bishop Mast informed them. "We've *kumm* from the town meeting this morning." He looked cold, cheeks bit harshly by the December tempera-tures. While he moved closer to the wood heat, Joel shrugged, shifting from one leg to the next.

"Us?" Hannah chuckled and when all eyes landed on her, she clamped her lips shut.

"You've captured my interest," Elli motioned for him to continue. "Go on."

"*Jah*, and half the proceeds will go to the new women's center. The remaining half, to our schools. All the Amish schools get part."

Having children of school age herself, Hannah's mouth fell open again. Each community did its part to support their school. Parents offered up a sizable donation each year for each child attending, and when times were tight, they had bake sales and auctions to help fund all the needs to keep a school stocked with supplies.

"That's *wunderbaar!*" Hannah abruptly said.

It was, Rachel considered as she let her fingers loosen around the tray. "How does this cookie tour work?" She was simply curious. She looked to the bishop, warming his hands and continuously frowning. She hardly believed he wanted to be part of something that sounded silly and *Englisch*. Bishop Mast preached often enough on being Plain and the importance of being separate from the world, even though most knew it was the loss of his son who now lived amongst the world that provoked the regular teachings on the subject.

"I'm glad you asked," Joel beamed a bright smile at her as if she alone was interested. She wasn't.

"It's a self-guided tour. Each business will sell tickets all week, start-ing Monday. They even plan on selling them off the internet. They're advertising," his grin grew wider, as the bishop made a snort.

The Amish didn't advertise, with exception of flyers or a rare newspaper advertisement of their business in the local paper. Rachel suspected the cookie tour would be on the radio, in newspapers, as well on the internet the *Englisch* were so fond of spending time on.

"Each ticket earns you a box."

"A box?" Elli asked.

"To fill with *kichlin*," he smiled and Rachel's stomach flipped over again. She knew better than to skip breakfast. It was the most important meal of the day after all. As he continued, Joel's eyes twinkled in the vast lighting flooding in through various windows. *Gott* was simply testing her. That's what it was. Elli had breathed silly notions in her head and now *Gott* was testing her.

Joel darted her another look. "And folks will be given a map of each of the stops on the tour. They will have two days to explore the communities, collect a sample of cookies from each business, and while there, hopefully pay for some of our handmade *guts* too."

"So everyone with a ticket," Hannah cleared her throat, "gets a box. They get free *kichlin* for being there, and all the money is split with the schools?"

"*Jah.* That's the notion all agreed on," Bishop Mast answered as he moved a little farther away from the stove.

"Which shops have you got so far," Elli prodded.

"The bookshop is selling hot cocoa, but she has plans for some locals to set up booths too. The local museum's selling ornaments and a bit of history but..." his eyes landed on Rachel once more. "She really was hoping someone else would do the baking."

Rachel blinked. Was he asking her? The idea was silly, she scoffed. He was probably thinking of just how horrible her *kichlin were*. She'd have no part of it, even if *kichlin* were involved.

"We are to be separate," Rachel spat out earning her an approving nod from Bishop Mast. "Not all the volunteers bake. Our sheriff especially," he said, paying her no mind and continued answering Elli.

"That is a splendid idea Joel. You can surely count on Schwartz Creamy to help," Elli shot Rachel a warning look. "We can make more baskets too." Elli said. Pleased with himself, his dark smile turned on her again.

"We have two weeks, but I could use help," Joel said and every eye turned on her.

Two heartbeats passed, and then three. Four. Great, they were all waiting for her to reply. Whatever happened to silence being a virtue?

"Rachel," the bishop said, drawing her glare on him. "You will help Joel with this. You can speak with some here and though Joel claims to know his way around a kitchen, I reckon you can help with baking a few batches of those peanut butter *kichlin* you always make for our gatherings. Some of those who offered to take part, have no baking skills at all for such an event."

The bishop loved her *kichlin*, but was he suggesting she work alongside the *Englisch* after losing a child to the world as he had? More so, did he want her to help Joel bake cookies?

"He bakes?" she said with a laugh, earning her a taken-back expression from the handsome Joel Wickey.

"All must do their part, and I feel you two would make a good match...for this."

Rachel stood, mouth agape. She stared at the bishop, his not-so abrupt request, and then to Joel, amusement in a cocky smirk.

Of all the stuff and nonsense.

"A *gut* idea Bishop," Elli too quickly added. "The schools will benefit, and it is nearly Christmas. What better time to bring folks together."

"I hope you can convince Ben Hilty to join us." Joel's voice was unnaturally calm. Surely he didn't agree with the bishop's thoughts of them working together.

"The buggy shop is a perfect location. Tourists can see the inside of how it is run and perhaps go for buggy rides."

"Freeman would be *froh* to show off all his knowledge of buggy riding," Hannah snickered.

"And be happy to charge for it," Elli muttered. Joel looked to the floor. "I just thought the buggy shop could offer rides, you know, to make it more of a draw for tourists."

The room went eerily silent. Rachel had to admit the buggy shop would be the best option as most of the cottage businesses in Walnut Ridge were simply bulk or fabric stores, or men's workshops.

"Rachel can speak to Freeman," The bishop once more replied in her shocked silence. "She has some practice with the stubborn-minded."

Rachel tried not to look affected. Her bishop was not usually one to feed his flock to the wolves, but clearly he was still raw that she had not convinced Martin to stay in Walnut Ridge all those years ago.

"I was hoping to tend to this today or tomorrow evening as I have to run the store early on. I'm pressed for time to let the chamber know which shops will be added to the list, so they can finish up with the flyers."

"She can take off tomorrow," Hannah volunteered.

"I'll pick you up in the morning," Joel said without thinking to ask her if she was willing. He placed his hat back on his head and turned to the door as eager to leave as she was for him to.

"Perfect!" Elli said with much enthusiasm. "I am sure between the two of you, this will be a success. It's for the good of the community, of course."

"I'm eager to see what *kichlin* you make, Joel. My *ehemann* has yet to boil water." Hannah aimed a thumb towards Rachel. "But our Rachel will be there if you have troubles."

She was a cheesemaker, not a baker she wanted to remind everyone, but kept her lips tight in case something else spilled out and tied her to spend any more time with Joel.

"If memory serves me well, you did make sugar cookies once," he smiled tripping up her thoughts once more before walking out the door...whistling. Bishop Mast bid the room so long, and in bishop fashion, lumbered out behind him.

Rachel was speechless. The last ten minutes felt like a bad dream. "He remembered the sugar *kichlin*," she silently muttered, and a wave of anger rushed through her. He probably had a sweet tooth which she was incapable of satisfying. The memory grasped her heart while the rest of her was still tingling. Clearly, the power of attraction was a very real and dangerous thing. Yes, she definitely should have eaten this morning.

"Perhaps Joel is your second chance," Hannah spit out. "He stared at her the whole time," Hannah stated as she worked a length of ribbon into a bow. "I think he still has stars for her,"

"He does not." Rachel blurted out, finally regaining some of her composure.

"*Jah*, he does." Hannah turned back to Elli. "Stared like a man who had nothing better to do with his life but stare." Hannah snickered amusingly.

"I couldn't be rude and not accept. The bishop insisted," Rachel replied, ignoring the humor dancing in Hannah's eyes while positioning another small butter spread container in a basket.

"*Nee*, you could have told him you had to buy thermals," Hannah dug into the box of ribbons to find another color, giving each basket a

Christmasy touch. "That would surely send both of them out the door and you wouldn't be shackled to Joel for the coming weeks."

Rachel wouldn't dare mention thermal underwear out loud. Hannah was being ridiculous. "He's not even from Walnut Ridge and trust me, he doesn't want to try my *kichlin* anymore than I want him too." She felt her pulse rising slightly. She straightened.

"Now Rachel, I was from a whole different side of the fence, and now here I am, happier than a bee in a honey hive

. Cherry Grove is not Siberia! It's ten miles away and any man would be blessed to eat whatever you make." One could only hope. "If *Gott* sees to bring love to your door, I say open it and run." Elli smacked her hands together to accentuate her point. "You deserve a good man who knows your worth. The bishop's son only knew north was thataway." Elli pointed north and Rachel felt a fresh fear. Helping Joel was not going to be an easy task.

Chapter 3

Friday morning the sun brought out a delightful wave of warmer air. Joel suppressed his disbelief behind a blank expression as Rachel waved farewell to the Hilty's and climbed into the buggy seat beside him. For a woman who was determined not to help, she had easily convinced both men to not only take part with the fundraiser, but volunteer to give buggy tour rides to any tourist willing. Willing, meaning willing to pay of course, but it was another Amish shop to scratch off his list of hopefuls and if the cookie tours became an annual event, Joel could see many happily being carted around in buggies through the countryside.

"You don't like Freeman, do you?" Rachel asked, turning to take in the snowy field and rolling hills around them.

Joel remembered well enough when Freeman tried his hand at courting his eldest *schwester*, Lydianne. Despite Lydianne having no interest in him, he kept showing up surprising her. *Daed* eventually had to forbid him coming about which had caused a silent rift between families. It was further widened when his parents bought his first buggy elsewhere and had it hauled all the way down here from Indiana.

"*Gott* loves everyone, and we are to be more like Him," Joel said grinning at her pink upturned face. She had clearly not forgiven his abrupt offer to court her the day her intended left, but she was here, next to him in the buggy seat, helping him. So there was that.

He pulled a list from his pocket. "I was hoping to add the Troyer's Orchard over in Miller's Creek to the list."

"The Fenders would be a good one too, Elli suggested it."

Joel hadn't considered the bed and breakfast, and immediately jotted down *Fenders* on his list. Beside him Rachel sat primly, waiting for him to hurry.

Despite himself and all the work that awaited him when he returned home, he was not rushing today no matter how many times she huffed. He had waited a good long time to spend time with her and she was no longer the willowy girl he crushed on. All those long limbs and straight up and down frame had filled in and it had taken all the strength he could muster not to drool. Even when she narrowed her eyes at him, Joel found her beautiful. Perhaps he would just have to invent new ways to light a match to the fire he hoped kindled inside her.

"*Mamm* insists on me stopping by Miller's Bakery too," he gladly suggested and waited for her to offer some smart reply. Rachel winced and he couldn't help but grin. The local matchmaker was one the unwed often avoided. Hazel Miller sought any opportunity to see who *Gott* had planned for ya, meaning who *she* saw fit to match one with. None were immune to how far out her reach was. She had even had her hand in seeing the good sheriff married. No, Hazel Miller didn't abide by hearts not being paired up.

"We can find others," she said swiftly, her posture tightening.

"Afraid to face the baker?"

"*Nee.* One of us at least is capable of seeing this done." She lifted her chin. "But I won't step one foot in that bakery and you shouldn't either, Joel Wickey. Hazel Miller will have you married by Christmas!"

Now that was a fine thought.

"I wouldn't mind, Rachel. If *Gott* sees fit to find the perfect heart for me." Amusement gone, he softened a look at her before clicking his tongue and giving Appletop a tap of the lines. They veered down the long winding drive of Hilty's Buggy Shop. It was rutted but scraped down to the dirt.

"Freeman could use the old matchmaker for sure. He used to like *mei schwester*." She stared at him for a moment.

"He gave Grace some troubles when she moved here, as he has most *maedels*, but he isn't so bad. Many are eager to marry."

Joel gave her a sidelong glance. Did that mean she was? "One should be patient in such."

"One should," she muttered and let out a sigh. "When he was a youngie, I caught him crying once. Crying because he thought he had no friends. I declared that day to be his friend. He's difficult, I know," she turned to him. "But we are all only human, none perfect."

Her mild rebuke carried over him. He admired her heart for others. If only she aimed some mercies his way.

"*Nee*, none of us are perfect," he replied.

"You should have to suffer sitting next to Dok Stella during gatherings. She isn't married and twice the age of the rest of us." Rachel used gloved fingers to count. "Doesn't live in a regular house and won't drink a drop of water that isn't boiled. She eats weeds, and even lets that beast of a dog of hers sleep on her bed, and," She laughed. "She is a remarkable woman." Her eyes twinkled at the admittance.

"Well, Rachel Yoder, if I ain't mistaken, I'd say you got a soft spot for the reckless. It's a wonder Freeman Hilty hasn't sparked you yet."

"Whatever. If I ever considered courting, it certainly would *naet* be Freeman Hilty."

Joel perked up at the link of hope carried within her statement. "So you are not against dating anymore?" he tempted and fastened eyes with her for more than three blinks. How a man could ever break her heart was beyond Joel, but it seemed Rachel Yoder might no longer be heartbroken.

"I'm not interested in courting you," she said smugly and pulled from his gaze.

She was as transparent as the wind, but he would not jump in with both feet and make a fool of himself again. With his free hand, he lifted a quilt from between them.

"*Gut*, because I'm not interested in courting you either." Her mouth rounded in surprise at his terribly convincing lie as he worked to unfold the quilt one-handed and lay it over her.

"Then what do you want Joel Wickey? No way Bishop Mast would force me to help you, unless you talked him into it." She jerked the quilt and spread it daintily over her. Did she think him so underhanded to seek help from the neighboring bishop for time with her?

"It was his idea, I assure you," he said flatly. "But I do want one thing" She looked at him suspiciously. "Sugar *kichlin*."

"What?"

"You make the best sugar cookies I've tasted yet, and I'm eager to taste those peanut butter blossoms the bishop spoke of too."

"You want my recipe, that's it," she snapped. "You mock me," she folded her arms. She clearly didn't understand him if she thought he'd mock her baking skills, but she'd be shocked to learn he was plenty capable of baking a few dozen cookies successfully.

"*Nee*, I have my own. If you're afraid you cannot do it," he hiked a grin and pressed it on her already rattled nerves. "I can bake them all.

Can't be too hard, I'm sure even *mei bruder* can bake them just as *gut*."
Rachel bristled. This conversation was going south quickly.

"I'll bake them. It's too important a cause," Rachel snapped again and all went silent between them.

Joel cleared his throat. "What kind of man would you consider courting?" He simply couldn't let the matter go.

"I told you I'm not interested. You don't have good ears, do you?"

"And I have no interest in courting you. That was almost two years ago." He reminded her. "Besides, you're not my type "

She gathered her black shawl in her ungloved fingers and stared at him. "We are both Plain. We are but one type."

"Yet, none of us are the same," he shot back. "I want a *fraa* who loves... baking, and *kinner*, and..." he sent her a serious glare. "me! Marriage is too serious to settle for less than that."

Her shoulders sank as she stared over a collage of *Englisch* homes to her right. "Well. You're not my type either," she muttered loud enough the cold wind didn't steal the sarcasm in her tone. If Joel wasn't mistaken, his words had bruised her and he immediately felt guilty for them.

Rachel straightened. "I need someone who doesn't make promises he can't keep, isn't afraid to speak his mind, and knows what he wants." She took a breath. Clearly he hit that nerve he had been searching for. "Someone who doesn't run away when things get hard, and someone who knows when the right time is to ask a woman to court him."

"Rachel, I'm sorry I asked you back then." He said, ignoring the premonition that she was determined not to forget his youthful mistake. She looked to the hillsides next, her lips pressed firmly into a frail line. *She said need, but what does she want?*

It was bitterness, that's what it was. His forwardness after Martin's leaving her, he guessed. Well, the fastest way to sweeten a bitter cookie was by adding just a bit more sugar to the mix and tossing it into a hot oven. Joel let his fingers relax on the reins as he contemplated what to do about the woman next to him. Because one thing was for sure, he hadn't gotten over her, and for the next of couple weeks, they would be spending a lot of time together.

"Why did you name your horse Appletop?" Joel cleared his throat when she finally spoke after twenty minutes of silence. The market came into view ahead, and he tightened his hold on Appletop's reins to keep the pace.

"I was a handful to my folks at nine." He smiled, recalling a childhood full of wonder and freedoms.

"Just at nine?" She sounded skeptical.

"*Jah*. I was given a slingshot that year for my birthday. I got mighty *gut* with it too," he winked. "Appletop was a youngie at the time, not even harness ready. *Daed* used to fuss that he was a poor horse, until I traded a slingshot for him."

"You bought a horse with a slingshot?" She tilted her head up to him. Under her black bonnet, blue eyes twinkled with curiosity. Joel smiled. She was simply lovely when she forgot she didn't like him.

"*Jah*, I reckon I did. I was practicing knocking cans off the fence one day and Appletop kept coming over and knocking them over before I got off my shot. I wasn't always of *gut* temper," he shared as he veered towards the market's driveway. Cars lined along the front, vans carrying Amish mothers to fulfill a day of shopping. More than a dozen buggies settled near the barn.

"So I tied him to the fence, put a can on his head, and shot it off."

Rachel's hand went to her mouth. "*Nee*, you did not." Her eyes rounded creating a dreamy pool of dew drops.

"He didn't move a muscle. After that, I practiced and not one time, even when I missed and shot an acorn up his nose, did he move." Appletop is the best horse in the world.

"You were a terrible *bu*," Rachel scolded as he brought the buggy to a stop along the east side of the market.

Joel set the break and quickly got out and moved to her side. He offered her a gloved hand, noting her cold fingers through the layers.

"*Jah.* That's what *daed* said when he caught me." He chuckled. "He said the horse was no good and neither was a little *bu* with a slingshot" he said, slipping off his gloves.

"I think your *daed* is a wise man but a poor trader." She said admiring Appletop. She tensed the moment he grasped her fingers and began slipping his warm gloves over them.

"*Nee*, it's still a *gut* slingshot. Alan played with it, but never got much *gut* with it." Considering Alan was the reason Joel had to go jail, he thankfully wasn't much into shooting cans anymore and preferred helping *daed* in the cabinet shop. Rachel stared up at him as he worked the material over her cold fingers, her bow-shaped lips parting. The thought of kissing her attacked his senses and he quickly let go. He wasn't sure if they were still fitted after all this time, but there was one way to find out.

"It's Laura who can knock a bug off the barn door with it," he laughed and to his surprise, Rachel laughed too. It was a sweet sound that filled his chest with happiness as he held open the door and followed her inside.

***

Troyer's Market was a long metal structure filled with various booths. In summer the outside was filled with wagon loads of garden vegetables and flowers. Fall brought out the pumpkins and of course bushels and paper baskets of apples. In winter, it was a sea of selections, everything from leftover summer honey to a three-piece bedroom suit. Rachel seldom wandered far from Walnut Ridge, but she had taken a stroll through the market with *mamm* on occasion.

"I'll go see if Leon is about if you want to check out some of the booths." She nodded, happy to put some distance between them. Her fingers tingled, going from cold to hot so quickly, and reminded her how much she had once wanted Joel Wickey to hold her hand. Still, she reminded herself, he was no more interested in her than she was him. A fact he had no trouble saying aloud.

Forgive and forget was what she had been taught her entire life, but Rachel couldn't just forget the fact that if Joel had simply asked to take her home that day, she would have never settled for someone else's offer. That all those years wasted on the wrong man would have never been suffered.

Removing her bonnet, she watched as he threaded his way through the booths to her left and then took in the aisle to her right. How different life could have been if he hadn't waited until the worst day ever to show an interest. If he had only approached her that day at the gathering, when her eager heart was on the cusp of womanhood.

Troyer's applesauce lined the first table, as well as their apple butter which Rachel had once discovered spicier than her *mamm's* own recipe. Not everyone understood the importance of balance, or when to stop adding cloves and maple sugar when plain ole cinnamon was capable of standing on its own just fine. An *Englischer* bartered over a few bars of sweetly scented soaps. Rachel gingerly slipped past them and the next three booths considering she wasn't in the market for furniture.

"You came with Joel Wickey?" A soft voice drew her around to find a young *maedel* near her in age staring at her as if she was a newcomer, and not from the next community over. She was dressed in gray with a black apron front and standing to the side of a small table filled with various sauces. Rachel lifted a jar, *Kick'n Sauce* it read, and sat it back down. She preferred sweeter flavors over the warmer ones.

"I'm helping him with some errands today," Rachel responded, but forced to help would have been more accurate.

"Your folks own the bakery at the top of Walnut Ridge, *jah?* I'm Arlene," wide brown eyes stared at her.

Rachel nodded. "I'm Rachel, *jah.*"

"I see it takes one who knows his ways to turn his head," Arlene sighed. "He seldom leaves his family's store, but rumor is he is as handy in the kitchen as he is outside of one." Rachel flinched. So he did know how to bake? Still, it didn't mean he should find other's baking so unsatisfactory.

Despite her mother's bakery, Rachel never liked spending her days waiting on customers. Working for Elli gave her a chance to try new things, without the watchful eye of her mother piercing her, and without sorrowful expressions every time someone looked at her and knew she was the girl the bishop's son rejected.

"Are you courting?" Arlene asked boldly. "Sorry, I tend to go straight to a thought and think to share it." Arlene lowered her gaze and began to rearrange sauces. One with a chunky mustard yellow made her stomach queasy.

"He is the most sought after here. All the single *maeds* spend a Wednesday at the Bulk Foods Store." She blushed and Rachel wondered if she was including herself. "That's the day the truck arrives and you can see him in the back... unloading it." Rachel's eyes widened at the open confession and clearly there were too many maedels with idle hands and thoughts in Cherry Grove. Sure, Joel was handsome, but the sudden thought that he was being spied on, onlookers waiting for his Wednesday shipments to arrive, sent an unreasonable unease through her.

"We are not courting, nor do I shop on Wednesday's." *Of all the stuff.*

"But he never spends time with any other maedel," Arlene titled her head suspiciously. "I won't tell anyone you're dating, but if you are…"

"It's not a date," Rachel scoffed.

A date, her heart whispered and she quickly tried warding off the idea. She refused to act like a desperate *maedel* again. If she hadn't been so eager years ago, so determined to marry and have *kinner* of her own, perhaps she would have noticed the first boy to ask to take her home, was not the best one for her.

"Excuse me. Have a *gut* day," flustered, she ducked away, moving past the next two booths. Around the corner, she spotted Joel. Hopefully, he was ready to go and she made her way to him. He was her only way home after all.

As she neared, Rachel tried not to flirt with the silly ideas Arlene planted in her head, but the image of Joel, unloading trucks, taunted her terribly. She tried not to imagine muscles under his long coat. Those fine looks and charm probably worked on all the *maedels* of Cherry Grove faster than a moth ate cotton, but anything that came easy or too fast, usually spoiled first.

"Hiya," he greeted as she neared. "Leon here is happy to help."

"I reckon anything for the schools would be appreciated, even if mine aren't ready to attend yet. I'll see some of the ladies make *kichlin*, and set up a booth at the door. We could use the traffic. Winter is not our best season here."

"*Danki,*" Joel shook hands with him and they made their way to the next stop. The last place either wanted to go to. Miller's Bakery. If Rachel made it out without a scratch, she would be very thankful.

Chapter 4

"We did it," Joel said, pleased as he pulled into the Yoder drive that evening. It had been a long day but Joel felt he'd made a better impression on Rachel than he had years ago. Beside him, Rachel looked just as unhappy to slip out of the blanket as he was. The heaviness of the quilt they shared as the day drew into a cold evening, matched with her warmth, had made him feel as if they weren't riding around all day in the cold at all. The Old Order open buggy was part of life, and though at times it made for some discomfort, other times…he looked to his side… other times it had its advantages.

"I never knew Hazel Miller to be courting." There were many things Joel suspected she had missed, keeping to herself the way she did. "But we made it out of the bakery unhitched." her voice lifted amusingly.

"Not on account of Hazel not trying," he laughed, recalling the look on Rachel's face when Hazel announced that it was about time they both found love. "You should have seen the look on your face when she asked if we were planning to live in Cherry Grove or Walnut Ridge."

"And we both answered, confusing her even more."

Her laugh swelled his affection for her. The sudden thought pierced him. Would Rachel ever consider living in Cherry Grove? Her heart was in the creamery. His was his parent's store.

"I should be sorry I kept you out so late." He turned to her, noting how the wind had kissed roses on her cheeks. He quickly exited the buggy and rounded to her side but she was already out.

"I suffered through it," she said, straightening her bonnet in careful fashion.

"I thought I was the one who suffered." She lifted a sharp brow. "I was the one holding the reins all day."

"You are impossible Joel Wickey." She huffed.

The way she said his name sent sparks into his chest. "Perhaps I should go explain to your folks, see they don't mind that I will keep you busy for the coming days." Winter sunset cast a violet hue over her, forming a glow of porcelain perfection. The attraction, the quick moving spark in his chest, was flickering. He had promised himself to be strong, but his heart and head were moving faster than he was accustomed to.

"*Danki* for helping me Rachel," he said in a low voice.

"You're different," she stared at him studiously.

"I grew up, as did you." He took a step closer than remembered it was only one day, a gift. "It will be fun to see whose cookies are gone first," he wiggled his brows.

"You should know men are terrible bakers." She tried to hold up her continued stubbornness, but as the hot breath escaped her, pushing a soft moving cloud between them, Joel could see he was not the only one feeling sparks. Her nearness was making him remember why no other had ever turned his head. His heart collected an extra beat.

"I'm not like most men," he reminded her. "I'll do half the baking. We cannot know if being a cheesemonger has made you rusty." Her eyes flickered challengingly.

"Are you challenging me, Joel?"

"*Jah*, I am," he continued with the dumb idea. "If tourists prefer my *kichlin*, then you have to go to dinner with me." Her eyes widened clearly not expecting an invitation to go on a date. In truth, he wasn't expecting to offer one up, but it was out there now and he waited for her response.

"Fine, and when mine are all gone and you still have *kichlin* left for the chickens, you have to …" Her confidence wavered.

"Let you pick the restaurant?" He tried.

"*Nee*," she quickly replied. "You have to admit that my *kichlin* are better than yours." That wasn't fair. Rachel was born of bakers. But that wouldn't stop a man from trying

"Nothing will make me happier than proving you wrong…about me." The air grew thick between them as awareness wafted over them. If she disliked him so much, then why was she looking at him in such a way and why did it feel as if she was getting closer?

"*Kumm*, you should get inside and warm up." He motioned her towards the house kicking himself for not finding better words. She was simply too beautiful, it muddled a man's thoughts. As he walked by her side, Joel couldn't ignore the slight hike of a smile when she realized he planned on seeing her right to her front door. They came to a stop at the steps leading to the long porch. Someone had lit a lamp, hanging it on the railing, for her return. They both hesitated. Proof she no more wanted the day to end than he did.

"We have a full list of shops. They're printing tickets, and if you don't mind suffering another cold day with me, we can deliver them together."

"It wasn't that cold," she shrugged. "And it is for the *kinner*."

Her pale gaze rose to him, causing his breath to hitch. The remembered sensation of her hand in his urged him closer.

"*Jah*, for the *kinner*."

She placed a hand on her chest to keep it still. Joel felt the same jolts, same erratic beats. He wanted to kiss her, but kissing her would certainly be a mistake. It would send Rachel Yoder into another two years of avoiding him.

Would one kiss truly create a fire?

"Rachel," his lips whispered and he watched her shiver.

"*Jah*," her voice trembled.

"I want to…"

He gathered her hands in his, stared at them, joined, and then looked at her again. She lowered her head bashfully and paused before looking up at him again.

"I need my gloves back." Joel managed to keep his calm despite his heart tripping over his rib cage.

"*Ach*," she shook her head and opened a gap between them. Quickly she hurried out of his gloves. "Of course…I'm sorry," she began rambling adorably. She handed him the gloves and he cupped her trembling fingers.

"I didn't mean to upset you, but if I dared steal a kiss, you'd only hate me for another two years." At his admission, he felt her sway slightly. That's why he moved closer. Why he placed a hand on her cheek to keep her steady.

"You were thinking about kissing me?" He smiled and lost himself in her sudden vulnerability.

"I have thought about that since I was nineteen."

"You have?" Her eyes widened as if the thought of him kissing her was lost on her.

"I would like to get to know you better, Rachel Yoder." There, he said it, and waited two breaths for her reply. She blinked and then bristled as if now remembering cookies left in a hot oven. They both jolted and turned towards the driveway as a car pulled in.

"Who could that be?" Rachel said, slipping from his grasp. Those glittering blue eyes, twinkling with excitement a moment ago, widened in a panic to match her kicked up breaths. She turned and Joel twisted and noted the stranger exiting from the car. *Blue jeans, a heavy cobalt coat, and a pale mess of curly hair.* That's when recognition hit with a solid punch.

And just like that, after two years, Martin Mast had returned to Walnut Ridge. On this day of all days.

Martin's matching blue eyes arrowed directly on the girl he left behind. Joel bristled, the fire in his belly extinguished. Words of an older *schwestern* rang in his ear. "A woman never forgets her first love."

"Hello Rachel." Martin said, cocking his head. Rachel's jaw dropped open and a rush of cold air rushed in. She looked suddenly ill which made Joel itch. Rachel had nearly melted in his hand just moments before, and now....

Joel soothed his temper and took a step forward. She had feelings for him, despite those stone walls she tried putting up. Joel needed to do was what was right. A man only had right and wrong to choose from. He had to be a better man and hope Rachel noticed that. What was important right now, was that a lost sheep had finally come home after leaving so many hurt by his going. Joel made the decision right then and there. He chose to be the first to welcome Martin home. Time for establishing boundaries would come.

"Hello Martin Mast," Joel reached out a hand. Martin had always been one to wander over fences and dare to do strange things, but *Gott* did have a way of reaching into a man's heart and bringing him home.

"Hiya, Joel Wickey. I remember you." Martin sat his bag into a mound of snow swept from the path, indicating this was truly his first stop in returning. The car backed out slowly, and disappeared into the darkness of evening. Both facts that sent two sharp stabs into Joel's gut.

Joel remembered him well too. Few could forget the *bu* who painted mailboxes and raced cars. Joel had only one smudge to his name, and that was for helping his *bruder* learn a valuable lesson. Joel lived as upright as he could. He didn't dally to join the church, or help others when he could. Martin Mast was a man who wanted to straddle the fence without choosing which side to bed down at night on. "Your folks will be *froh* you have *kumm* to visit."

"I'm home for good," he said sharply before turning his attention back to the beauty between them. "I came to see you first of course. You still look...*schee* as I remember." Joel would have agreed if not for the man stating the obvious.

Beside him, Rachel trembled. There was history here that Joel knew little of. He wished he knew what to say to help this shock, but some heart matters had to be dealt with alone. And the last time he helped another out of trouble, Joel had to spend a night in jail.

We all have choices to make, the voice in his head reminded him. Loud enough that Joel looked about, almost expecting to see his father in the shadows somewhere. Rachel had the same free will to decide her next words. Being a good guy really was hard. He ground his molars silently. Rachel had his heart, and only she could decide what would happen to it.

"Why?" Rachel finally spoke, her narrowed gaze piercing.

"You know why," Martin said.

"*Nee*, I do not." Martin looked from Rachel to Joel and slow disappointment replaced the cocky grin Joel remembered.

"I can see I've *kumm* at a bad time. I should get to my folks place." Martin lifted his bag.

"You should. Your *daed* has missed *du*, and your *mamm* has cried plenty tears since you left."

"Are they the only ones?" *Of all the stuff.* Joel stepped forward.

"Martin, things are the same as when you left them." Joel said in her silence. It wasn't interfering, it was honesty. Actions had consequences.

"I see," Martin narrowed his gaze. "*Vell,* some things… can never change. *Gut nacht* Rachel," Martin tipped his straw hat and aimed down the lane. Joel watched just as Rachel did, in silence until he disappeared around a plot of barren trees eerily standing under a half moon. When he looked down, Rachel turned to him. She was on the verge of tears. On instinct Joel wrapped an arm around her.

"It's okay Rachel." To Joel's heartbreak, Rachel burst into tears. Fifteen minutes ago he was about to kiss her, now he was soaking up her tears for another in his coat, again. This was not how he imagined the day ending at all.

The timing was the worst, but Joel was known for his ability to finish a chore. He would just have to show Rachel that love could be something worth counting on, worth staying for. Joel had to put his faith in *Gott,* and in Rachel. They had only just started getting to know each other, but was it enough to help her leave yesterday behind?

"I'm sorry," Rachel said.

"We cannot know what a day may bring for us to deal with," he said quietly. He certainly had no foresight in how the day would roller-coaster.

"I never expected to see him again. I thought the ocean was bigger than his feelings for me," She wiped an angry tear away. "He said nothing here could hold him." Tears continued to glisten in her eyes. "That I wasn't enough." Joel shifted uneasily. Recognition flickered over her. "*Ach,* Joel, I shouldn't be saying these things to you."

"*Jah,* I'm glad you can talk to me. That you don't keep your thoughts from me, and Rachel, you have always been…enough. Some need oceans and bigger waters." He placed a hand on her arm again. She pushed her coat sleeve under her nose and nodded. "The rest of us find joy in what is right here about us." He sounded more like *daed* than the man plotting new ways to win her. "I want us to be honest with each other."

"I..."

"I have no plans of letting you... outbake me," he smiled tenderly and brushed her damp cheek. "I like Mexican food too much to risk it."

"You cannot make a better gingersnap or sugar cookie than me, and Mexican food sounds...too spicy" she forced a smile.

"It is late, and you're *kault*," he took a step back. "I will see you tomorrow, *jah*?" He waited two heartbeats, not a lot of time, but if it was your heart, it was a chock full. She nodded. "He was right about one thing," Joel added. "You are still as beautiful as I remember too." With that, Joel made his way back to his buggy.

Appletop snorted. "*Jah*, I know," Joel mumbled as he turned in the wide drive and headed for the long cold ride back to Cherry Grove. He was nineteen again. So close to what he wanted, and Martin Mast was there to stand in the way of his future, again.

Chapter 5

Rachel woke early and stared blankly out the kitchen window, looking over a gray morning rising over Sugar Mountain. She had barely slept a wink all night. *Martin was home.* How long had she waited for his return, and oddly felt nothing but surprise after nursing her heart all this time. Not the reunion she had hoped for, but clearly he didn't hold the place within her as much as the memory of him had. Perhaps her heart was ready for second chances.

All day, Rachel fumbled through work. She misplaced the food thermometer, forgot to rinse out all the cheese cloths, and ruined a full batch of farmer's cheese. It was the easiest of all the cheeses. But who could make cheese during these confusing times?

And Joel.

If only…she bit her lip trying to let old hurts die. He had changed, she'd admit, thawing out a coldness she had wrapped around her heart too long, but he was still the man who hated her *kichlin*, and had the worst timing…ever!

Last night Rachel was certain she had been given that second chance Elli spoke of, but now confusion thrashed at her perceptions. What second chance had she been given exactly?

Standing, once again, waiting, in front of the same window, staring at the same gloomy valley she woke to, Rachel pondered on what Gott's plan for her life was as she waited on Joel to pick her up. *What if he didn't kumm.* Would he think Martin's arrival had changed her heart? Rachel was shocked, but she didn't feel love had returned to Walnut Ridge for her in Martin's arrival. She felt...nothing. The revelation of that surprised even her.

"You are pacing *dochder*," *Mamm* said carrying a basket of laundry in from the back porch. Laundry didn't wait for sunshine and breezes. No, perfect conditions didn't always come when one needed them. She inhaled a long breath. Cold wind could see a pair of trousers stiff and dryer than after they ran through the ringer. No matter how bad today was, it could always be worse.

"Let me help," she began to re-hang the clothes near the wood stove to finish out.

"So what has you looking like you lost a dear friend?"

"I ruined a batch of cheese today." Rachel shrugged and unhinged the drying rack secured to the wall, letting it level out before pinning a pair of trousers on the first rung. Beside her, *mamm* stilled at her confession, but as usual, she showed no surprise.

"None can make the best cake in all weather." Spoken like a true baker. "Does it have to do with the nice young man who has been sharing your time?" Her thin dark brow lifted as a grin tugged at her lips.

"I know how love can muddle the senses."

"Love?" Rachel stilled at the four-letter word that had been her yoke long enough. *Mamm* hung a freshly cleaned dress on a hanger and reached up to secure it.

"This makes me *froh* to see he has caught your eye. Verna Wickey raised *gut kinner*," she nodded her head, agreeing with her own words. "*Yer daed* would approve, I reckon."

"He didn't like me before, but now..." Now things were different. Rachel decided not to share how he looked at her like she was the sweetest sugar cookie. "He's *verra* kind."

"*Jah?*"

"Too kind."

Mamm waved a hand in the air. "No such thing as too kind.." *Mamm* scoffed.

He thinks I make terrible cookies and likes to rile me. But he also stood by me when Martin arrived, and let me cry without saying a word. There was something to be said of that too. "He didn't even get upset when I cried."

"You cried?"

"It's complicated, *mamm*," Rachel finished hanging the last pair of trousers. The scent of laundry soap and wood smoke filled her nostrils. *Mamm* drew quiet, a habit she had when she hoped to encourage one to spill their guts. Oddly, it worked every time.

"Martin is back in Walnut Ridge."

"*Ach?* It is *gut* for his folks, *jah?*" Rachel agreed, but more than the bishop's family was affected by his sudden return. What if Gott wanted her to try harder this time, to keep Martin in the fold.

"I see your thoughts getting crowded, *dochder*. It is best to focus on a task at hand, than on yesterday's mishaps. The two are very different situations Rachel. Getting to know Joel, if that is what pleases you, has nothing to do with Martin returning. You cannot know if he plans to stay, or if he is ready to join the church."

"He came to see me before his parents. I am confused over it."

"You do not know if you want to spend time with Joel and an uncertain future, or pick up a past with Martin, who left you?" It was a trick question but the right one, she concluded. Rachel didn't know which man *Gott* wanted for her.

"This is all Joel's fault." She declared shaking out a poor stiff shirt.

"How so?"

"He knew I liked him, his *schwester* told him such. He...noticed me too."

"When you were youngies," *mamm* nodded. "I see. A young heart has much to learn."

"Well, Joel thinks I am a horrible baker." *Mamm* lifted an amused brow but focused on the laundry. "He thinks no one will even eat my *kichlin* on the Cookie Tour, yet, wants to take me for a spicy Mexican supper."

Mamm paused again with that little tidbit of information. Rachel may have said too much, but little affected *mamm*. Unlike Rachel, she remained the same calm person in a thunderstorm that she did on a spring day.

"So you have had eyes for Joel Wickey? I did *naet* know this."

"He came to the bakery with his family a time or two, and I saw him at my first gathering with the neighboring communities. I made a new dress for it." Oh how foolish she had been as a teenager to sew a new dress in hopes to catch his eye.

"I remember."

"But he never asked. So Martin asked, and I accepted. He was the only one who wanted me." What was she supposed to do, be alone with no possible chance of a future?

"I see."

"See what? I don't see anything."

"You blame Joel for your impatience. It was your first gathering. Why would you think to find a husband so quickly? Love has to grow first. Are we not responsible for our own choices?"

"A choice I made because he didn't leave me any."

"Must you have answers to all your questions on a fast breath?" *Mamm* huffed. It was a common quarrel between them. Rachel's hasty choice to work at the creamery had been one decision *Mamm* believed made in haste, but Rachel had found her passion there, had she not?

"You have certainly put yourself in the middle of a mud puddle."

"One that might drown me." Rachel said on a huff. *Mamm* picked up the empty basket and placed a hand on Rachel's arm.

"My *kinner* all may be short on patience, but are all *gut* swimmers," she winked. "Follow *Gott's* plan for you, and you shall not fail."

With that, *mamm* disappeared into the summer kitchen leaving Rachel more confused. Why did mothers talk in proverbs and riddles? Weren't they supposed to tell you what was best? *Gott* didn't provide burning bushes or send angel messengers to relay His wants. If Rachel had one path, sure, she would trust herself to follow it, but Der Herr had given her two and both were as crooked as a willow stick. On the left, a man who made her palms damp and her heart excited, but Rachel had no way of knowing Joel's heart. On the right, a second chance. Martin was home, but did she dare try to rekindle what they shared and risk failing again?

No less frustrated than before helping her mother, Rachel returned to the window, as just as he promised, Joel's buggy was working its way up the slight incline of the driveway. Instantly smiling, Rachel quickly grabbed her coat, shawl, and slipped on her bonnet before rushing outside.

"I wasn't sure you would *kumm*." She hoped she didn't sound like one of the desperate *maedels* who spent their Wednesday shopping at Wickey's Bulk Food Store.

He climbed down from the buggy and walked around a frozen puddle below the porch steps. He wore a black fleece headband under his hat to ward off the cold. Rachel noted the stack of blankets, and all thoughts of Martin Mast returning vanished in the warmth of Joel's smile. She wanted to sit in the buggy seat next to Joel. She wanted to hear more about his *mamm's* store and his *schwester* Mary's new *boppli*.

Mamm was right. She was blaming Joel for her fast choices. She wasn't even certain he was capable of making a bad decision. Rachel suspected Joel, though he might not understand the proper way about women, was the kind who rescued baby birds and tickled young *kinner* into laughter.

"I told you I would." She was discovering that. Joel was a man of his word. He offered her a hand. Helping her around the icy puddle, she felt a renewed hope in her heart.

Chapter 6

Leaving Troyer's market Joel shifted in his seat, anticipating the next stop. Rachel sat beside him, a blanket draped over both their laps, as the sun finally cleared out from behind the parade of gray clouds that had been looming all day.

"I saw you talking to Arlene again," he said coolly.

"She could use *freinden*," Rachel replied. Joel doubted that as he knew good and well she had plenty when they all did their weekly shopping every Wednesday at the Bulk Store.

"Did you know she has twenty siblings?" He laughed and nodded.

"*Jah.* I grew up with her *bruder* Aaron. Amos Graber is a blessed man," Joel laughed. "I think a dozen would be right."

"A dozen? You only need half that many Joel Wickey, or you best start selling lots of slingshots at your family's shop." Whatever had sparked her good mood, he was thankful for it. Perhaps Martin's return had not affected her like he feared.

"I thought you were going to buy those wooden ornaments from Hank Fisher's booth," Rachel laughed as temperatures warmed despite the evening approaching.

"They were handmade and exact replicas of all four covered bridges. I can appreciate a man who takes time to create something beautiful," he gave her a long look.

"Or woman?" She asked playfully. "You know cheese is a delicate process too."

Joel knew so little about the process of making cheese he trusted that was true enough. Aiming for Walnut Ridge, Joel grinned thinking of their last stop of the day. He planned it intentionally. The tree farm was not only closest to Rachel's home, but one of Joel's favorite places in all of the county. When the steep hill appeared before them, Joel veered right onto Hungry Holler Road.

"*Ach*, I forgot the tree farm. Are we going there now? I haven't been before." Her voice was laced with childish enthusiasm as she squirmed in the seat beside him.

Joel concealed a laugh. "You have lived here all your life and yet never been to the tree farm before?"

"*Nee*," she replied, eagerness gone. Bishop Mast's words filled him then. She had become a recluse aside from her job at the creamery.

The buggy bounced over the uneven road. A crusty sheet of wintry mix glistened as they dropped over the slight slope. A large lake welcomed visitors, a sea of trees in its backdrop. Joel maneuvered over the narrow road that was also a dam built to keep the lower section of the valley from being flooded.

"You have missed a great place, but I'm *froh* to be the first to bring you." Joel was happy that they could make this one memory, together. He looked to the sky. The sun was low-hanging, sitting in a dull yellow with pinks under a cloud skidded sky. Another inch of snow was expected by morning. "Today we will remedy that." Her lips lifted just a little looking over to him.

The tree farm was abuzz with activity. As far as the eye could see, trees filled the sea of rolling landscape. A wooden shop had a long porch, decked out in pine boughs and red ribbons and candles that used batteries, not flame. Glen and Charlotte Newsome were in their late fifties and had taken over the farm when Glen's father passed away a few years ago. Joel always loved coming here. As a youngie it was for a day's wage, cutting trees, wrapping them in green, frail netting, and loading them for customers.

"That's Hope Miller," Rachel said and waved towards the large windows of the Santa Shop. "Grace's *schwester* is even more stubborn than Grace was." She laughed. "I didn't know the Amish worked here too." Two other Amish *maed*s worked making wreaths, but Joel didn't recognize either of them.

"Each year the owners hire extra help for the season," he informed, helping her out of the buggy and noting she wore her own gloves today. Scents of pine and fir and wood fire filled the air. The fire pit was ablaze where two men were laughing and warming their hands. The door of the Santa Shop opened and Charlotte appeared wearing a Santa hat for warmth.

"Joel, I was wondering if you'd show," she met them halfway. "I have already been getting calls, folks wanting to know when they can pick up their boxes and tickets. I hope you brought the tickets." He reached into his coat pocket and presented the long envelope the tickets were stored in.

"Sorry it took so long. We had many stops to make." Charlotte nodded and then paused.

"Put us last on the list did ya?" Her laugh was booming, turning heads her way. Beside him, Rachel was still taking in the vast view of snow-covered hills and trees. It warmed his heart to see she was enjoying it.

"*Nee*, saving the best for last," he countered, earning him an appreciative smile.

"That's more like it," Charlotte looked to Rachel. "You must be the one helping Joel bake for the Sheriff and Vicky."

"*Jah*, I am," Rachel replied after a short hesitation. Competing was a more appropriate word. The very thought she'd accepted his spur-of-the-moment thought brought a warm smile to his lips.

"With the event just a week away, I was hoping you could make some for us too. Sugar cookies, unless everyone else is making the same." She turned to Joel, "We can't all make the same cookies or folks won't like it." She faced Rachel once more. "Maybe some recipe cards? Folks love that sort of thing. We have a few specialty items to sell and I'm making my famous chocolate chip, but I could never make a sugar cookie to melt in your mouth like you folks do." Charlotte frowned.

"I would be happy to help," Rachel beamed. "I'm making ginger snap and candy cane cookies for the sheriff."

"And peanut butter for the animal rescue farm," Joel added.

"And what will you be making young man?" Joel nearly forgot he too had an extra role in making the cookie tour a success, as well as finally getting a date with Rachel.

"Snickerdoodles," he replied. Charlotte patted his shoulder.

"A man who can bake. Don't you let this one out of your sight." She said to Rachel.

"That's what I keep telling her," Joel teased.

Rachel looked about, having no comment to add to their playfulness. "I can make sugar cookies shaped like trees."

"I like her," Charlotte gave two thumbs up. "You should take your girlfriend on a sleigh ride. It's…romantic. Glen should be back any minute with the last group." She glanced down a snowy lane that disappeared within the trees.

Joel turned to Rachel who was turning a pretty shade of pink. Nothing would make him happier than a romantic sleigh ride with Rachel Yoder, but he could tell she wasn't quite favorable of the idea. Looking about, Joel noted two half-grown boys sledding on a hill nearby.

"I've got a better idea," he smiled.

***

It was the glint of his eyes that prompted her to be part of the childishness. Rachel hadn't ridden on a sled since the age of fourteen and Elis and Enoch Schwartz ran her over, racing. It was still just as dangerous, but sitting between Joel's legs, her skirts tucked protectively beneath her, his warmth and strong hold all around her, nothing in the world could be better than this moment.

"Relax," Joel whispered in her ear. The plastic sled molded to their frames as they took to the snow-covered hillside.

"Easy for you to say," she bit out as he gave them a slight nudge. Who could relax sitting in the full body hold of a man and about to careen over a hillside. He was all around her, his smothering warmth making her stomach refuse proper digestion of the turkey sandwich she managed to nearly finish earlier today. And then she squealed as the wind took them over.

By the third trip, the jostling no longer disturbed her. They tilted and tipped, Joel's legs clutching so tight she was certain nothing could shake her off the sled. And just when she was finding her wings, the sled veered and struck something solid.

"Hold on," Joel called out as they plowed into a snowbank. Rachel groaned, the sudden impact taking her breath. Joel's arm quickly reached out to her, though he too was sunk deep into the snow plowed into a massive mound.

"Rachel, are you alright?" His wide eyes and struggling to break free from his own wedged in state, had Rachel gurgling for air as Joel fought his way back to freedom.

"You're hurt!" He rushed over to her.

"*Nee,*" she took a breath and burst into ridiculous laughter. "You were stuck *gut.*" She took in another deep breath. "Your face..." Oh, it was no use and she surrendered to the silliness and let go.

Joel stared at her for a moment, until his own laugh burst out of him. "Liked that, did you?" he said brushing snow from his trousers before helping her out of her own fixed state. Rachel worked a clump of wet snow from the underbelly of her coat and tried taming down her amusement.

"Are you sure you are alright?" Joel gripped the sled string in his gloved hand and inspected her. Sprinkled with snow, cheeks bitten by the cold, and being stared at with eyes sparkling with affection, she wasn't sure she would ever be alright again. Then just as her heart was about to soar with fresh delight, he leaned in and kissed her right on her frozen cheek.

"Sorry," he said, pulling away. "You look adorable after crashing into the snow." Taken back by the abrupt kiss, Rachel touched her cheek, the tingling rushing through her whole face, and she tried to muster an equal reply.

"Perhaps I should learn to be clumsy then," she said looking up to him, not typically one to succumb to flirting before.

"Clumsy or *naet,* you're always beautiful Rachel." And there he'd gone and made her heart skip. Speechless, Rachel ducked her head and tried working off the remaining snow on her dress.

"*Kumm,* let's get you home before we both turn to snowmen."

The ride home was awfully quick in Rachel's opinion. She wasn't sure she wanted the day with Joel to end, having as much fun as she was. It was the least Rachel could do, offering Joel a fresh cup of *kaffi* and time to warm up before his long drive home. He sat next to her on the couch. Her parents had been welcoming, but let them be alone in the dim sitting room while they worked on a list of *kichlin* for the cookie tour. Her cheek still tingled in the place his lips touched her.

"I can make thimble cookies too. Most love them with raspberry jam."

"I love them with raspberry jam," Joel said, setting his cup down on the side table. "I'll make gingerbread then. Though I'm not as skilled at making them look like goats or cats," he laughed. Rachel added it to the section for the animal shelter.

"I can see over the baking," Rachel offered. "You came up with the idea, put this all together. You don't have to try baking too."

"Try," his voice lifted in amusement. "I can handle cookies, and how else can I take you to try Mexican if I don't show you my cookies are better than yours," he winked.

The challenge no longer riled her. Rachel was looking forward to spending more time with him and was grateful Martin had kept a distance since his sudden appearance two nights ago. But she wasn't about to hurry into a relationship even if she had to add fancy sprinkles to each cookie to beat him.

"Sounds dangerous. What if I want pasta?" She teased in return. Someone snickered in the next room, indicating their playful banter was being listened to. Rachel sat down the list as Joel got to his feet. "I hate to think of traveling all the way home. It's *verra kault*."

"I think that kiss will warm me for the whole ride," he whispered. "I have to tend over the store most of the week," he shifted facing her.

"We're hosting church services Sunday and I promised *mamm* I'd help get ready for it."

She might not see him again for a week. Rachel surprised herself at how much that bothered her. It had been a wonderful day, full of laughter and…snow, and a soft kiss. *Patience. Mamm* was right. It was time to be patient.

"I have work as well, and there's much baking to do."

"And recipe cards," he added, making his way to the stove to collect his damp coat and boots.

"*Jah*, and recipe cards." She watched as he worked his feet into his boots and added, "It is our free Sunday here. *Daed* likes to visit neighbors then. It is not easy, belonging to different communities." She bit her lip on that thought.

"Or perhaps it is better." Joel quickly countered. Lamplight flickered in his chocolate eyes and beamed on his pearly smile, but it was the tone of his voice causing her to shiver just now.

"Next Sunday, I can attend *gmay* here. Then you can attend mine after that." She stared at him blankly. "Perhaps it is too soon for me to…"

"*Nee*," she placed a hand on his arm. "That would be nice," she smiled wider. It was a beginning, a proper one. She truly needed to let go of the past as *mamm* insisted.

"I will see you Friday I hope." She ducked her head in the bold request. "We can deliver *kichlin* before the shops open." He worked into his coat and scarf.

"If they *kumm*," she muttered. It would be terrible after all the work Joel was putting into raising money for the schools if it didn't do well.

"They will *kumm*." He was always so positive. She admired that about him. "No one can resist my snickerdoodles," he chuckled.

"*Ach*, you are impossible Joel Wickey," she gave him a playful slap on the arm. Rachel walked him to the door as he placed his black hat over his thick hair.

"You will be going out with me even if I have to bake ten batches to get it perfect," he leaned in and kissed her cheek again, just as he had at the tree farm.

"That should keep me warm all the way home. *Gut nacht* Rachel Yoder."

Chapter 7

Rachel had collected all the ingredients she needed to oversee dozens of Christmas cookies. She had also purchased a few dozen blank recipe cards from her parent's bakery. Charlotte had a good idea when she had thought of that.

Outside a winter storm thrashed, the howling wind like an animal begging for its freedom. She finished the last of the supper dishes, thankful for sturdy walls and a warm house.

"Let me fetch those recipes," *Mamm* said, walking to the corner cabinet and pulling out the worn book, a handwritten collection of Yoder's recipes generations long. A knock at the door had both of them lifting their heads.

"Now who would be out in such weather?" Her mother disappeared into the next room. When she reemerged, Rachel froze solid, a heavy sugar container wrapped in one arm and resting on her hip.

He was the only man to ever dare travel in such weather. Martin had at least abandoned his *Englisch* clothes, resembling the man from memory. Clean-shaven, he looked like the boy she remembered, the one she had long hoped to marry. She shook off the caring.

"Martin has asked to speak with you," *Mamm* said, her lips pinched into the makings of a frown. Rachel nodded, inwardly wincing.

"I'll just be in the next room, with your father." *Mamm* left without giving Martin a full look, but her warning tone wasn't ignored.

"Some things have changed," he grinned playfully.

He had changed so little in two years. He was still strong with eyes the color of a summer storm, but something had dulled in them. The eagerness of a boy aching to see oceans was replaced with disappointment as if out there, the world he had chosen over marrying her, had not been kind, tossing him about to survive each rock-bashing wave. Rachel pushed aside the sudden sympathy worming its way into her heart.

"I have much baking to do. It would be best if you didn't dally long," she sat down the container and turned to find her favorite mixing bowl. "I would offer you something, but…"

"But you have a lot of baking to do, *jah*, I heard you." He stepped further into the room, his gaze taking in everything. "*Daed* said you were helping with the Cookie Tour for the *Englisch*. Not sure he liked the idea of it."

"Yet he was the one who insisted I help," she snapped. "The *Englisch* are a part of it, *jah*, but we all will benefit, and it was Joel's idea to help raise money for the schools." The tour was a great idea, helping many.

She found the measuring cup and spoon and the remaining utensils before going to the propane refrigerator and pulling out butter and milk. On the table between them sat the notebook. Great, now she would have to turn around and deal with him to get any baking done.

"I'm sorry Rachel," he said. "I've only *kumm* to ask for forgiveness."

Just like that, he was sorry. She blinked. Seconds sped by as she debated a reasonable reply. Yes, he looked haunted, and sad. Maybe he was being sincere, but… "It's been two years. No reason for leaving. No letters. We got nothing."

"You know how it was for me, Rachel. *Daed* was impossible. Rules..." Martin waved his hat in the air. "Always the unbendable rules."

"Our rules have always been there. It serves a purpose...to those willing to follow them. You cannot jump back and forth over the fence." She reached for a fresh apron hanging on the pantry hook nearby, determined to get busy for the sake of the cookie tour despite the visitor currently making a chore of her evening. She had promised Joel, and unlike the man awakening old hurts, Rachel kept her promises.

"You sound like *Daed*," Martin mumbled.

"*Danki*," she nodded proudly. Being compared to a man who didn't waver in his faith was a high compliment. "I can't talk of this now. I have dozens of *kichlin* to ready for the morning, and you should be home with your family...not out in this weather," she pointed towards the back door as the wind smacked the small glass pane with snow. He moved to the table and inspected all the ingredients.

"Let me help you. The storm is near over. Let me at least help you with these while I wait it out," he motioned over the table.

Another howl outside jolted her. Rachel didn't want his help, she wanted him gone, but what kind of Christian would send another out into the storm? He lifted up a jar of peanut butter and inspected it.

"I remember once baking peanut butter blossoms with you," he chuckled a soft laugh that she had once found endearing.

"You nearly caught them on fire," she said, recalling the day he had kissed her. Just as she was explaining the importance of timing, of how to never distract a person mid-chore, Martin had kissed her.

"But as always, you made more and no one was the wiser that following Sunday." He shrugged. "Without you, I burn everything. Without you, I get lost." The words tore a fresh thread from her heart. No longer the cocky *bu* of her youth, but a man lost, regretful, and needing forgiveness.

Pity tugged at her heartstrings. There were times in a woman's life when she had to choose to hold on to the past, or simply step into a fresh future. She couldn't simply let Martin return to his worldly ways.

Oh help, she was hopeless.

"I'll bake, you can write recipes," she handed him a pen and a stack of recipe cards. It was forgiveness she was offering, a friendship. No, she would not let him beyond those walls he created around her heart. A heart she was losing to someone else.

For the next hour, they worked in mutual respect. Rachel mixed the batter for her peanut butter blossoms, pushed the first sheet of cookies into the oven, and quickly refilled the flour and sugar containers for the next batch. Then she retrieved the sugar cookie dough from the refrigerator. She worked the chilled sugar cookie dough, half red with simple food coloring, the other plain. Each would be twisted and curved to mimic a candy cane. Once the tray was full, she slid them in the oven and cut out the remaining dough delicately with the tree cookie cutter *mamm* unearthed from the back of the cabinet. Martin rambled on about life outside of Walnut Ridge as he worked on the recipe cards, but Rachel's thoughts drifted to Joel, the sled ride, and found herself smiling.

Removing the first tray from the oven, she slid another in its place. She worked with precision, seeing all was done before the hour grew late. She prepared dough for thimble cookies next. The simple shortbread recipe was a Christmas favorite, especially with *mamm's* summer jams. She loved the process and the way the house filled with the sweet aroma.

At the table, Martin continued to talk about how different some communities were, but spoke nothing of the ocean he had always spoken of. Rachel wondered if he had even made it there, but then decided she didn't want to know.

"There are many bakers there too, but I only saw one cheese store," Martin smiled up at her and went from copying recipes to fiddling through ingredients. She really wished he would focus on the task at hand over rearranging her orderly ingredients. Next she saw to the gingersnaps, a forever favorite.

"I think you would love it there, and you'd have plenty of business if you wanted to have your own cheese shop," he said. She had loved him for two long years, pinned over him for two more, and yet, as her womanhood matured so did her interpretation of what love truly was. Love was steady, dependable.

Joel. He was patient; even welcoming Martin home despite what he had felt. He was attentive, and an anchor to a woman who had felt lost at sea. And she cared deeply for him. The thought stirred inside of her shockingly. She loved Joel Wickey. A man made for a woman who never wanted to see oceans.

"I love my home," she replied. Yes, everything she loved, needed, was right here.

"Let me help box those," Martin said, taking the cooled down cookies and arranging them in easy carry-on boxes from the bakery while she continued to mix dough and bake.

"I could take you to deliver them," Martin suggested toying with a can of cream of tartar. Rachel swiped the can from him.

"I already have plans," she informed him.

"Joel?" she nodded.

"Do you have feelings for him?"

"We are becoming dear *freinden.*" That was a lie. She cared for him deeply, and not like just on the surface. "I do have feelings for him." Martin's gaze jerked up and landed on her.

"I'm surprised your *daed* allows that." His jaw tightened.

"He's just from the next community. There are no rules against that."

"*Nee*, but courting a man who's been in jail? Many will gossip."

"Martin Mast, what a thing to say. Joel's never been in jail. That's *narrisch*. He would never bring such trouble." Rachel stomped a foot loud enough the whispering in the next room quieted. It was a ridiculous statement. Joel was the epitome of an upright man.

"*Nee*, only I do that," he said more like a question. "I am not the *bu* I was, and he is not the man you cast him to be."

"I cannot believe you!"

"He spent two days in jail for destroying his neighbor's property… with a gun. Killed the fella's dog too." Rachel's shock couldn't be contained and she gasped.

"I remember it well enough because *Daed* used to tell me if I didn't wise up, I'd be just like him."

"I cannot believe…" she clutched her chest. "Joel is a *gut* man," she said aloud.

"And I am a bad one? *Kumm* on Rachel, you know me." He reached out and took her trembling hand. "We grew up together."

"He wouldn't keep that from me," though Martin had planted the doubt and Rachel wasn't so sure.

"People hide things, and I'm certain he wasn't eager to tell you about it. Rachel, I love you and even if you no longer have feelings for me, I care too much to let you make a mistake in courting a man unworthy of you."

"A mistake?" her voice wavered. Was she making yet another bad and hasty decision? This was too much information to process in one setting.

"I have never stopped caring for you. Can you just give me a chance to make things right between us? I have never cared for another, and I am ready to settle down now. I'm ready to give you what you always wanted."

He was ready to marry, and on the heels of that knowledge, a terrible ache pierced her temple. Sensing she had no response to his weak proposal, Rachel ached to hide up in her room.

"I told Joel this too," Martin informed.

"You did what!" Could this day get any worse? In her abrupt shock, Rachel grasped the table so hard, cookies scattered all over the floor. Marty quickly went to recover them, but sure enough, her first two batches were a crumbled up mess good for nothing but a snack for hounds.

"I can help you make more, but even he understands we share a history, and that no one is better suited for me than you." Rachel remembered to breathe, and inhaled a hard breath. It was too much to think of. She lifted the full sugar container.

"Let me fetch more sugar. I'll have to start over...again." She slipped from the room under the false excuse for privacy and burst into a thousand tears.. Joel was nothing like Martin Mast. He couldn't be. Joel said honesty was important to him. Then she smelled the burning sugar cookies and, setting aside her current turmoil, rushed back into the kitchen just as Martin was slipping the gingersnaps into the oven. On the counter were two dozen crisped to a-point singed trees. Ruined, just like her budding romance with a man who might be a criminal.

"It's getting late and I have upset you plenty," he reached for his hat nearby. "I'll let you get to doing what you need to without bothering you." She noted the thimble cookies were all filled with jam. "I will give you time to think." He walked to her, leaned in and kissed her cheek. "We can start right where we left off. There is a reason I never found another, and why you haven't either. No one will ever care for you...like me."

Then he was gone, leaving her twisted into a thousand impossible knots.

Amish Christmas Cookie Tour

Chapter 8

Moonlight glowed over the white landscape in pale violet as Joel made the short walk from the house to the bulk store next door. He'd barely slept, working late into the night to ensure the next batch of cookies was even tastier, softer, and chewier than the last. He'd wager a few more sleepless nights if that is what it took for a date with Rachel Yoder. Six days and he was already aching to see her. Perhaps love did smack a man hard enough to knock him a bit senseless.

All that aside, he reined in his thoughts to focus on the day before him. The Cookie Tour had been his idea and right now, he needed it all to go off without a hitch.

Inside his family's bulk store, he quickly stroked the fire to life again, adding two dry logs to the heap of embers still glowing. When a hiss and pop sounded, birthing a hot glow against the early morning chill, he closed the door. It would be toasty and warm by opening. He began his morning routine, a little quicker today so he still had time to fetch Rachel so they could distribute their cookies together.

Turning on the battery-operated lights hanging overhead, Joel moved through the store until all four were on before moving to the front of the store. He turned on the light over the counter. Fetching the bank bag hidden in the clever compartment below, he had begun adding cash to the register, small bills and change, when his father walked into the shop.

"Thought you'd be sleeping yet by the looks of the kitchen this morning." David Wickey looked younger than his fifty-two years, a gift he often contributed to having a firm faith, work he enjoyed, and an endless supply of cherry fry pies.

"Wanted to see over the morning doings before heading out," Joel replied, tearing the orange paper wrapped around nickels. "The Cookie Tour doesn't start until ten."

"You have enough *kichlin* to feed a whole town," *Daed* jested.

"Hoping the whole town shows up." *And takes every last one...of mine,* he silently mused thinking of his and Rachel's arrangement. It was a terrible thought, wishing his were favored.

"I'll go see to the phone messages while you finish up here." David took up a notebook from nearby and one of the freshly sharpened pencils *mamm* was adamant about keeping ready, and stepped out of the back of the store where the phone shanty sat a hundred yards away on the neighbor's property. A few local widows had come to appreciate calling in orders ahead of time, though Joel suspected many did so to get fresh baked goods his *mamm* often made before they flipped the closed sign to open.

Joel continued to finish readying for the day as *Mamm* and his *schwesters* came in carrying all his cookies to wrap. They flipped the closed sign to open.

"It's to be a *gut* day for all," *Mamm* said in her always cheerful tone. "You must have baked through the night *sohn*," she sat down two plastic containers he suspected were his snickerdoodles.

"Had to get it right," he winked.

"Because?" his elder sister Lydianne queried. Thankfully Joel didn't have to explain as *Daed* appeared, notebook in hand and two worried brows bending towards one another.

"I have two orders needing filled," *Daed* handed two slips of paper over to Lydianne. "Hope we have four bread loaves left," he shot *mamm* a brow.

Of course they did, as *mamm* often over-baked. *Except for last night when he was doing all the baking.* Hopefully the baked goods table still had plenty from yesterday.

"She always has plenty." Lydianne, a mother of three, was happy to help for the next two days to ensure all went well with the cookie tour. Joel was thankful that even twelve-year-old Laura was here to help in his absence today. He wanted Rachel and him to deliver cookies to the few shops needing them, but Joel also wanted to visit the shops, check in regularly to ensure the event carried on without a hitch. All had to go well. .

"I have a message for you too Joel," *Daed* said a little quieter and handed over a third piece of paper.

Scribble in his father's hand Joel read.

Rachel will not need you today.

Going alone.

"I'm sorry Joel." *Daed* winced and Joel felt his happy mood plummet.

"Did she say why?"

"Only that…she'd made a mistake ."

A mistake.

"I understand," but Joel didn't. Staring at the words scribbled below him, he puzzled about what could have happened between Saturday and today. Had not Rachel found herself just as happy with him as he was with her? Had six days been all it took to forget the sparks between them? *And what of the Cookie Tour?* Rachel believed just as strongly as Joel did about raising money for the schools.

Mamm offered a sympathetic look as two *Englischers* strolled inside and veered towards the laundry detergent aisle. There was only one explanation for Rachel's change of heart that Joel could think of.

Martin Mast!

His head and heart both agreed. Martin's worldly charms had clearly stripped away the start Joel had waited so long for. With frustration punching his ribs, Joel took two calming breaths. Seemed the good guy didn't always get the girl and anger had no place in a man's heart.

Behind him Laura was arranging cookies on green plastic trays and wrapping them securely while Lydianne went straight to mixing dough, for pies he assumed. Suddenly the Cookie Tour, his hope for bringing communities together and raising money for the Amish schools, seemed unimportant. Without Rachel... he gritted his teeth and tightened his grip on the counter, nothing felt as it did.

Another jangle of the door pulled his attention as Grace Graber walked in carrying two boxes.

"I thought I would help out, considering it's for such a good cause," she presented his *mamm* with two boxes and one looked a whole lot like the white boxes from Yoder's bakery in Walnut Ridge, Joel puzzled.

"That is *verra* kind of you Grace.," *Mamm* lifted the lid on the first box. "Joel made some, but not cranberry. They will be *appeditlich*."

"*Jah*, they will be," Joel added. He lifted the lid on the next box and felt his heart sink at the peanut butter blossoms and gingersnaps arranged orderly within. "You made gingersnaps too?" He tried not to sound judgmental, but as the sweet scents of both cookies filled his nostrils, a vision of blue eyes and blonde hair filled his head.

"Those are from Rachel. She and Martin Mast worked late into the evening on them. She dropped them off this morning and asked that I deliver them to save her making so many stops." Grace smiled, happy to help, and unaware she had just confirmed Joel's biggest fear. All eyes landed on Joel. Even Lydianne froze in her dough making.

"Here Laura, add these to the trays for the ticket holders." Joel said in a sharp tone. Laura accepted both boxes and skidded away to display them with the ones already waiting to be devoured.

"It warms my heart to see so many helping, even those wandering astray." Bless *mamm* and her ability to sweeten a bitter tea.

Rachel's message had said she had made a mistake. Joel inhaled a slow breath, succumbing to the fact *he* was that mistake. A relentless heat crawled up his neck that had nothing to do with the freshly stoked fire nearby.

"Whatever," Lydianne muttered from behind him. He didn't want to believe it either, but Grace was not one for untruths. Admittingly, Joel held concern from the day Martin returned that he would have competition to win Rachel.

"I have spoken too quickly," Grace replied with a worried expression. "Cullen says I tend to speak my thoughts."

"*Nee*, Grace. You are just speaking truth, ain't so? I'm sorry too *sohn*. It looks like he has come between you and Rachel," *mamm* said in a tiff.

"Her happiness is all that matters. If she has chosen him, I cannot quarrel with that. They do have a history." He refused to say more on the matter with Grace there. In truth, Rachel had waited two years for Martin to return. Perhaps it was *Gott's* plan all along. Lydianne laid a gentle hand on his shoulder. He should have known the women would make this torturous.

"But you have had stars for that one since you were a youngie. I say do not give in so quickly *bruder*. At times you are too easygoing. He might hold some of her history, but you, *bruder*, can be her future." Lydianne was only being encouraging.

"She doesn't think so. I should go. I have deliveries to make." Joel turned to gather up all the boxes. He would go alone, supervise the tour for the next two days. "Martin probably got a pocketful of *kichlin* already," he mumbled under his breath, punishing himself further.

"*Mamm*, these are terrible," Laura said, spitting into a nearby trash can. Everyone turned as Laura held a partially eaten gingersnap, her face soured.

Joel shot his sister a disapproving scowl for her dramatics..

"What's wrong with them," *Mamm* walked to her, inspecting the cookie.

"They *geschmack*…." she rubbed her tongue on the roof of her mouth and swallowed. "Like someone added cornstarch to the batter. A lot of cornstarch."

"But ginger snaps don't have cornstarch in them," *Mamm* scoffed. "Lest no recipe I have ever made. Perhaps she was heavy on the baking soda." *Mamm* took the cookie from Laura and nibbled on it. Her immediate frown, partnered with two sorrowful brown eyes, confirmed Laura's need to quickly spit food out of her mouth. Cleary they did taste awful.

"You can't offer them up to the tourists. It will only make folks think she can't bake. What if someone falls ill?" Lydianne insisted.

Joel had never heard of cornstarch poisoning before, but Lydianne was right about one thing. If Rachel's cookies became the center of attention in the wrong way, she would be heartbroken.

"It's cornstarch or cream of tartar one or the other. No matter, it's horrible."

"Rachel knows ingredients by heart. She has given me a dozen of them straight from memory. I don't understand," Grace said just as shocked as Joel. Rachel was born in a house of bakers. Joel couldn't help but wonder...

"Rachel is a fine baker, but...she didn't bake these alone!" Joel's temper flared. Perhaps he was thinking wrong. It was best to not have ill thoughts towards others, but Joel had a dozen already of Martin Mast, the *bu* who could out-prank a prankster. But if he was hoping to win Rachel's affections once more by ruining the cookie tour they had worked hard together for, Joel had to do something.

"That's terrible," Grace said. "Verna, use mine for the tour, and hurry and get rid of those. Rachel doesn't have to know you didn't use hers. Accident or on purpose, we cannot let her be shamed by this."

Joel reached for his coat. She wasn't going to be happy to see him, but Joel needed to find Rachel and stop her from delivering any more of those terrible cookies.

"*Jah*, Joel you should get going and deliver your cookies, especially now. The poor thing. I hope she didn't bake too many."

"She baked as many as me," Joel said grimly.

"*Ach*, that's a lot," Laura said.

"I need to call Dan, our driver, and get all those cookies before someone tastes them."

"*Jah*, that is a *gut* idea." All heads nodded . "How will you get rid of hers without her knowing, and before anyone tastes them?" *Mamm* said with a slight flicker of concern.

"I'll think of something." He'd steal them right out from under her if he had to. No way would Rachel become the center of gossip and amusement if he had a say in it.

"You best hurry," Grace urged. "She's already delivering them."

This morning all he could think about was out-baking Rachel Yoder so he could spend more time with her. Now Joel was going to have to ruin her chance at a fair game. Being a *gut* guy was hard work.

Chapter 9

Joel watched Rachel's buggy leave the Covered Bridge Museum. "Pull the car over there," he pointed and Dan flipped the signal and found an empty spot. "I hope you don't mind carting me around all day," Joel added. He probably shouldn't have rambled on so much about Rachel with the man on the way here, but Joel was still torn up about the fact Martin was out to sabotage Rachel's reputation as a means of winning her heart. It was the most foolish thing.

Sort of, yet, Joel winced, was that not what he too was trying to do?

"Don't mind at all," Dan said with a raspy chuckle. "The wife will think I'm romantic, helping out you young folks, and I would do the same for my Greta, if she ever decided to take up baking that is."

Joel scooped up a tray of chocolate crinkle cookies and snowball cookies he hoped would be enough. Inside, Brenda, the museum curator, smiled up at him.

"Joel, so glad to see you. Your girlfriend was just here." She motioned over a beautiful display of cookies and fresh brewed *kaffi*. There were four trees covered in twinkly lights with the covered bridge ornaments she hoped to sell. Every wall was adorned with newspaper clippings and portraits of historically important folks linked to Pleasants County. Above, a clock chimed, announcing he had one hour before the tour officially started. He had to make this quick. No way was he going to get to all the stops in time.

"I was hoping you would accept these, and..." he pointed at the gingersnaps arranged nicely nearby. "Well, I need those. Please don't ask." He let out a breath. Brenda stared at him, and then the cookies.

"I won't, though I suspect it's for the best. You have done a good deed for our community, and whatever you need, I'm happy to help, but I imagine a young woman might quarrel with you stealing her cookies." That was stating it mildly.

"*Danki* Brenda," he sat down his boxes and scooped up the gingersnaps, racking them back into the white box they were delivered in.

"You seem very concerned. Is there something I can do to help?"

Joel hesitated. It would be to his benefit to have a little help. "You could help, but it might cost you some trouble." Her eyes twinkled instead of narrowed. Lord forgive him, but he was recruiting an accomplice.

"Sounds fun, what can I do?"

"Steal all of the cookies from the same white box and put these in their place." He presented her with a dozen snowball cookies that he worked on all night.

"Where?" Brenda looked ready to commit a crime.

"The sheriff's office." Joel winced. Asking someone to steal from a sheriff was probably going to get him arrested again, but these were dire circumstances. Brenda surprisingly didn't flinch at his foolish request.

"Oh Joel, this is gonna be fun, but I have to ask. What is wrong with these? I thought your people were great cooks and bakers, that's why I asked for help."

"Rachel is a *wunderbaar* baker, the best, but she had help recently." He offered her one of Rachel's cookies. It had to be done if he were to get to all the stops in time. Brenda bit into the cookie, taking a large bite, and made a face.

"Oh yes, I'm on it. These are terrible."

"The worst," Joel thanked her again before rushing out of the museum.

At the light just a hundred feet away, Joel saw Rachel's buggy and quickly plastered himself against the museum wall, as thin as paper. From his position he had a full view of Dan behind the wheel of his van, laughing. Hearing the buggy take off, he blew out a hard hot breath and made his way to the van. The things a man did for love, for a woman, who loved another. It was disgraceful. He climbed inside and felt as if today was going to be a test that might just cost him more than his heart. But she is worth it.

"Where to next, Bond?"

Joel shot Dan a quizzical look, but ignored the name. Dan was a playful fella, and obviously, Joel reminded him of some poor fool named Bond.

"From here," he considered Rachel's next stop which would be the sheriff's office, but Brenda was tackling that switch. "The rescue sanctuary, but you stay far from her or we will both be found out. She has a stop to make first, and then she'll be heading to Vicky's busy barnyard."

Dan let out a booming laugh and put the car in gear. "This is the most fun I've had in years. No worries my friend, I raised two teenage daughters. I know how to stay in the shadows. Let's get a quick snack first. It's gonna be a long day. "

Indeed, it was.

***

Rachel felt a strange unease ever since she had left the museum. Brenda was warm and kind. The museum had been filled with twinkling lights, trees draped in fancy *Englisch* ornaments, and the whole room smelled like cloves and cinnamon. She nearly bought one, considering how much Joel seemed to like bridges and things of beauty, but then remembered him for the man that he was and decided her money would not be wasted.

She turned at the light, but couldn't shake off the eerie sensation that eyes were on her. She veered onto the next street, cars as thick as brambles on the edge of summer fields, but Jiffy was a good horse and experienced in traffic. Near the sheriff's office, she found a safe place to park under a naked persimmon tree bare of fruit and leaves. She gathered up the candy cane and gingersnap cookies marked, Sheriff, and made her way inside.

It was no warmer inside than out, with gray walls and a coldness far from the welcoming of the museum.

"Hello," her trembling voice called out, bouncing off walls and floors. The sheriff lifted his head from behind a tall counter, the desk behind strewn with papers. He was a mountain of a man. Some say he had come from the south. Rachel only knew him as the keeper of peace, for he cared for everyone no matter which side of the fence they lived on.

"Joel felt sorry for me did he?" the sheriff laughed and Rachel forged a smile.

She didn't want to think of Joel currently, not standing in a place where he once spent two nights. "I made candy cane sugar cookies and ginger snaps." She offered them to him. She still had two more stops to make and should be on her way, but as he inspected the contents, Rachel paused.

"I feel you have something to ask, and no, I cannot bake worth a nickel. My wife isn't much at it either, though neither of us starves."

Rachel fiddled with her *kapp* strings. She wanted to know if Joel truly had done as Martin said. What if she had been too quick to believe someone prone to lie. She bit her lip.

"I..."

The door to the office burst open and Brenda, the museum owner barged in, her breathing fighting to level. She looked flushed despite the December cold.

"Brenda?"

"Hi Sheriff," she stilled when her gaze locked onto Rachel's. "I see you are nearly ready for tourists."

"I was just about to taste the goods first," the sheriff opened a box of ginger snaps, selected one that looked to his liking, and lifted it to his mouth.

"No!" Brenda swatted the cookie away. "I mean, those are for the tourists, you shouldn't be greedy, and now you have fingered them." She clicked her tongue disapprovingly. Rachel was confused by her sudden change from bubbly sweetness to stern schoolmaster behavior.

"Here, you can use these. I have more than enough, and these I can take with me," she swiped both boxes of Rachel's cookies out of the sheriff's hands, and before Rachel could even protest, Brenda marched out of the office as if she had just saved the world from utter destruction.

"Well, I guess she worries I'm packing germs." The sheriff shrugged as if it was not strange behavior. Rachel scowled at the door in utter confusion.

"Perhaps she didn't like the ones I baked," Rachel lifted her chin. There was nothing she could do without causing a scene, which she wasn't inclined to do. She had two more deliveries and she was certain Brenda the museum owner didn't know where they were.

"Wedding cookies," the sheriff said, lifting a white cookie from the box.

"Those are snowball cookies," Rachel corrected in a shocked tone. *Snowball cookies were what Joel was baking for the museum.* This day was getting stranger and stranger by the minute.

Chapter 10

Rachel spotted the large red barn of the local animal recuse sanctuary ahead. She veered toward the drive; her confusion over the day's oddness hadn't abated as she muddled over the strange account at the sheriff's office. Brenda's odd behavior, her insistence to see all of Rachel's cookies switched with Joel's, was still perplexing. Perhaps Rachel was looking at it all wrong and Brenda adored her baking so much, she wanted all the cookies to herself.

That had to be it, Rachel gathered and sat a little straighter in the buggy seat. All that mattered was that at the end of the day, not a *kichli* was left even if Brenda swiped them for herself. She had promised to go out with Joel if more folks preferred his over hers after all. That Rachel couldn't do. Rachel couldn't allow herself to be seen in public with a criminal!

The round graveled parking area was already filling, indicating that it had to be near time for the tour to begin. Families milled about along the fences surrounding the barn, feeding goats, donkeys, and at least a half dozen chickens scratching for whatever fell. Rachel never understood the interest others had in petting animals for fun.

Working the reins, she found a turnaround and pulled off in the snowy field and set the break. She scooped up two boxes of Christmas

Tree cookies, dodged two large snow mounds, and weaved around a silver van she recognized as Dan's, the driver many of the local Amish used when taking a buggy wasn't an option.

"So many tourists," she muttered as she reached for the decorative side door of the barn. It was a beautiful sight, seeing the community all out supporting each other this Christmas season. Joel had done a good thing, insisting on the cookie tour. Rachel still couldn't imagine him the sort to get arrested, but Martin had insisted it had been all the rumor at one time. Considering Rachel had never bent an ear to gossip, she had to believe him. There was no cause for Martin to simply make it up, not now that he had returned home and was planning a life dedicated to his Amish roots.

Inside, the smell of fresh hay, winter's chill, and hot chocolate permeated the air. The crowd inside was twice the size of those outdoors. A rooster crowed, spurring laughter. To her left, a manger scene, much like the one described in Luke, only instead of a baby Jesus, Rachel watched a young boy playfully work his younger sister into the hay. Tied to a stall, a donkey, happily enjoying grain from palms and wasn't opposed to having his picture taken.

Rachel weaved toward the counter where Vicky stood.

"You're here!" Vicky said much too loudly.

"I'm sorry if I'm late," Rachel offered. At a long table she noted the tray of slightly burned, lumpy *kichlin* shaped like birds, dog bones, and something else she couldn't make out.

"These are for the pets," Vicky said revealing a tray was labeled *Animal treats, not for humans* with a smiley face. Rachel smiled and began helping to set out the cookies. She remembered how Joel worried over making gingerbread chickens and goats. She quickly pushed the sweet memory out of mind.

"Okay folks…" Vicky began, when suddenly a side door opened and a parade of animals came running into the room.

"Oh no!!!" Vicky cried out as goats of all sizes and colors poured into the crowd. An Emu darted between bodies and pushed his way to the table, attacking the lumpy animal cookies and scattering them in various directions. A child's cry filled the air, as three small pigs ran between legs but clearly uncertain which direction they should go.

"Hank!" Vicky called out over the chaos just as a small white goat with horns curved in perfect symmetry set his sights on Rachel.

In an attempt to heed the warning tone in Vicky's voice, Rachel cradled the box in her arms and took a step back. Not to be deterred from his purpose, Hank the goat showed his goaty side by lowering his head. Even Rachel knew a threat when she was faced with one. Without flinching, Hank charged and head-butted Rachel's hip. The impact caused her to stumble backwards, but thankfully two women quickly gripped her to stay upright. Before she could reprimand the terribly rude intruder, a long muzzle moved over her right shoulder, in a second attempt to win over the box.

"Clyde, no!" Vicky cried out this time in hopes of convincing the hungry spotted pony to stand still. Vicky's cries clearly were in vain, as not one animal was determined to listen. Seeing as Hank the goat wasn't getting his way, he chose then to make a meal of Rachel's coat. The tug-of-war went on just long enough, Clyde was able to knock the box from her grasp and Rachel's cookies went flying. Somewhere in the collision, her bonnet had fallen and disappeared under the trodding of feet and hooves. The rescue animals had gone crazy, and Rachel felt as if she was the one in need of rescue now. Chickens appeared as well as one old red *hund* to get their share of her *kichlin*.

The next twenty minutes was utter chaos. Tourists, clearly not as afraid of thieving farm animals as Rachel, quickly began helping wrangle and herd flocks of poultry and lost pigs. Poor Vicky was nearly in tears as she held a hen under one arm and a bawling goat under another. A man with a heavy gray coat slid on his knees to keep hold of a small pig, while another man was trying to coax Clyde the spotted pony back out with a stalk of straw. Someone should tell him straw was bedding not food, but Rachel was currently in her own troubles in a corner as Hank the goat eyed her challengingly. For a little fella, he could sure leave a mark on his target, and she was certain climbing into the loft in her dress with so many about, wasn't proper.

In one corner, high on a stack of bedding straw, a young boy sat holding two white boxes tightly in his arms and laughing uncontrollably at the whole mess. Rachel paused and took in a long breath. She knew the look of a mischief maker sure enough. It wouldn't surprise her if the child wasn't responsible for opening the gate leading to the outside pasture. Someone had to have let all these animals in had they not?

"I'm so sorry folks. Someone must have opened the gate. I promise you none will harm you or will purposely hurt you," Vicky said loudly, though a short-haired hound with two black ears was growling to keep everyone at bay while he devoured all of Rachel's beautiful thimble cookies. Her stomach instantly knotted as she helplessly watched her peanut butter blossoms become nothing but chicken scratch on the floor.

It was a disaster and for the second time today, her cookies were gone.

While a few helpful patrons assisted in ushering animals back outside, Rachel felt something touch her leg and brush the material of the thermals she wore under her dress. The cat looked up, and then went back to purring. If he wanted a glass of milk to go with the mess here, he was purring up the wrong leg.

"Someone thought turning them all loose would be funny I guess. And today of all days. I'm so sorry everyone." Embarrassment seeped over Vicky's already flushed face. To Rachel's own disappointment, it was a shock that folks seemed to find the whole catastrophe amusing.

"I was told to give you these," a boy she had spotted on the straw earlier emerged.

"Kenny, what have you got there?" A woman asked. Rachel could only assume it was his mother.

"I dunno. The man said to hold on to them, and not let the animals have any, but once all the animals were up, he said to give them to you," he offered the box to Vicky who carefully opened the lid as if she feared another trick was being played on her.

"Oh! Well now, I guess we still have cookies to hand out after all."

Vicky tilted the box out for everyone to take one and Rachel felt her heart plummet as gingerbread cookies in the perfect shape of chicks and goats were being distributed to everyone. Worse, they even looked like perfect replicas of goats and baby chicks.

"Who gave those to you?" Rachel asked the boy, not meaning to sound so stern. "Did he wear a black hat?"

"*Yeh*, and gave me five whole dollars to hold a box," Kenny beamed, proud as punch to be part of the calamity.

"Of all the stuff," Rachel stomped her foot. Joel had been there and not only had he caused the trouble Vicky was facing, but made certain his cookies were the ones being eaten. Never before had anyone gone to such measures to secure a date. A date Rachel was not going to let him have.

Suddenly Rachel recalled the silver van parked outside and quickly ran out the door just as it raced out of the parking lot. The same van she'd seen in town when she was delivering to the museum. Rachel wasn't one who believed in breaking promises, but as soon as she found her bonnet, and delivered her last *kichlin*, she was going to do just that.

***

At her last stop, Rachel took the hill leading to the tree farm and man-made lake. She recalled how excited she had been when Joel first brought her here. Thick ice had covered the lake's edges, but cold blue waters pooled in scattered places. Snow dotted the landscape just as it had when Joel had awakened her young heart to joy again. Love was such a trickster, making one foolish and too blind to see clearly.

Beside her, two boxes of sugar cookies shaped like Christmas trees remained. Determination filled her to see them delivered. She veered her buggy near the barn, letting it blend in with the other buggies there. Pulling her cloak around her tightly, she pushed down her bonnet a little firmer in hopes of hiding under the plainness. No way would she let Joel Wickey take this last stop from her.

Cautiously Rachel made her way around a few tourists near the fire pit. Children's laughter filled the air as Glen was returning from one of the sleigh ride tours the tree farm always offered. Up the wooden steps, she paused at the large window giving one a perfect view of the inside. Seeing no threat of a cookie thief inside, Rachel stepped into the Santa Shop.

"These look beautiful. You really have outdone yourself Rachel. The tourists will love them." Charlotte accepted the cookies and a stack of recipe cards she hoped were readable and copied correctly.

"Little trees indeed. These are simply precious and the recipes will be gone before you know it."

"I see Joel has already delivered his too," Rachel glowered over four dozen snickerdoodles nearby. More than enough for two days.

She looked about as people milled about the long narrow shop as they browsed displays and Christmas fancies.

"He did. I still find it fascinating that he bakes" And loves stealing everyone else's *kichlin*, Rachel wished to add.

"He brought so many I know me and Glen will have some to eat after."

"Or not. Hopefully they are all gone by the end of the day." *Because obviously that is his reason behind stealing all of mine.* The urge to cry grew. There was no way out of the mess she had gotten herself into. She would be known as the *maedel* who went on a date with a lawbreaker and ate Mexican food.

"I should go, but I do hope you have a great turn out." Cookies safely delivered, Rachel quickly left before her emotions got the better of her in front of Charlotte. Rounding the Santa Shop, she watched as Glen pulled another clutch of eager riders away from the barn and her heart sank. She would never ride on a sleigh, even a horse-drawn one, ever again. Suddenly Rachel realized that Joel had broken her heart worse than Martin ever could, because…

Rachel sucked in a hard breath. *Because she loved him.* She had fallen *kapp* over shoes for Joel's attentiveness and charms. It wasn't eagerness from a young *maed* hoping to find a husband, but the beginning of what love truly was. But it wasn't real, she silently scoffed.

Lifting her gaze to the landscape, Rachel caught sight of the silver van parked down by a small building where trees where wrapped in netting by a loud machine.

"*Ach, nee* he will *naet!*" Marching back up the wooden porch steps of the Santa shop to confront Joel, she paused at the window.

Joel held a tray of her sweet Christmas Tree Sugar Cookies in one hand while seriously talking with Charlotte. Whatever he was saying must have worked, because Charlotte then took the tray and tossed all of Rachel's cookies into one box and handed them to Joel who tucked them securely under one arm and disappeared from her sight.

Of all the stuff.

"He's a thief! A cookie thief!" Hot anger warmed her face. There was no doubting it now. Joel had let out all the animals at the rescue sanctuary, and bribed a child, an innocent, to help him. He probably convinced the museum owner to throw out all her cookies too.

As much as she wanted to get into her buggy and go home to cry away this horrible awful day, she had a man to confront. She would not lose this way.

Chapter 11

Joel stepped out of the back door, convinced he managed to save Rachel's reputation despite what it would cost him. With the white box tucked under one arm, he took the steps two at a time, glad he'd confiscated every last cookie she baked.

"You are a thief Joel Wickey!" The angry voice had him pivoting around. And there she was, the most beautiful woman in the world, snarling. By closer inspection, she looked a little...unmade. Her bonnet looked slightly pushed down on one side. Her coat had been shredded at the hip. By closer inspection, Rachel looked like she had rolled down a hill of briars, and was madder than a cat stuck in a rain barrel.

"What happened to you?" Joel reached out to her and to his heartache Rachel jerked from his touch. He knew he would have to face her, admit to sabotaging her part in the cookie tour, but it was her own disheveled state that currently had him concerned.

"You. This is all your fault. If you think I will be going with you anywhere after what you've done, you are *narrisch*. You are a thief...and a felon!"

Joel flinched at the latter. Of course he was holding the evidence of his thievery currently, but he hardly believed stealing cookies was a felony.

"Rachel, what happened?" He prodded further.

"First you try to convince me you have feelings for me when you clearly can't even stand to stomach my baking, then you ruin all my hard work by dumping it in the trash. You paid a *bu* to set free all the rescue animals. Hank nearly killed me!"

Joel didn't know Hank, but he immediately felt the wind push out of him knowing his attempt to help her, had nearly gotten her killed.

"I had to,." he pleaded. If she only understood it was for her own good that he had crossed the line. "I never thought any harm would come to you, or I would have just told you what Martin did from the start. Rachel, you must believe me, I would never let anything ever happen to you."

"Whatever. You had to beat me and your reason for it is to blame the innocent?"

"He's not so innocent." It was not proper to speak ill of others, even if they had made a mess such as this.

"It took me all night to bake those." She pointed an angry finger at the white Yoder's Bakery box under his arm.

He was aware how much work she put into helping him. Had too he not worked just as hard, and alone? "Well, you did have help," he reminded her with an equal snap and watched the evidence of him knowing such wash over her in a sudden surprise. "And have you even tasted one that you made?"

"Martin didn't help me," she said, then quickly let her shoulders slump. "*Ach vell*, he did…but he only copied recipe cards for Charlotte." Joel wondered how he had managed to sabotage her cookies then, but realized the man was far more clever than he was.

"It doesn't matter Rachel. For what has happened to you, I am wonderfully sorry." Joel handed her the box and backed away. "I know you don't believe me, but I promise not to interfere in your life any longer.

You are free to choose who to give your heart to." Knowing he had done all he could do, Joel turned to walk away.

***

And just like that, Joel turned and walked away. Rachel watched him stroll toward the van. Her arms hung heavy in despair. It was all too confusing. Martin informing her Joel had broken the law and was once arrested, Joel claiming he had only taken all her *kichlin* because of Martin and not to ensure he won the wage between them. Joel didn't seem like a man who would bribe *kinner* to do wrong and she believed he would never intentionally bring harm to her, yet, he had. Rachel lifted the lid on her box of *kichlin*. The fact she hadn't tasted them, wasn't the point. Joel hated her baking despite telling her otherwise. To prove him wrong, that she was a fine baker, Rachel reached for one, snatched a tree shaped sugar cookie, and took a tentative bite.

"*Ach* no!!!" She spit and glared into the box. "Cream of tartar!!! That man." She had been terribly wrong to think Joel would have gone out of his way to hurt her. In her heart, she always knew it was Martin who was more prone to doing the wrong thing out of selfishness. She had to apologize.

Rushing around the Santa Shop, in hopes of catching Joel before he left, Rachel saw him running at full speed into the trees.

"Wait!" she heard Joel call out as he raced off. Then she saw it, the child, a boy of no more than six or seven, clinging on for dear life as Glen drove further away. Everyone was singing, paying no mind that a child had fallen off the wagon and was now being dragged behind. Rachel dropped the box and instinctually took off toward the wagon too.

When Rachel cried out, a few heads turned her way. Two men ran past her in a rush to help, waving their arms in earnest. But it was Joel who reached the boy first, chasing down the tractor and scooping up the child before Glen could even bring the ride to a halt.

Out of breath, Rachel slowed and watched as the child's parents jumped from the wagon to see to their son, the father, as well as the others, thanking Joel for his heroic feat.

Rachel worked to slow her racing heart and fast breaths, when his eyes landed directly on hers. Yes, she had been terribly wrong to trust Martin and any tale he was trying to weave to put a wedge between her and the man she had come to love.

When all finally settled, Joel walked her way.

"You saved him," she muttered. Joel said nothing and she knew it was time to give him the apology he deserved.

"I'm sorry. I should have never doubted you."

"I'm sorry too. I should have told you instead of trying to make things better without you knowing."

"Why did you not tell me about being arrested?" She moved closer, waiting to hear how a man such as this one could ever find himself in such a fix.

"It was one night, because my *onkel* the Bishop thought it would be a gut lesson to Alan. Not something one chats about."

"Alan? You spent time in a jail because of your little *bruder*?"

Joel shook his head. "This is all coming out wrong. I agreed to spend the night, and deserved it for my part in it all." He gave his neck a full rub, and Rachel could see the tension growing there.

"Alan wanted to practice shooting. He'd gotten good with the BB gun, but I told him I was busy. He hit one of the neighbor's *hunds*. When I heard the dog crying, I scolded Alan *gut*. I took the gun from him and went to see the over the *hund*, to be certain the animal was all right, but old man Barbour came out of his house threatening me. He called the law and as it's a crime to shoot neighbor's dogs. I was arrested." She stared at him for at least five blinks, clearly deciding if he was lying or telling the truth.

"You let them take you when it was Alan who did it?"

"He was ten Rachel." He snapped "He wasn't aiming for the *hund*, but cans *daed* lined up for him. An accident. How could I let him go through that?"

"But his accident to face Joel," Rachel said, just as the days of life were examples of her own decisions too. "A lesson for him to learn ain't so?"

"How well I know that…now. I should be careful about helping others in the future," he winked. "I agreed to stay all night for my part in it, and Alan… he suffered more thinking I was being treated badly because of him."

"Well, that still doesn't explain why you followed me around all day stealing my cookies. Despite what you think, I'm a *gut* baker."

"I always thought so," he squinted at the thought he didn't like her baking.

"Yet, the first time I saw you at the seasonal gathering, you tasted the *kichlin* I brought and then carried them inside so no one else could have one." Rachel had waited a long time to hear his reasoning for that one.

"So this is why you get your feathers ruffled each time I say you make *gut kichlin*," he chuckled. "Rachel," he drew close, so close the collision of cold December air and her hot breath formed a cloud between them. "I took them because I liked you. I took them so that no other would even get one. I feared if they knew what a fine baker you were, I would not have a chance."

"But you never asked," she squeaked out.

"I wanted to ask you out then, but you were sixteen and me three years older. I couldn't take my eyes off you," he admitted. "I was clumsy and just a *bu*. When I decided that your age didn't matter, Martin had beaten me to it."

"I thought…" she sniffled and ducked her head.

"We both have thought too many things. I say from now on, we share our thoughts with each other. Keeping those to ourself tend to end in wrong conclusions."

Rachel agreed. It was all a matter of miscommunication. How foolish she felt. Joel had only stolen her *kichlin* to help her, thankfully so. Then she realized, there was one other batch of *kichlin* not accounted for. "Joel, I had *mamm* drop off some to the Fenders Bed and Breakfast."

Joel smiled, flipping her heart over, and touched her arm every so lightly.

"They tossed them after the first bite," he assured her. He certainly had seen to his job. "Rachel, I know you have been…" he looked to his boots, the slick icy patch to his right, before looking back at her.

"Foolish. Blind. Untrusting," she said on an eye roll. They were a pair indeed. However, every wrong step and mishap, had brought them right here. He was her second chance, and there was no doubt in Rachel's mind that Joel Wickey was the man who would love her for as long as *Gott* allowed them.

"I was going to say, cautious, kind-hearted, beautiful, and waiting." Like a pedal to the sun his body leaned closer, unable to stand still. He was going to kiss her, and Rachel wasn't pulling away or stepping back.

"Perhaps your thievery wasn't so bad," she muttered." She lifted her chin a little higher and Rachel saw nothing but hope and a hundred tomorrows in his eyes.

"You're more important than where I plant my feet. More loved than I have words to say," he leaned closer, aching to touch his lips to hers. "You are… my ocean, Rachel Yoder."

There were times when a woman had doubts. When she battled with confidence and felt small in a big world that was made up of acres and oceans. Rachel had learned *Gott's* path wasn't sugar-coated or sprinkled. But there were also times, when a woman simply knew she didn't need sprinkles or sweet Christmas icing for the cookie to taste good. That sometimes the plain version was the best.

The kiss wasn't tender or sweet, but hurried and anxious. He smiled before deepening his part of the collective love of lips touching. When he pulled away, Joel smiled down at her.

"I want to ask you something Rachel," he said, still working to slow his breathing. "Will you court me?"

"Joel Wickey, it's about time you asked."

The End

Peanut Butter Blossoms

1 ¾ cup of flour

1 tsp baking soda

½ tsp. salt

½ cup of butter

½ cup of sugar

½ cup brown sugar

½ cup peanut butter

1 egg

2 Tbsp milk

1 tsp vanilla

Hershey kisses

Sift flour, soda, and salt together. In a separate bowl, cream together butter, sugars, and peanut butter. Add your egg, milk and vanilla. Blend well. Add dry ingredients. Shape into balls and place on greased cookie sheet. Bake at 375 for 8 minutes. Remove from the oven and place a Hershey kiss in the center and press down to secure. Return to the oven for another 3-5 minutes.

Yields: 3 dozen cookies

Made in the USA
Middletown, DE
01 November 2023

41797221R00166